BOOK 3

DIMWORLD SERIES

INSIDE THE MACHINE

Books by J. Boyd Long

THE DIMWORLD SERIES

Genesis Dimension

When Good Plans Go Bad

Inside The Machine

BOOK 3

DimWorld SERIES

INSIDE THE MACHINE

J. BOYD LONG

Inside The Machine, Book 3 of the *DimWorld* Series

Inside The Machine is a work of fiction. All characters in this book are fictitious. Any similarity to real persons, living or dead, is coincidental and not intended by the author.

Copyright © 2019 Justin Boyd Long

Written by J. Boyd Long

www.JBoydLong.com

All rights reserved.

No part of this book may be reproduced in any form or by any electronic or mechanical means, including information storage and retrieval systems, without permission in writing from the publisher, except by reviewers, who may quote brief passages in a review.

Published in the United States by Mad Goat Press

Gainesville, Florida, USA

www.madgoatpress.com info@MadGoatPress.com

Cover Design by: My Custom Book Cover

Limits of Liability and Disclaimer Warranty:

The author shall not be liable for your misuse of this material. This book is strictly for entertainment purposes.

First edition printing August 2019

ISBN 978-1-948169-12-7 (Ebook Edition)

ISBN 978-1-948169-13-4 (Paperback Edition)

ISBN 978-1-948169-14-1 (Hardcover Edition)

Library of Congress Control Number: 2019905454

Printed in the United States of America

For Erica, who showed me the stars.

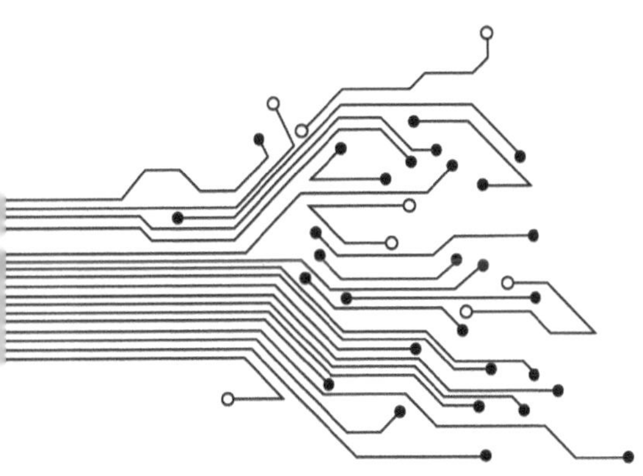

CHAPTER 1

Quentin rolled over and glanced at the clock. The novelty of having electricity in the island cabin hadn't worn off yet, and he grinned as the automatic coffee pot kicked on out in the kitchen. Having coffee ready and waiting was really living in style, compared to getting up and building a fire to heat water. He stretched luxuriously for a moment, then melted back into the bed. The mattresses were a new addition as well, and not having to share a bed with Eissa was nice.

The injuries that Bob and Tocho had sustained as prisoners of Vincent Macalister and DimCorp had prompted them to make some serious improvements to their living arrangements. Solar power came first, for lights, cooking, and coffee, along with good beds for everyone. The beds took up a lot of space, so they added on to the cabin. It had taken a couple of months, but they now had an indoor bathroom, and they each had their own small bedroom. Quentin felt guilty for thinking it, but Bob's injuries had come with a silver lining. If he hadn't been hurt so badly, they probably would have gone on living the way they were, all cramped up in one room.

He made his way out to the kitchen and poured a cup of coffee. The sun was just peeking through the trees, and the birds were chirping in the bushes on the other side of the open windows. Bob shuffled into the kitchen a moment later, rubbing the sleep from his eyes.

"Morning."

"Hmm," Bob grunted, noncommittally.

Quentin poured him a cup of coffee, and they moved out to the front porch. They sipped their coffee in silence for a few minutes as the island slowly woke around them. Tocho came through the door just as Quentin was finishing his last swallow.

"Are you ready to go for a run?"

Quentin groaned. "I'm still sore from Monday. Getting that water tank on the roof just about killed me."

Tocho began stretching. "Exercise will loosen up your muscles, make you feel better. Sitting around makes you stiff."

Eissa staggered out onto the porch in mid-yawn. "It's too early for this shit. I just got a nice, comfy bed, and I need more time to get to know it." Her hair was pulled back into a pony-tail, and she was wearing the new running shorts and shirt she bought in Dimension 443 the week before. The island diet and exercise plan that Tocho had them on was melting the weight off her, and she'd had to replace her wardrobe completely.

"Don't bother arguing," Quentin said, pointing at Tocho. "I've already been rebuffed by the torture maestro."

"I'm not arguing," Eissa said, leaning forward into a calf stretch. "I'm just saying, I carried a thousand pieces of lumber through the DimGate last month, and I didn't use micro-movers to do it."

"That's not even an argument, and it has nothing to do with what we're talking about. That's you trying to make fun of me for using my brain, instead of my back."

Eissa switched legs, a smug look on her face. "Huh. So it is. How about that?"

Quentin shook his head, setting his coffee cup beside his chair. "You are incorrigible. I hope we run all the way around the island today."

"Well, if we do, I'll probably beat you, and then I'll use all the hot water, so there."

"Hey, hey, now we're all getting dragged into this," Bob said with a chuckle. "I'm glad I'm still on the injured list, so I can get ready while you go chase each other around. Don't stay gone too long, we've got a full day ahead of us."

"That's right." Tocho descended the steps and walked towards the beach trail. "Let's get moving. We'll see who's talking tough in an hour."

Quentin chuckled as he followed Eissa down the steps. She probably would beat him back, truth be told. He might have been in better shape than her when they started this whole adventure, but he had only improved slightly compared to Eissa, who had transformed completely. He was secretly proud of her, despite the ribbing she gave him about it. They broke into a light jog as they made their way to the beach to begin their workout session.

With a three-mile run and breakfast behind them, the four lined up at the DimGate. Today was a scheduled fun day, a reward for all the hard work they had put into remodeling the cabin. They were going to take a tour of the Armstrong Spaceport in Dimension 443, which was right outside of Las Vegas, and follow that with a nice dinner.

"Fire in the hole." Bob activated the DimGate, and Quentin opened the door, glancing around the other side.

The roar of wind and traffic assaulted his ears, as it always did, but the roof of the Diablo Tower was deserted. He stepped through, checking behind the door, and waved the others over. "All clear."

Once they were all through, Bob pulled a fuse from the control panel and closed the door, and they headed over to the airlift at the edge of the roof.

"Alright, listen up. We're going to take a taxi to the spaceport tram station. Think about everything you say. We don't want Quentin to have to rip the car door off again." Bob winked at Quentin. "Just be a tourist today. Have a good time, don't think about DimCorp, don't talk about anything illegal."

"Here, here," Eissa said. She pushed the call button for the airlift. "Once was quite enough for me with all that excitement."

An older couple stood inside the airlift when the door opened. They shuffled over against the rail as Eissa entered. "Ground floor?" the woman asked.

"Yes, thanks," Eissa said.

"What's the roof like? Is there a restaurant up there?"

"Oh, no," Eissa said. "There's nothing to see up there. We thought we'd take in the view, but it's too windy to enjoy it."

The woman nodded and gripped the rail with a grimace as the airlift plummeted down the side of the building. Once they reached the ground floor, she gave Eissa a tight smile. "Have a good day."

"You, too."

They filed out of the airlift and gathered on the sidewalk as Eissa hit the button for a cab.

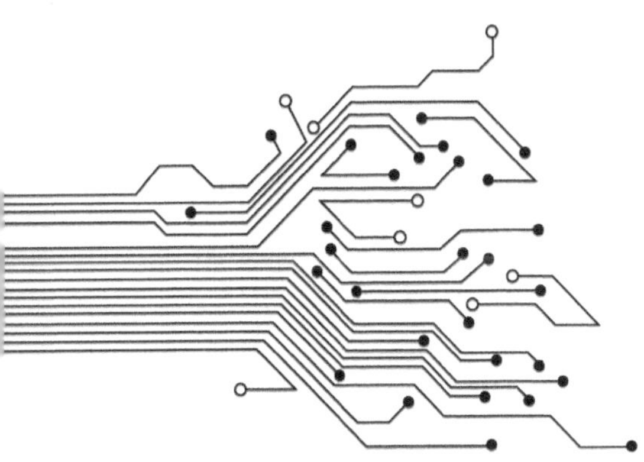

CHAPTER 2

Carl Holt leaned back from his desk and stretched, his fingers brushing the bulletin board on the wall behind him. His desk was overflowing with reports from various dimensions, demands from various CEOs, complaints about service, complaints about guards, complaints about schedules, and if he dug deep enough, there were probably complaints about complaints. His secretary screened out the unimportant stuff, but he liked to at least glance through them and see who was bitching about what. Sometimes it was someone who could scratch his back if he scratched theirs, in which case he might do something about the complaint, but most of them went in the trash.

Amid the piles of complaints and reports were actual things he needed to work on, or was in the middle of working on, or intended to work on, but hadn't found the time yet. He still hadn't wrapped things up with the IBZ employee who went rogue in Dimension 165, there was a mounting pile of evidence that one of the contractors at the spaceport in 443 was stealing materials, there was a missing recon team in Dimension 60, three separate worker rebellions in three different dimensions, and who knew what else. Even if he could figure out a way to stop sleeping and work 24/7, he wouldn't be able to get everything done.

The fluorescent bulb overhead flickered relentlessly, and he glanced up at it, irritated. There was always something falling apart in his office, whether it was an outlet that stopped working, or a pipe leaking in the wall. DimCorp had spent 65 million dollars renovating the corporate offices across the street after the terrorist attack, but it was never in the budget to even get a fresh coat of paint on the peeling concrete block walls over here in the security building. Funny how that worked.

He pushed a stack of reports out from in front of his monitor and shook the mouse to wake up the screen. Their computers were ancient too, now that he thought about it. Everybody wanted Security to work miracles, but they didn't want to spend any money to give them the necessary resources. They didn't even have holo-links, even though the civilian market had been using them for ten years. Instead, they were still using cellphones on the old network. Funny how that worked, too. As the Director of Security, he had over five thousand people under him in a hundred different dimensions. He had a Special Operations team that cleaned up all DimCorp's messes. He arguably had more responsibility than anyone else in all of DimCorp. And here he was, sitting in a dank basement office, trying to work with old equipment under a faulty light fixture.

He opened his email, hoping for something from Sergeant Anderson, his rescue scout in Dimension 60. If they were going to have to escalate that to a full-scale rescue mission, he needed to start the ball rolling ASAP. There was a list of new emails, but none were from Anderson.

The intercom on his phone buzzed, and he punched the button. "What?"

"Mr. Zimmerman on line three for you, sir," his secretary said. "From Dimension 165."

He sighed, rubbing the bridge of his nose. "Yeah, yeah, I know who Zimmerman is. And get a work order filled out for this damn light in here, it's driving me crazy."

"Yes, sir."

He picked up the phone. "Holt here."

"Good morning, Carl. It's Gerrard Zimmerman. How are things in the Genesis Dimension?"

Fucking peachy, he wanted to say. *Still working on cleaning up your mess.* The truth was, he wasn't actually working on Zimmerman's mess. They didn't have enough manpower to do more than a minimal investigation into Zimmerman's case, but Zimmerman seemed to think they should be putting everyone they had on it. It made Holt mad before Zimmerman even said anything about it. "We're plugging along. What can I do for you?"

"I've got a detective from the FBI calling my office wanting to talk to you about the protester shooting from last spring. Says he's doing a follow-up investigation at the behest of the Indian tribe."

Holt was silent. These things happened sometimes, but it was usually a county sheriff's department, which he could bullshit his way through with a phone call. Dealing with the FBI was going to be more of a pain in the ass, especially in Dimension 165. They were all about redundancy and paperwork.

"Well, what do you want me to tell them?"

"I'll come over and give them a call, but it won't be until tomorrow. I've got to deal with something at the Spaceport in 443 today."

"Alright." Zimmerman paused. "Any progress on finding Quentin James and his mysterious accomplice?"

"Not yet," Holt said, trying to suppress the rising irritation that always seemed to come with this subject. "They've been in three different dimensions that we know of, and one of them doesn't even host any DimCorp operations. Last sighting was months ago. If you can spare me enough people to search three planets, then maybe we can wrap this up by the end of the day."

"Alright, Carl, there's no need to get aggressive with me," Zimmerman said, his voice rising slightly. "I'm just trying to keep up with the situation, that's all."

Holt shook his head. He had to end this call before he crossed the line, and every time Zimmerman wanted to talk about Quentin James, he got perilously close to losing his cool. Zimmerman acted like James's defection had been some sort of failing on Holt's part, when it was Zimmerman's impatience that had started the whole thing. If he had just waited a day, and let Richard North open that damned email for him, none of this ever would have happened.

"I'll let you know if something changes," he growled. "Tell your FBI agent I'll call him tomorrow."

He hung up the phone. There was a time, years ago, when he had worked under a guy like Zimmerman. It was just one company, four locations, maybe a thousand employees. Holt didn't know how good he'd had it back then, running security for something so small and uncomplicated. Back then, he thought that moving up the ladder would be fulfilling, rewarding. If only he had known how stressful it would be to have a couple hundred CEOs and Project Supervisors to work for, each with impossible expectations, and the complete inability to listen to anything he said.

He turned back to the computer and opened the folder titled, *165 James, Quentin*. Speaking of pains in the ass, this guy was something else. 41 years old, single, worked in the IT department at IBZ for years without any issues. He had a few disciplinary write-ups in his file, all for petty insubordination to his supervisor. He opened one of the file attachments showing the supervisor's write-up.

> *Quentin James was caught with his cell phone at work, which is a violation of the employee conduct regulations as described in the IBZ employee handbook. When challenged, Mr. James told me: "You're a fucking asshole, Richard. You think you're a drill sergeant or something, but you're just a computer geek like the rest of us. Get over yourself." I suspended Mr. James for 1 day for his insubordination. He refused to sign this statement.*

Holt chuckled. As much as the James situation drove him crazy, reading his discipline reports was always good for a laugh. The smile faded, as he again thought about all the unknowns in the situation. How did James access the DimGate? He never should have gotten into the room, much less been able to activate the Gate. Why did he go to Dimension 444? And who was the woman with him?

That was the most troubling part of the whole thing. James and this mysterious woman manage to gain access to Zimmerman's office, then his DimGate, and vanish into Dimension 444. A month later they turn up in the Genesis Dimension with Spartacus, a known terrorist who had been presumed dead for three years. Not just in the Genesis Dimension, but in the DimGate Control Center, which had to be one of the most secure places in existence. However, the woman has documentation verifying her status as a DimCorp lawyer, with a writ of authority from the fucking DimCorp board.

No one that he could talk to knew who she was, but it wasn't a situation where he could just stroll through the C-Suite across the street with a grainy black and white security camera picture of her, asking if anyone knew her. The guard on the desk that night had dropped the ball in every way possible, which put him in a very awkward situation as the responsible party for the security department. They didn't have a copy of the letter, they didn't have her name, they didn't even photograph James when they booked him. Fucking botched in every way possible.

There was also the clandestine nature of DimCorp. There were so many secret agents running around, doing God knew what for God knew who, there was no way for anyone to know if she was a legit DimCorp operative or not. If she was, she might be using James to get her into the terrorist ring to take down a cell, and if he screwed that up, the political fallout would be very dirty. But how in the hell did James fit into the picture?

James wasn't the kind of guy who did any of this stuff. He didn't belong to any social organizations except Mensa, which was some high IQ club. He was single, lived with his sister, wasn't interested in moving up the ladder at work, had a boring Facebook page, the posterchild for benign. How could an email with a picture of Holt beside a couple of dead protesters turn him from that guy into this guy?

None of it was cut and dried, but Zimmerman didn't seem to understand that. He also didn't seem to understand that whoever James was with had their own DimGate, however the hell that had happened. When they walked out of DimCorp Security three months ago, they could have gone literally any-where. How the hell did they expect him to just find them?

He closed the folder with a sigh. They might catch James eventually, but it was unlikely unless he fell into their lap. They just didn't have enough people to bother with him. There were more pressing things to deal with, like this situation at the Armstrong Spaceport in 443. Someone was stealing truckloads of copper wire, and the onsite security chief was ready to burn them. The problem was that some of the security people were in on it too, and possibly even some bean counters in the office. Holt was going to help them set up a sting operation, and he had a meeting over there in an hour. It was time to move.

He shut down his computer and stood up, adjusting the pistol on his hip. With one last glance around the office, he shut the door and locked it behind him. His secretary looked up as he walked past her desk.

"I'm headed to Dimension 443 to meet with Captain Young. I'll be back late this afternoon."

"Okay. Did you assign someone to investigate the death of the site supervisor in Dimension 214? You asked me to remind you about that."

"Shit." He glanced at his watch. "Remind me again tomorrow. Speaking of tomorrow, I have to run to Dimension 165 and talk to the FBI about the pipeline protester thing. I shouldn't need more than an hour. Can you put that on my calendar?"

"Yes, sir. Have a safe trip."

He stepped out into the hallway and set out for the DimGate floor. So much to do, so little time.

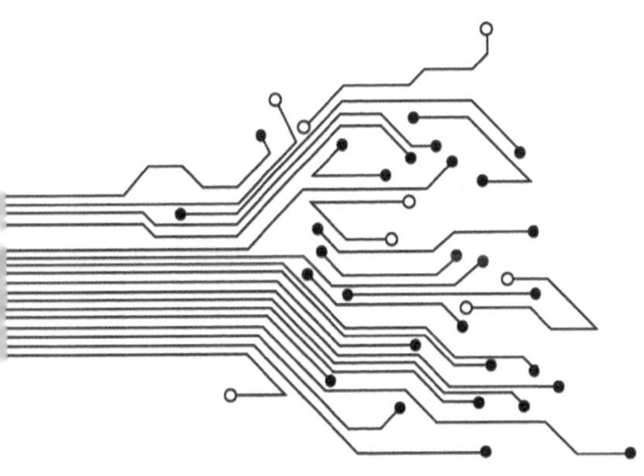

CHAPTER 3

Quentin stared at Eissa with a mixture of pity and exasperation. They were only thirty seconds into their first flying car ride, and she was already on the verge of panic. Tocho and Bob sat across from them in the rear-facing front seat. Bob was peering out the window as they cruised along in the fifth row up from ground level, but Tocho leaned forward and patted her knee.

"It just takes some getting used to," Tocho said. "When Bob found me, the only vehicle I'd ever seen was the train that carried the ore out of our mine. Trust me, I was terrified the first time Bob took me on a car ride."

Eissa shook her head. "I was a flight medic in the army. I've got over two thousand hours in a helicopter, okay? I'm not scared of flying. It's this fucking car. It's too small, it doesn't feel stable, and I'm pretty sure there's something wrong with it. It feels like the motor's skipping a beat, or something."

Quentin stared out the window, trying to ignore her, but it was impossible. There was no point in trying to reason with her, but it was the only way he knew to handle things. "Look, it's an electric car, right? It doesn't run on internal combustion like our cars, or a helicopter. You're probably feeling the generator kicking on and off, topping up the batteries. It's fine."

"Oh, so now you're a flying car expert?" Her knuckles were white as she clenched the armrest. "Just for your information, Mr. Know-it-all, a helicopter has a turbine engine."

Quentin shook his head and looked back out the window. "I can't believe I'm the rational one in this conversation. Look, we'll be there in five minutes. You can do this for five minutes, right?"

Eissa clamped her mouth shut, tightening her lips into a firm line. The skyscrapers outside the window began to give way to smaller buildings, and a moment later the cab banked to the right and dropped in altitude as it merged into a new line of traffic going north on the outer edge of town. Below them, Quentin recognized the building they were passing.

"Hey, there's Prepper's Paradise." He glanced at Bob. "That's where we got the bulletproof vest and the micro-movers."

A minute later, the cab dropped down to the lane below them. Quentin's stomach flipped, and Eissa grabbed his arm in a vice-like grip. Just as it settled out, the car dropped again.

"Oh, I don't like that," Eissa muttered through gritted teeth.

Quentin looked down. "We've only got one more level and we'll be on the ground."

She squeezed her eyes shut, keeping the firm grip on his arm as they waited. Bob and Tocho watched them in amusement as the car made its final descent. There was a light bump, and then they were cruising down the street like an ordinary car. Quentin pried Eissa's fingers loose from his arm.

"There, that wasn't so bad, right?"

Eissa glared at him. "Kiss my ass. This tram to the spaceport better not leave the ground."

Bob burst out laughing. "Don't worry, it doesn't. You can see it right over there."

He pointed out the widow to a monorail train that was slowly pulling into a station to their left. A moment later the taxi turned into the parking lot beside the building and coasted to a stop at the curb. The doors unlocked as a chime sounded.

Thank you for using AirCab. You have arrived at your destination.

The ticket line was short, and twenty minutes later they were sliding across the Nevada desert on the small automated train. Quentin marveled at the landscape. They were in a broad valley between two low, barren mountain ranges. The land was flat, and the only vegetation to be seen was sagebrush and tumbleweeds. A few hundred yards away, a paved road ran parallel to the train track, with occasional large trucks going by in the other direction. It was hard to guess at their speed with the lack of reference points on the near horizon, but they were clearly moving fast.

Suddenly, Eissa grabbed his arm and pointed out the window above the train. "Look, there's a ship coming down!"

Quentin spun around and pressed his face against the window. Sure enough, he could just make out a streak of light, like a daytime meteor. As it dropped through the atmosphere, the glow receded, and it began to take shape. Massive parachutes deployed, slowing its decent to a crawl. Just before it dropped out of sight, the parachutes released and drifted away. Thrusters emitting a blinding blue light engaged, and the ship slowly lowered itself over the horizon.

"Wow," Quentin said. "That was awesome! Good eye, Eissa."

She smiled. "Maybe that will even out my bad attitude in the AirCab."

"Definitely, all is forgiven." Quentin pulled a brochure from the rack on the wall beneath the window. "I gotta know what that thing runs on, though. That wasn't like anything we have in our dimension."

He flipped past the announcements for kids' entertainment and museum hours, and finally found something about the operations. The Armstrong Spaceport was the center of operations for AMP, the Asteroid Mining Program. Automated shuttles arrived hourly, carrying refined ore from the Lagrange Point 5 orbital storage facility. The brochure didn't discuss the shuttles themselves. Quentin folded it up and put it back in the rack.

Buildings appeared on the horizon, and the train began to slow. The recently-landed shuttle was nowhere to be seen, but it made sense that they wouldn't be able to get very close, in case something went wrong. Massive warehouses soon blocked their view. Every building in sight was tan, though whether they were painted that way or just coated in dust from the desert was impossible to tell. The train slid smoothly into the station and came to a stop. Bob and Tocho stood up from the row behind them, and they made their way to the door at the end of the car.

The exit walkway funneled them across the platform and into the visitor information center and museum. It was filled with people admiring the displays of old space technology, their holo-links providing personal hologram presentations at each station. There were rock samples from every planet in the solar system, and details about the missions to each of those planets.

"Dude, look at this." Eissa pointed to a large display case behind them. It contained a series of model rockets and ships, showing the chronological advancement of technology in space travel. "They stopped using solid-fuel rocket booster technology back in the 1970's."

Quentin made his way over to the case. This was exactly what he was interested in. A placard beside each model described the features of the technology. He tried to glean more information from a child's holo-link playing beside him, but the audio was playing over the kid's earbuds, and the silent movie told him nothing except that there had been some spectacular failures as they had developed the technology. Even without sound, the 3D spaceship crashes were impressive. He returned his attention to the placards.

"There it is," he whispered excitedly. "QID, or Quantized Inertia Drive, a fuel-less propulsion technology. Huh." There were six different model ships with the QID from 1972 to 2012. Of the most recent, one was a human transport, and the other was an automated cargo shuttle, like the one they had seen land.

"I wonder how they're so far ahead of us with this stuff," Eissa said. "I don't get it."

Quentin pointed to one of the QID models. "It says the technology was pioneered by the Global Collective for Technological Advancement. I bet that's what Bob was telling us about, where all the countries pool resources to figure this stuff out."

"Do you think they'll ever figure this out in our dimension?"

"Oh, eventually," Quentin said. "It's physics. It's not so much a matter of *if* they'll get it, it's *when*. Right now, there's probably thirty people trying to figure it out, but they're in different labs working for different companies or governments, so they each have to find it on their own. It looks like they put them all in the same room in this dimension."

They moved on to the next exhibit, which had a chronological display of the evolution of spacesuits. Quentin was almost disappointed to find them quite similar to the ones he was familiar with. There appeared to be some universal constants, and protecting people from the harsh extremes of space was one of them.

"If you all want to take the bus tour, we'd better get in line." Tocho pointed to the ticket counter. "The next one leaves in ten minutes, and there's six seats left."

"Yes, let's do that," Quentin said. "We can finish looking around here when we get back."

———————•———————o

Quentin was disappointed to find the tour bus was driverless, and there was no tour guide. Instead, as they left the museum, a video recording began to play, narrating their route through the spaceport. It was informative, but he had no way to ask questions.

To the right of the bus is the warehousing complex for Dimension Resources, or DimRec. DimRec holds the government contract for the Asteroid Mining Program, and has been operating AMP since its inception in 1998. Up next is the Space Vehicle Refurbishment Building.

Quentin and Eissa stared at one another for a moment, then simultaneously turned to Bob, who was seated across from them.

"Did she just say DimRec?" Quentin asked.

"That's what it says on that building," Bob said, pointing out the window.

Quentin turned and looked. They were passing an office building with a giant mural of the solar system painted on the side, and *Dimension Resources* was emblazoned across the center of the image.

"Is that what I think it is?" Quentin asked. "Because that name is too similar to be a coincidence."

Bob shook his head. "I don't know. I haven't been here before, and Tocho and I never leave Vegas when we come to 443."

Next to the DimRec office building was a smaller, single story structure. There was a large badge on the front door, and a line of security vehicles parked in front. A dusty black SUV pulled up and parked on the other side of the narrow strip of grass as the tour bus stopped at the traffic light, and Quentin glanced at the four men climbing out of it. The one on the front passenger side looked strangely familiar, but it took a moment for Quentin to identify him. The bald head, the wide jaw, the uniform… suddenly it clicked. This was the guy that was holding the rifle in the picture, the one who had shot Bonner and Whitefoot at the pipeline protest.

Carl Holt.

He was standing less than ten feet away, separated from them only by the window of the tour bus. Quentin froze, his eyes fixed on Holt. Holt glanced up at the bus as he adjusted his pistol belt, and for a fraction of a second, their eyes met. Holt's brow furrowed, and he raised his hand to shade his eyes as the bus pulled away from the intersection. Quentin flopped back in his seat, his heart pounding.

"Dude, what the hell is wrong with you?" Eissa asked.

Quentin resisted the urge to panic. *Think, Q. What is the situation? What are the facts?* He was trapped on the tour bus in the middle of a DimCorp operation. Their DimGate was sixty miles away, and the only way to get to it was on a train. He'd just come face to face with Carl Holt, DimCorp's head of security. Holt knew exactly who Quentin was, had undoubtedly been in Quentin's apartment, seen everything on his computer, grilled his sister for information, and watched the surveillance video footage of him and Eissa sneaking into Zimmerman's office and discovering the DimGate. This was beyond bad.

"Hey, Q, are you still here?" Eissa waved her hand in front of his face. "You're starting to freak me out a little bit."

Quentin nodded dumbly. His thoughts were sluggish, as if he had just awakened from a deep sleep. "Carl Holt. That guy back there was Carl Holt. He saw me."

Eissa's eyes widened in shock. "Holt? DimCorp Holt? Are you sure?"

"Positive." He cleared his throat. "We've got to get out of here with a quickness."

Tocho leaned across the aisle. "Calm down, Quentin. We can't do anything but ride this thing out. Don't make a scene."

Quentin took a shuddering breath. Tocho was right. If he somehow managed to get them off the tour bus, he would be effectively stranding them right in front of the security building, deep inside the spaceport. He just had to hope that Holt wasn't sure about who he had been looking at. It was possible that he hadn't seen Quentin clearly. Unlikely, based on his reaction, but possible.

Eissa extended her hand in front of him. "Here, do you want to squeeze my arm?"

Quentin chuckled, despite the knot of dread in his belly. That was one of his techniques for getting her through an anxiety attack, and she generally squeezed the shit out of his arm. "I'm okay. I just wasn't expecting to see him here. I mean, who would've thought we were walking into the enemy's lair?"

"Right? I guess that confirms our suspicions about the company name, huh?"

Quentin sighed. So much for the designated fun day. The tour bus continued its loop around the spaceport, and they got a glimpse of the shuttle sitting on the landing pad. There was a flurry of activity around it, and he tried to relax and listen to the video explain what was happening.

Each shuttle carries fifteen thousand kilos of refined metal ingots. This metal is mined in the asteroid belt and refined in space to reduce costs. The refined metals are warehoused at the Lagrange Point 5, and shuttles ferry them to Earth here at the Armstrong Spaceport. Each shuttle is unloaded, inspected, and relaunched in thirty minutes, and the pad is prepared for the next arrival. Shuttles arrive every sixty minutes, 24 hours a day, 365 days a year.

The bus moved on, and Quentin peered back the way they had come, trying to see if they were being followed by a security vehicle. As they turned a corner, he had a clear view. The road behind them was deserted. Of course, Holt could just go to the Visitor Center and wait for the bus to bring them back. There was just no way to know if they were in trouble or not.

The minutes crawled by, and Quentin was unable to enjoy the tour of the high-tech spaceport. It should have been the most fun he'd ever had, but seeing Holt had robbed him of the joy he'd started out with. It brought the ever-present thoughts of Vincent Macalister to the surface. Vincent Macalister, staring at him with eyes full of rage and contempt. Vincent Macalister, shooting Quentin in the chest. Vincent Macalister, bloody and dead by Quentin's hand. The wound was still raw, and running into Holt picked off whatever scab had managed to form. At last, the bus pulled back into the Visitor Center. Bob stepped past Tocho into the aisle and leaned towards them.

"Listen," he whispered. "We're going to get off the bus and walk right over to the monorail platform. If there's security looking for Quentin, we let them take him. Don't fight, because there's no way for us to get out of here. We're stuck in the middle of the desert, alright? We let them take Quentin, and we'll go back and figure out a rescue plan. If there's no security, we get on the train and go home. Alright?"

Quentin nodded, and looked out the window. There was a security guard on the sidewalk giving people directions and keeping the line moving. Bob stepped back, motioning for Quentin to go in front of him. He stood and moved slowly down the aisle, watching out the window. There were only three people left in front of him when a second security guard walked up and joined the first one. He showed him a piece of paper, then pointed at the people getting off the bus, and Quentin's stomach rolled.

His feet were heavy as he stepped down to the sidewalk. He fought the urge to puke, and then fought the urge to run. He looked down, wishing he wasn't so tall. It was impossible for him, at six feet two inches, to blend into a crowd. The guards were still waving the people through, but stopped the man in front of him.

"Excuse me, sir, can you come with me, please?"

Quentin's heart stopped, but the man in front of him seemed unperturbed. "Sure, did you guys find my camera case?"

"Yes sir, someone turned it in at the desk while you were out on the tour."

They walked towards the door, and the remaining guard waved Quentin past without so much as a glance. He walked to the monorail platform on the other end of the building, trying to be casual. His legs were shaking, and he jammed his hands in his pockets so no one would think he was having a seizure. He risked a quick glance at the windows beside him, and saw in the reflection that Eissa, Bob, and Tocho were all behind him. He put his head down and trudged forward. The train wasn't there, so they weren't out of the woods yet.

Bob caught up and walked beside him, but he kept his head pointed away as he spoke softly. "We're going to split up and pretend we don't know each other. You find a bench to sit on, maybe next to someone else, while we wait on the train. We'll sit separately on the train, and link back up once we get out of the station on the other end."

Quentin didn't say anything, and Bob moved on past him. There were several people milling around the departure area, and he sat down on a bench next to an older couple.

"Did you folks have a nice tour?"

"Oh, yes," the lady said with a smile. "Herbert's been talking about coming here for years. It's a lot of walking though, don't you think?"

They were happy to tell him all about their tour, and he let them chatter away, nodding occasionally and asking questions. There were sure to be cameras everywhere, and if Holt's security team was looking at them, he wanted to look like he belonged with them. The platform continued to fill with people. He could see Eissa up at the rail, peering down the track. She turned to him after a moment and gave him a discreet thumbs-up. A moment later the train glided silently into view, a faint vibration in the concrete the only giveaway that it was there.

Quentin stood and helped the elderly couple to their feet. "Let's get you up here in the front of the line, so you can get a good seat."

"Thank you, young man. You're very kind." The woman took Quentin's arm, and they slowly made their way to the yellow square painted on the platform. The train was still unloading people at the other end, but the overhead display showed that loading would commence in three minutes.

Quentin glanced around. Bob was walking over to get in line, and Eissa was coming up from the other side. The train began to move to their end of the platform, and the security guards moved up from the unloading area and directed people to line up at each of the yellow squares. Eissa got in line for the second car. His gut tightened as the last security guard came up and stood directly in front of them and unclipped the gate chain as the train came to a stop. The elderly woman still clung to his arm, and he slowly helped her climb the steps onto the train.

"Make sure you've got all your belongings," the guard called out. "Please don't leave anything behind, especially your children."

A chuckle rippled through the crowd waiting to get on the train, and Quentin relaxed slightly. There were three seats on each side of the aisle, and he settled them into the front row. It would become the back seat once the train started moving. He settled into the window seat, staring nervously out over the loading platform. The car slowly filled up. He saw Eissa as she got on the second car, and a moment later

Bob climbed up the steps, briefly making eye contact with him as he made his way by.

At last, the door closed with a pneumatic hiss, and Quentin let out a deep breath. Maybe Holt hadn't recognized him. Maybe he had, but he hadn't placed him yet. He probably had a catalog of hundreds of people in his head that he was watching for. It was possible that Quentin had dodged a bullet on this one.

A chime sounded overhead, and the lights dimmed briefly. *Ladies and gentlemen, the tram will depart for Las Vegas in one minute. Please remain seated during acceleration.*

Movement on the platform caught his eye. Three security guards were running past the museum towards the train, led by Carl Holt. He was shouting into a radio as he ran, his face red. Quentin scrunched down in his seat, willing the train to move.

"I wonder what's going on," Herbert said, pointing out the window. "It looks like they're after someone."

Quentin tried to remember if he had been able to see inside the train from the outside. Were the windows tinted? Mirrored? It seemed like something he would be able to recall, but as Holt raced up to the train, he had no idea if Holt would be able to see him or not. Holt jammed the radio onto his belt and cupped his hands around his eyes as he leaned up against the window.

He was three rows down from Quentin. He looked the other way first, then swept his eyes over the car. They came to rest on Quentin, and Holt slid down the car until he was directly in front of Quentin. He pointed his finger at Quentin, jabbing the window, then pointed at the platform. His mouth was moving, and while they couldn't hear him, he obviously wanted Quentin to get off the train.

The elderly couple turned to look at Quentin. "It looks like he wants to talk to you," Herbert said. "I wonder why?"

Quentin's mouth was dry, and he was dizzy from the overdose of adrenaline pumping through his body. He tried to think of something to say to them, some benign explanation, but all he could think about was what was going to happen when the train door opened, and Holt came on and dragged him out. Bob had told him to just go along with it, but what if Holt didn't take him back to the security building? For all he knew, Holt might take him straight to a DimGate, cross to another dimension, and just kill him as soon as they were out of sight. His bloody body would just be the latest photo in a large file on Zimmerman's computer back at IBZ.

Holt pounded on the window with his fist, then ripped the radio off his belt and began shouting into it again. A moment later, the train began to move smoothly out of the station. Holt ran beside the car, still pounding on the window, but fell behind as the train picked up speed. As they left the station behind, Holt turned and ran back the other way. Within moments, they were hurtling across the desert, the spaceport dwindling in the distance.

Quentin finally turned away from the window. Everyone in the train car was staring at him. He had to say something to calm them down, or they would think the worst. The last thing he needed was for them to form a vigilante justice mob and turn him over to security at the other end. Now that Holt wasn't on the other side of the window, he could think again. He stood up and faced the crowd, bracing himself against the accelerating train.

"Folks, I'm sorry about that. There was an incident in the museum, and an elderly woman tripped over a little kid. I was able to catch her, so she's fine, but my elbow hit a display case and cracked the glass, and that set off an alarm. I didn't want them to think I was trying to steal anything, but I've heard stories about the security out here, and I panicked and left. I just wanted to get home." He looked around and shrugged. "I just didn't want you all to think I was a bad person."

A few people chuckled, and they visibly relaxed.

"Hell, I would have run, too," Bob said, from the other end of the car.

A few heads nodded, and the hubbub of conversation began to fill the air. Quentin sank back down into his seat in relief and cast a furtive glance and Herbert and his wife. She reached over and patted his knee.

"It sounds like you were being a gentleman. Those security bulls just like having someone to bully, that's all."

Quentin grinned. "Yeah, I think they do. That guy looked really upset. I'm glad he didn't drag me out and beat me up."

Herbert chuckled darkly. "He looked like the kind of guy that would kick you while you were down."

Quentin's hands were shaking, and he forced himself to relax, straightening his fingers. He leaned his head back and tried to focus on something positive. *What did you learn from this experience?* For one thing, he learned that DimCorp was either running a spaceport, or had a big hand in it. There was also the fact that Holt hadn't been able to stop the automated train. That was good to know. There might be a platoon of soldiers waiting for him at the other end, but for now, he was safe.

His heart finally slowed to a normal rhythm, but his stomach was still churning. Holt definitely knew who he was, and where he was, and it wasn't likely that Holt was going to just drop it. That meant Dimension 443 was no longer a safe zone, or more accurately, that it had never been a safe zone. Vegas was a big city though, and there was a reasonable amount of security in that. Holt probably didn't spend much time in Vegas when he was here, so the odds of running into him on the street were low. Still, they were going to have to be much more cautious with their movements in this dimension.

Bob's hand on his shoulder startled him, and he stifled a scream as Bob squatted down beside him.

"Jesus, Bob, you scared the crap out of me."

Bob gestured out the window. "Well, that scares the crap out of me."

Quentin followed his pointing finger. Three black vehicles with flashing blue lights in the grills were racing down the highway, slowly gaining on the train. They had to be traveling over a hundred and fifty miles an hour as they passed a transport truck like it was standing still. A greasy ball of dread formed in his stomach.

"That's bad."

Bob nodded. "There's an emergency exit on the other side of the train, away from the road. I think you could jump out when the train slows down and head into town on foot."

Quentin turned and looked behind him. A few rows away there was a big red sticker on the window, and a red handle on each side of it. If he used it, it would mean jumping out the window of a moving train. It didn't sound very appealing, but the alternative was much worse.

"Okay, so assuming I don't break my neck, how do I get back? There's only one credit card."

"There's a neighborhood right beside the station. We'll get a cab and cruise through there. Flag us down when you see us. If you have to keep going, stay in a straight line parallel with the main highway and we'll find you. That's the best we can do."

Quentin nodded dumbly. This day was not going according to plan at all, and he was totally unprepared for this turn of events. He wasn't wearing his bulletproof vest or his micro-movers, since they were supposed to be having fun in a safe place. The black vehicles were even with the train now. They couldn't be far from Vegas.

The chime sounded overhead. *Please brace for deceleration, and collect any loose items. Restrain small children and strollers until the tram is at a complete stop.*

"We have to move," Bob said. "It's now or never."

Quentin stood up and followed him back to the emergency exit. "Folks, I'm sorry to do this, but I need to get out that window."

The man in the aisle seat stood up. "Hey man, no problem. We'll block the view so the fuzz can't see what's happening." The two men with him stood up and moved into the aisle. They grabbed the overhead rail as the train slowed rapidly, and caught Bob as he crashed into them.

"Thanks guys, I owe you." Quentin slid into the seat and grasped the handles on the sides of the window. With a sharp yank, the window came loose and tore out of his hands in the rushing wind and disappeared. He stood up on the seat and poked his head out the window.

The train was approaching the edge of town, and the rocky track bed was giving way to concrete. He gripped the side of the window frame and turned around, putting one foot up onto the sill and then the other. He crouched, gripping the sides of the window frame for balance as the train continued to slow. He wiped his sweaty hands on his pants one at a time, and with a final nod to Bob, he hopped his feet out the window and dropped his hands to the bottom of the window. His knees bashed painfully into the side of the train, his fingers protesting as he hung from the window. To his right, he could see a patch of grass approaching, bordered by a wall with a neighborhood on the other side.

"That's it," Bob shouted out the window. "Go, go, go!"

Quentin pulled his feet up and braced them on the side of the train, and just as they reached the grass, he shoved himself off the side of the car. He hit the ground hard, tumbling head over heels. Momentum carried him back up to his feet, and he ran forward a few steps, trying to regain his balance before falling and rolling again. He came to a stop and did a quick damage assessment.

Nothing seemed to be broken as he moved his limbs experimentally, but the wind was knocked out of him. He lay still for a moment until he could breathe again. He could hear sirens now that he was outside the train, and panic shot through him. He struggled to his feet and glanced around. The train station was still a mile away, too far to see what was going on. Soon, the train blocked his view as it slid into the distance, and he turned back to find an escape from the wide-open monorail track.

On the other side of the track, the open desert stretched into the distance, with only the highway to break it up. That was definitely not an option, as he would be visible to anyone who happened to glance in that direction. He turned to the wall between him and the neighborhood. It was about eight feet tall, and there was no gate in sight. There was a small tree, though, and he jogged over to it. The lower branches were thick enough to support him, and he quickly climbed up and grabbed the top of the wall. On the third try, he was able to swing his leg up and catch the edge, and he scrambled over the top and down the wall, dropping gracelessly to the ground on the other side.

Rather than someone's yard, he was relieved to find himself in a small, deserted park. Empty swings and jungle gyms sat idly in the hot, dry stillness. At least he didn't have to worry about someone reporting him to the police. He headed for the gate on the far side, determined to put as much distance between himself and the train track as possible before Holt and his team showed up looking for him.

His knees were sore from slamming into the side of the train when he hopped out the window, and everything else was sore from hitting the ground at thirty miles an hour. He reached the sidewalk on the other side of the park and hobbled across the street. The neighborhood wasn't run down, but it was aging. Its residents probably worked the casinos or at the hospital, making enough money to avoid living in the apartment buildings that covered the city, but not enough to run the sprinklers and keep the grass green all summer.

Quentin trudged down the sidewalk, trying to assess each house as a defensive position as he walked by. They were mostly single-story brick homes, with a low wall separating the back yards. If he had to get off the street in a hurry, he might be able to hide behind a bush in front of some of the houses, but that would leave him with no place to go if he was spotted. His best bet was to get into the back yard and pray they didn't have a pack of dogs waiting there to eat him. Hopefully it wouldn't come to that, as the possibility of someone calling the cops and reporting a burglar would become a problem. It didn't seem like Holt would get the local police involved in trying to find him, but a little old lady watching him through the curtains certainly might.

There was only one house left before he reached an intersection, and he slowed down. If this had been Florida, he probably would have had a yard full of trees and bushes to hide behind and check the crossroad for the black vehicles. Instead, there was a vast expanse of open space between the house and the street. The only thing taller than the dead grass was the stop sign. There was no safe way to scope out the road to see if it was clear. He crept forward, craning his neck to see past the house on the other side of the street. So far, so good. He took another few steps, pausing to glance behind him. The streets were deserted.

It seemed like hours since he had jumped out of the train, but he knew it had probably only been ten minutes or so. Holt and his team would have searched the train by now and determined he went out the window, so it was safe to assume they were descending on this neighborhood, or would be in the next few minutes. There was nowhere else that he could have gone, and they would know that. He just had to hope that Bob could get a cab that he could cruise around in without giving it a specific destination.

With one last look over his shoulder, Quentin jogged across the street. Now that the adrenaline rush was wearing off, the bruises and scrapes from hitting the ground and climbing the wall were starting to make themselves known. He checked both directions as he ran, hoping for a flash of a yellow cab, but there was nothing in sight. To his right, the street ended in a cul-de-sac a few houses down. To his left, it went up two blocks and turned to the right. He had no idea how big the subdivision was, or which road was the artery into it from the highway. He reached the other side and continued to jog. Maybe Holt would go to the wall by the tracks, hoping to catch him hiding in place there. The park was falling into the distance behind him, but not fast enough. He stepped up his pace.

He slowed to a walk again as he approached the next cross street. This house had a low decorative wall all the way around, and a variety of plants and cactus in the gravel yard. He could hear something coming down the cross street to his left, and he jumped over the brick wall and dropped flat to his stomach, praying there was no one home. He crawled forward through the gravel, the rocks biting his hands and knees, until he could see out the gate at the walkway. Two black SUVs were stopped at the intersection. He jerked back from the gate and pressed himself up against the wall, his heart pounding. If they turned, he was good, but if they went straight, and happened to glance into the yard, they would see him lying by the wall, clear as day. *Hold it together, Q. Think, don't panic. Make a plan.*

He could hear one of the vehicles turn and slowly cruise past him. He held his breath, staring at the house through the branches of the giant prickly pear cactus in front of him. He could just make out the reflection of the SUV in the bay window as it passed. The windows were down, and he could see faces staring out from the front and back seats. If one of them looked in the same window he was looking at, would they see him in the reflection? The SUV kept moving and disappeared from sight. He rolled back onto his stomach and craned his neck forward, trying to see out the gate without exposing himself. He inched closer, cursing the noise of the gravel as he scraped across it. Who ever thought gravel yards were a good idea?

The second SUV was turning left, and he watched as it moved up the street in the same direction he had been going. Now he knew where two of them were, but there was a third vehicle unaccounted for. It was possible that it was outside the subdivision, patrolling the highway, or perhaps out by the monorail track watching for him. It was decision time. Stay here, or try to get out of the neighborhood?

He rose to his hands and knees and cautiously peered over the wall. The first vehicle was nearing the park, two blocks away. The second one was at the next intersection up, and he watched as it turned right and out of sight. He glanced back just in time to see the first one turn left. They were flanking the blocks, which gave him an opening to move. He got to his feet and shuffled to the corner, staying hunched over behind the wall. He crouched down behind the column at the corner and checked the street in all four directions. It was clear, and he hopped over the wall and raced across the street that he had been walking down.

The cross street was wider than the others, so it was probably the main road that came in off the highway. He decided to get closer to the highway, since Holt was working his way to the back of the neighborhood. He felt horribly exposed running down the sidewalk, but there wasn't a better option available. The dry desert air burned his nose as he ran, a new and unexpected discomfort. He crossed another street, holding a fast jog, and came up to an elderly woman out walking a tiny dog. He paused, running in place, trying to look like he was just out for a run.

"Looks like a manhunt going on," he said, nodding his

head up the street. "I saw a bunch of black SUV's cruising around looking for someone. You might want to go inside where it's safe."

"Oh, my," the woman said. She tugged on the leash, and the dog looked up at her. "Thank you! We don't want any trouble with anyone, do we, Princess?"

"Me, either," Quentin said. "I'm headed home as fast as I can get there." He flashed her a smile and took off down the sidewalk. Hopefully she would be out of sight by the time Holt and his crew came back, as they would be sure to stop and ask her if she'd seen a tall man go running by.

As he crossed the next street, a yellow car turned the corner a few blocks ahead of him. It was headed away from him, and he jumped in the air, waving frantically. He couldn't be sure that it was even a cab, much less the one with Bob, Tocho, and Eissa in it, but he wasn't about to take a chance on missing them. He sprinted forward as the car came to a stop. The door opened and Eissa stepped out, gesturing frantically to him.

"Run!"

Quentin raced towards her, pumping his fists to gain every bit of speed he had. If a person were driving the cab instead of a computer, it could back up and keep him from having to run so far. He shook the thought off and focused on running. Their exercise program on the island included a lot of jogging, but sprinting was making an entirely different set of demands on his body. The cab was still half a block away when he heard squealing tires and the roar of an engine behind him. He surged forward, ignoring the stitch forming in his side. He ran harder than he ever had before, and a horn honked behind him, making his heart miss a beat. The cab was five steps away, then three, and finally one. He dove into the car, gasping for breath. Eissa slid in behind him, slamming the door.

"Hello, taxi, Diablo Tower, please." Bob grinned at Quentin from the back seat. "Nice of you to join us."

Quentin looked over Bob's shoulder out the back window. The black SUV was still a few blocks behind them, but it was closing the gap. His chest burned, his lungs protesting the unreasonable demands he put on them with his sprint. He wiped the sweat off his forehead with a sleeve and glanced over his shoulder.

"It's good to be here, assuming this motherfucker can fly. We're about to get–"

Bob raised his hand. "Think before you speak. Remember, words matter, especially here." The taxi turned the corner onto the highway, and a moment later it left the ground, accelerating up into the lanes of flying cars above. Bob grinned as the black SUV fell away behind them. "How about that?" His eyes twinkled below his bushy white eyebrows. "Pretty good timing, eh?"

Quentin managed a smile as he collapsed into the seat. "I'll take it. And I'm never leaving the island again, assuming we get there in one piece."

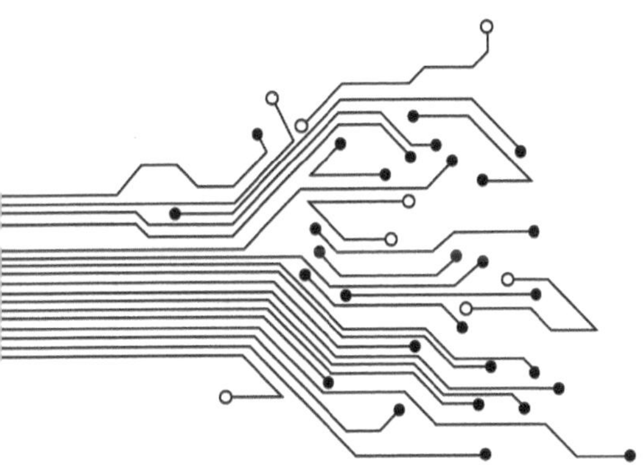

CHAPTER 4

Carl Holt was livid. He stared out the window as the empty desert rolled by. The only sound in the vehicle was the rush of cold air from the vents. There was no one to blame but himself. No one in this dimension had any idea who Quentin James was. They couldn't be expected to read his mind.

The ten minutes he had spent trying to put a name with the face was where he'd lost him. Instead of going inside the office to finish the meeting with Young, he should have gotten everyone right back in the vehicle and pursued the tour bus. He had just looked at James's file before coming over here, so there was no excuse for the delay. It was just so unexpected. Why would James pop up here, of all places?

They could have had him at the train, though, which would have made his delayed identification a moot point. James sat on the monorail and stared at him through the window, and the fact that no one could get the doors open or stop it from leaving was unacceptable. That was going to change.

"Captain Young." Holt flipped the sun visor down so he could see Young in the mirror.

"Yes, sir."

"After Action Review. When someone calls your office and says they need to stop that train and open the doors, what is the protocol?"

"The desk sergeant confirms the identity and authority of the caller, then calls the monorail control center. They do a password authentication, then engage the safety shutdown."

Holt nodded. "How long should that take?"

"No more than a minute on the communication part, sir." Young returned his gaze confidently. "If I may speak candidly, I'll tell you what I think happened."

Holt flipped his hand up from the center console, waving it in a circle. "By all means, please explain to me how our fugitive sat on a train and calmly rode away, and nothing happened."

Captain Young cleared his throat. "First off, there were four security personnel on the platform responding to orders to get the train stopped. That means multiple people trying to talk on the radio at once. We lost some valuable time there."

I did that, Holt realized. *Goddammit, how did I fail at basic situational management? I wrote the book on this stuff.* "Alright, go on."

"The train was probably already moving before Security ever established contact with the MCC. The rest of it is just the monorail system. Once it gets going, you can't just stop it right away. It's all computer sequences, and it has to do things in order. You can't stop it during acceleration, and you can't stop it during deceleration, which only leaves a six-minute window out in the middle of the run."

Holt drummed his fingers on the armrest. He wanted to tell Young to get a shutdown button installed at the security desk, but it wasn't realistic. He was just trying to find ways to shift the blame away from himself, and that was bullshit. Leadership was about owning your mistakes.

"Alright, I screwed the pooch on this one. I should have told one person to make the call. What else could we have done differently?"

The driver and the other rear passenger remained silent, but Young spoke up again. "This all went down in about five minutes, if you take out the drive to Vegas. I think we did everything we reasonably could on that part. The only thing we could have done in Vegas would be to involve local law enforcement, but we don't even have a picture of this guy to give them."

Holt nodded. Getting the LEOs enough information to go on would require a call to his secretary, and there were only two phones in the spaceport that he could use to do that. By the time she could email the file through, James would've had time to get to Canada.

The driver spoke up. "Do you think he's part of the copper theft?"

"It doesn't make any sense if he is," Young said. "Why would he be on a tour bus?"

"Yeah, I don't see it," Holt agreed. "The only reason he'd be on a tour bus is if he's scoping out the place for the first time. We need to put the entire spaceport on high alert. When we get back, I want to look over the camera footage and see who else was with him. I don't know what in the hell he was doing here, but he's obviously up to something. I want to know what."

●———○

Carl Holt and Captain Young stood behind the video technician, staring at a row of monitors. On the left screen, the tech had isolated a loop of Quentin James exiting the monorail, followed by the mysterious woman and two unknown males.

"Freeze the frame," Holt shouted. He peered closely at the screen. He didn't recognize the dark-haired man, but the one with the white hair was almost certainly Spartacus. "Fuck!"

He jammed his fists against his legs, overriding the urge to punch something. Spartacus was the name they had assigned to The Terrorist, lacking any other means of identification. He was an incredibly elusive fugitive, wanted for inciting riots and revolts in the workforce in at least ten different dimensions. He had popped up in a variety of places over the years, but most of them didn't have cameras, so all they'd had to go on were vague physical descriptions and a few low-quality images. A couple of DimCorp Security field units had even arrested him a few times in more recent years, so they had better pictures of him now, but he always managed to get away before anyone realized who he was. To find out that he had been right there in front of Holt, and he hadn't even known it, was maddening.

He composed himself, stifling his rage. There was nothing to be done about that now, other than to play the tape and gather intelligence. He gritted his teeth and indicated for the tech to play the video.

The four of them appeared to be together as they walked toward the museum, but it was possible that the unknown male was unaffiliated. He was clearly talking to Spartacus, but that didn't necessarily mean anything. James and the woman were heavily involved in discussion, though, and she elbowed him in the ribs as they passed the camera. James was smiling.

The next screen showed them entering the museum. They stayed together for the first three exhibits, all of them talking and pointing at things. After that, James and the woman paired up, and Spartacus and the dark-haired man split off to a different display. The four of them were almost certainly together.

"Try to get a decent face shot of this guy," Holt said, tapping the screen with a pen. The dark-haired man looked old, but if he was with Spartacus, he was probably worth looking into. "I'll take it back to the Genesis Dimension and run it through the system and see if we know who he is."

"Yes, sir."

The tech put up a video on the third screen, showing the loading area for the monorail. This was after Holt had seen James on the bus, but before they had arrived to try to catch him. James was sitting on a bench next to an elderly couple, and they appeared to be talking. Spartacus walked by in the background, ignoring James, and disappeared offscreen.

"What other cameras do we have of this area?" Holt asked. "Can we see the whole platform at the same time?"

The tech pointed to a projector screen on the wall. "We've got four cameras on the platform. I'll bring it up over there so it's big enough to see."

Holt waited impatiently as the screen lit up and the videos loaded. The top left showed the tour bus unloading. He watched as people filed off the bus. The image was a bit grainy, mostly due to the contrast between the areas of sunshine and shade, but when Quentin James finally appeared, Holt had no trouble identifying him. The dark-haired woman was right behind him. "Pause that," he snapped. The frames froze as a security guard was leading the man in front of James away. "The woman behind him on the top left, try to get a good still shot of her, as well."

The tech nodded, making a note.

"Okay, roll it."

James walked out of view on the top screen just as Spartacus appeared at the bus door. There was a gap in video coverage as they moved from the tour bus platform over to the monorail platform. James appeared first, with the dark-haired woman trailing behind and off to his left. He sat down next to the older couple, and she continued on to a bench a few yards away. A moment later, Spartacus showed up, with the unknown man walking a few paces behind him, talking to a young woman pushing a stroller.

They were trying to make it look like they weren't together now, but when they arrived, they hadn't been worried about it. That was interesting. They weren't trying to disguise their identity, and they weren't worried about the cameras. Not until they had run into Holt. Up until that point, they either thought they were anonymous, or they didn't know where they were, and that seemed unlikely.

"Do you know who the woman is?" Captain Young asked.

Holt shook his head. "We don't have an ID. She might be a DimCorp operative. On our previous contact with her, she had papers from someone at the top giving her clearance."

Young glanced at him, and Holt could sense the questions in his eyes. He took a deep breath and let it out slowly.

"I'm 99% sure the older male with the white hair is Spartacus. We don't know his name. We have his fingerprints, but he's not listed in a database anywhere. He's known to have been involved with ten different worker uprisings over the last twenty years, suspected at a whole lot more, and we think he might be the one that blew up the DimGate Control Center in the Genesis Dimension."

"Really?" Young's eyes grew round. "Damn. That makes this even more confusing. Why didn't we apprehend him at the monorail station in Vegas? I saw him in the crowd, but I didn't know who he was."

Holt closed his eyes for a moment before responding. "I didn't know he was there. I saw James on the bus, and then on the train. That was it. The first time I saw Spartacus was here, on the video."

Captain Young looked down. "I'm sorry, sir. I didn't mean to imply anything."

Holt reached over and patted Young on the back. "I'm not mad at you, Captain. I'm mad at myself. If I'd handled this properly from the start, we'd have them all in a cell right now."

Young nodded. "I understand."

"Alright." Holt clapped his hands twice, trying to banish the negative energy. "Let's get images of these four suspects to everyone. I don't think they'll try to come in through the front door again, so we need to crank up our border security. They may have a DimGate, so we need to be ready for anything. Make sure the facial recognition system has the best images we have of them to work with. If they pop up somewhere, I want to know within two minutes, understood?"

"Yes, sir." Captain Young clapped the video tech on the shoulder. "We have the best people in the business here. If they show up, they won't get away a second time."

Holt smiled grimly. "I hope not. Don't underestimate them though, they're surprisingly slippery." He glanced at his watch. "I've got to get back to the Genesis Dimension. I'll have my people over there working on ID's for the two unknowns. If anything happens, call me directly on the squawk. I'll have the Special Ops team on standby to assist."

He walked briskly down the hallway to the secure DimGate room. Quentin James and Spartacus presented a puzzle that didn't make any sense, and he was the kind of guy that wouldn't be able to leave it alone until he figured it out. Maybe Spartacus had recruited James, and the email thing was coincidental timing. Maybe the mysterious woman was a bounty hunter, trying to set up a sting operation that netted her several wanted posters at once. Maybe all three of them were in cahoots to blow up a spaceship, for some reason. Whatever it was, they would tell him all about it in a sound-proof room in the sub-basement of the security building. Of that much, he was certain.

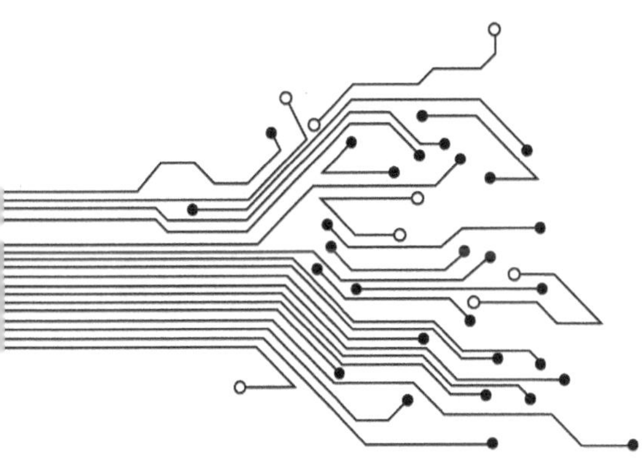

CHAPTER 5

Quentin and Eissa lounged in the shade under a huge dead tree, which lay on its side on the beach, a victim of erosion and saltwater. The return to Dimension 107 from the spaceport fiasco in Dimension 443 still hung on Quentin, despite the serenity of the empty ocean in front of them washing into the shore. He watched as a tiny crab popped out of the sand and scuttled out into the water.

"We need a way to get online," he said. "I want to do some homework on the spaceport."

Eissa was lying back on a towel, and she leaned up to look at him, propping herself up on her elbows. "What do you mean?"

"I mean that it sucks not having a computer. I like being able to Google something when I want to know more about it."

"This is the Universe trying to help you become less of a dork. Just embrace it."

Quentin picked a small shell out of the sand and threw it at her. "I'm being serious. We need a way to get on the internet."

"I don't think that's going to happen. Not here on the island, anyway. Maybe you should go to an internet café or something. I'm sure there's a place to do that in Vegas, assuming you're crazy enough to go back there."

Quentin shrugged. It wasn't as if DimCorp could deploy a bunch of guards to perform a manhunt in Vegas. They were powerful and had good connections, sure, but they still had to play the game in developed places. Vegas was just as safe, and just as dangerous as it always was. That wasn't to say he wouldn't be a nervous wreck the next time they crossed over. Emotion always trumps logic under stress.

"Now that you mention it," Eissa said, "I wouldn't mind getting on the internet in 443 myself. They're more culturally advanced. Maybe they've got better online dating options for lesbians than we do in 165." She pushed herself up to a seated position, crossing her legs and brushing the sand off her toes. "Why do you want to investigate the spaceport, anyway? What kind of ideas are cooking in that crackpot brain of yours?"

He doodled in the sand, drawing lines with his fingers as he avoided looking at her. "I don't know. Maybe I want a shot at Holt. I never really got to thank him for fucking up my life."

Eissa laughed. "You had every opportunity to kick his ass yesterday, and you didn't do it."

His face turned scarlet. "I'm not talking about kicking his ass, I'm talking about putting him in jail."

Eissa reached over and squeezed his arm for a moment. "I'm sorry, that was a really shitty thing for me to say. I meant for it to be funny."

Quentin gave her a small smile and tried to shake off the hurt feelings. She wasn't trying to make him feel bad, and he knew that, but sometimes she still cut him deep when he wasn't expecting it.

"Okay, so how do we do this? What's your idea?" She spun on the towel to face him, a clear sign that she was extending the olive branch.

"I have no idea. That's why I want to do some research, see what all goes on at the spaceport. Maybe Holt spends a lot of time there, who knows? Even if you take him out of the equation, the fact that DimCorp is involved means someone is probably getting screwed."

Eissa nodded. "That's a fair assumption. So, do you want to go hit up an internet café?"

He hesitated. While that was one way of doing it, it wasn't a very secure way. It wouldn't be hard for DimCorp to watch the activity at an internet café, and there probably weren't very many of them in Vegas, a city where most people had their own computers. If DimCorp had a decent IT guy working on it, they would know in seconds if someone started snooping around, and Holt and his black SUVs would be out front before he knew it.

"No, I think it's too risky. We need an inside guy in Dimension 443, somebody who already has a computer and flies under the radar."

"Well, that's a problem, because we don't know anyone in 443."

Quentin smiled. "Actually, we do. He's a bit of an asshole, but I would almost guarantee that he falls into the category of 'my enemy's enemy', which makes him a friend."

Eissa stared at him, her brow furrowed. "Are you talking about the dude from Prepper's Paradise? What was his name, Jack? Jake?"

"Ding, ding, ding, we have a winner!" Quentin clapped his hands. "Jake. He's perfect, think about it. He's probably a borderline anarchist, so he's not going to call the cops on us, and if we explain who Carl Holt is, he'll probably volunteer to help us take him down, just to stick it to The Man. Also, he has access to a lot of useful stuff that might help us out. He's the perfect inside guy."

"Hhmmm, that's hard to argue with." She stood up, shaking the sand out of her towel as she folded it up. "We're losing the shade, let's head back to the cabin. So how does this work? Do we just go back to Prepper's Paradise and ask him if we can borrow his laptop?"

"Pretty much, unless you have a better idea. Maybe you can bake him some cookies, a little deal sweetener."

Eissa flipped him off, draped the towel over her shoulder, and began walking down the beach towards the trail to the cabin.

Quentin stood in front of the DimGate control panel and adjusted his shirt collar to hide the bulletproof vest underneath. Lessons learned hard were lessons learned best, and he had no intention of going anywhere unprepared, ever again. The micro-movers were strapped to his wrists, covering the pink scar tissue from the burns they had given him a few months before.

"Remind me when we get there to get the coordinates for a safe place nearby, so we don't have to keep going all the way across town."

Eissa nodded. "That's a good idea. We need to get a good GPS so we can start adding jump points to the list. It looks like we're going to need some new ones."

"Great idea." He pulled his notebook out and jotted it down on his shopping list. "I'm sure Jake has plenty of them." He finished setting the controls on the DimGate.

"I don't trust the map on this thing to be up-to-date, and it could put us inside a building that wasn't there five years ago."

"Exactly." She picked up her backpack and slung it over her shoulders. "Ready when you are."

Quentin activated the DimGate. A moment later it clicked, and he gave her a nod. "We're hot."

Eissa cracked the door open while Quentin waited with his hand on the emergency kill switch. The noise of the traffic in Vegas drifted through the opening, and Eissa peeked through the gap before sticking her head through to the other side. She leaned back and gave him a quick thumbs-up before crossing over. He closed the panel and followed her through.

The traffic flying past them was light, but the cool wind still whipped around, making them uncomfortable. Quentin pulled a fuse and closed the panel, and they hurried across to the airlift. The doors sealed off the wind, and Eissa rubbed her arms vigorously.

"Damn, why is it so cold? What month is it?"

Quentin thought for a moment, but before he could answer, the floor of the airlift fell out from beneath his feet. Caught by surprise, his arms flailed, clawing the air for something to hold on to. Eissa was holding the handrail, and he swung his arm out, trying to catch it. The micro-movers picked up his intentions, and he slammed into the clear wall face first, as his hands crunched into the rail. Stars spotted his vision for a moment. He shook his head and pulled himself upright just as the lift began to slow.

"I really gotta get the hang of these things, or they're going to kill me." He used his sleeve to wipe the drool and smudged faceprint off the window. "I hope nobody saw that from the outside."

Eissa shook with laughter, her face red and eyes watering. "Oh my God, that was the best thing I've ever seen!" Her breath came in gasps. "We've got to find a video of that. Fucking spectacular."

Quentin's face reddened, and he turned to the door. "Yeah, yeah. Have your fun."

Out on the sidewalk, Eissa walked over to the taxi stop and hit the button on the pole. Quentin glanced over the stream of people moving up and down the sidewalk. It was early yet, so the streets weren't as crowded as they would be later. There was no sign of Holt or his team. He didn't think there would be, but he had to check.

"Remember to watch what you say in the cab." He gestured to the yellow car dropping down from the row of traffic above them. "It's doubly important now. DimCorp might be able to monitor what local law enforcement is doing, for all we know. We've got to stay invisible."

Eissa opened the door to the cab and gestured for him to enter. "Look here, Mister Man. One of us gets into shit on a regular basis, which is you, and one of us gets you out of shit on a regular basis, which is me. Get in the car."

Quentin grinned sheepishly and climbed into the cab, pulling his credit card out and swiping it across the ceiling as he slid into the seat. "Hello, taxi. Prepper's Paradise, please."

The cab moved forward on the ground a few blocks until it reached a turn-around point in the street. Once it was pointed back the other direction, it rose smoothly into the air and merged into the traffic lanes overhead, continuing to rise until they were in the tenth row up. Quentin looked closely at the roof of the Diablo Tower as they passed by slightly above it. The DimGate was almost invisible, blending perfectly into the dirty concrete and tarred gravel. He wondered if anyone had ever noticed them coming and going from there, or if they were just as unnoticeable as the DimGate. Most people were probably too busy looking at their holo-links to pay any attention to passing buildings or people walking around on them. Still, it was an exposed location, and it wouldn't hurt to have another place to cross dimensions, somewhere a little more secluded.

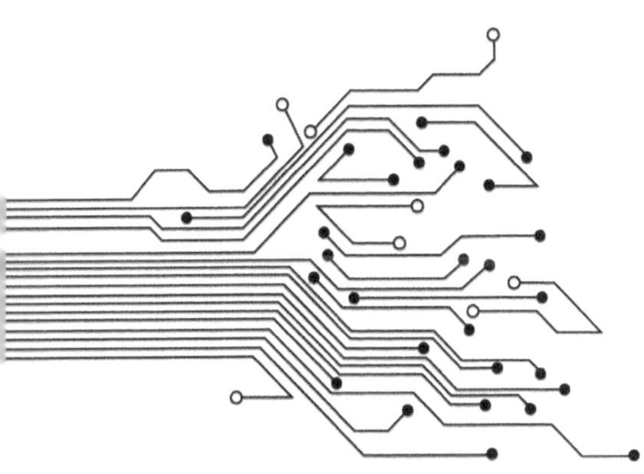

CHAPTER 6

Quentin pulled open the door at Prepper's Paradise and held it for Eissa as the chime dinged, announcing their arrival. The cool wind tried to rip it out of his hands, but he managed to get it closed without incident. A giant box of green canteens sat in the middle of the entryway with a sign on a pole sticking up from the center, announcing a clearance sale. They made their way past it and turned left down the main aisle, heading for the back of the store.

Jake was stocking pocketknives when they found him. He closed the display case as they walked up, a smile of recognition crossing his face.

"Hey, it's my micro-mover guy. How'd the vest work out for you?"

Quentin patted the front of his shirt. "I took two rounds in the chest and lived to tell about it, so I'd say it did pretty good."

Jake's eyebrows shot up. "No quix? Can I see the vest?"

Quentin shrugged, and unbuttoned his shirt. The slugs were still embedded in the mesh, two big silver splotches clearly visible against the white fibers.

Jake whistled, leaning in for a closer look before stepping back. "I bet that hurt like hell."

Quentin nodded, chuckling ruefully. "You can say that again. It took a month for the bruises to go away. No broken ribs, though. This thing is worth its weight in gold."

"You need to get a new one if you're going to keep wearing it. If you get shot again in the same spot, or even right next to it, it might go through. The rest of it's fine, but you don't want a compromised area right on your chest."

Quentin paused. He hadn't even considered that the vest might be weakened. "Alright, we'll add that to the list. I need to get a few other things too, and I wanted to talk to you, if you have a few minutes."

"Sure, come on over to the vest aisle. What's on your mind?"

Quentin fell in behind Jake as they walked around the corner. He had rehearsed several versions of this conversation in his head, but now they all sounded ridiculous. How do you explain to a relative stranger that you're not sure how the internet works in their dimension without sounding like a maniac? He abandoned his planned speeches and decided to wing it.

"I'll start by saying that this is going to sound cryptic and weird, and it's going to be complicated, but it will all make sense in the end, okay? But you'll have to bear with me, because it's really hard to explain."

Jake glanced back at him with one eyebrow raised. "And I'll start by saying if you're trying to recruit me to your church or your political group, I'm not interested. Just to save you some time and me some irritation." He stopped in front of a rack of vests and pulled one out. "You were a large, right?"

Quentin nodded. "Yep. And don't worry, this has nothing to do with religion or politics. Well, perhaps politics, but not in the way that you're concerned about."

"Okay, lay it on me." Jake put the new vest on the counter and turned to face him.

Quentin took a deep breath and blew it out. "Okay. Let's start with terminology so that we're communicating clearly. Do you have internet here? Do you know what that is?"

Jake's eyes narrowed. "Are you making fun of me, or do you just think I'm an idiot? What kind of an asshole question is that?"

"Slow down," Quentin said, raising his hands. "I'm asking because we're not from here, and I don't know if you call things by the same names as we do."

Jake shook his head. "Vegas might be different than most towns, but this is still America. We use the same language as everybody else, eat the same food, use the same internet. You must be from New York, thinking nobody outside the big city knows anything."

"It's not like that at all, quite the opposite. I need to use a computer and get on the internet, but I don't have any idea how that works here. I don't know what stuff is called. You probably have a lot of technology that I've never heard of. I'm hoping you might be a source of information, someone who can help me figure this out and find what I'm looking for."

"Why don't you just go buy a computer? You don't seem to have any money problems."

Quentin nodded. "That's a fair question. The answer is, even if I bought a computer, which I can do if we decide that's the way to go, I need help navigating it. When I say I'm not from here, I don't mean Vegas. I mean I'm not from this country. I speak the same language as you, but I don't know anything about how things work here."

Jake relaxed slightly. "You were right, this is weird and cryptic. Why are you asking me for help with this? I sell tasers and survival knives, man. You should go to an electronics store for this."

"We came to you because we made some guesses about the kind of guy you are based on our experience with you before, and what you do for a living. Your tattoos, the beard, the attitude, all that tells me that you're a guy who likes being out on the edge of society. Not an outlaw, per se, but someone who doesn't want someone else telling him what to do and how to live. Would you say that's a fair assessment?"

Jake grunted. "Sounds about right. Are you fugitives or something? Trying to fly under the radar?"

"You could say that, although we're not running from the law." He patted his chest. "There are people trying to kill us, obviously, but they work for a big company, not the military or the cops."

"Alright, you've piqued my curiosity," Jake said. "So, what is it you're trying to find on the internet?"

They were rapidly approaching the point when they were going to have to take Jake into their confidence, and once they did that, there was no going back. They would be vulnerable, at his mercy if he decided to report them to the police. Even ignoring the danger aspect, he was hesitant about sharing his newfound world of alternate dimensions with someone. It was probably ridiculous to be so possessive of it, but it felt like a secret world that only the four of them shared, and he was loathe to let anyone else know about it. The need for information and resources outweighed his desire to keep the DimGate to himself, but only just.

Quentin glanced around the store, but there was no one in sight. He leaned in slightly anyway, and lowered his voice, just to be on the safe side. "There's a company out at the spaceport called Dimension Resources. I'm trying to find out what I can about them. I'd also like to see a satellite view of the spaceport. Where we're from, we can use something called Google Maps on a computer to zoom in and look at satellite imagery of just about anywhere. Do you have something like that here?"

Jake's eyes lit up, and a smile tugged at the corners of his mouth. "You're fucking with DimRec? Is that who shot you?" He burst out laughing. "Quix, man, why didn't you lead with that? I used to work for those assholes, I know all about them." He shoved his hands in his pockets, grinning through his beard.

Quentin glanced at Eissa, then back at Jake, his mouth hanging open. "Seriously? You worked out there?"

Jake nodded. "Yeah, I was a guard for a while, couple years ago."

Quentin's mind was racing. This was an unexpected development, and he wasn't sure how to proceed. If Jake was sympathetic to DimRec, they were already in trouble. It didn't sound like he was, but they needed to be sure about where he stood.

"Our altercation wasn't there, it was at another site where they operate. I don't want you to think we're fighting with your friends."

"I don't have any friends at DimRec. If you were going to blow that place up, I'd light the fuse for you. It would be good riddance to a bunch of pricks, if you ask me."

"Well, I guess we're all on the same side of this." Quentin's shoulders sagged with relief. "That's a great start." He wiped his hands on his pants. "So, what do you think? Can you help us out?"

"Well, I can tell you that yes, we have SatelLife, which is a map of the whole planet." Jake walked around behind the counter and sat down on the stool by the register. He pulled a bottle of water from below the counter and took a slow drink, watching them with guarded eyes. "Now I know who you're after, but I don't know who you are. You don't sound like you're from another country. I've got some questions of my own before I commit to anything. First one is, are you cops? Do you work for the government?"

Quentin shook his head. "No, we don't work for anyone. We're independent."

"Huh," Jake grunted. "Last time you were here, you told me your boss had deep pockets, and you spent a lot of money on a whim. That doesn't add up."

"Like I said, it's complicated. I'm going out on a limb, here. I'm willing to let you in on a secret that will blow your mind, but before I do, I need to know that I can trust you. We're in a serious war against DimCorp, which is the parent company of DimRec and a whole lot of other companies. Whatever's going on out at the spaceport is just a tiny fraction of what they do. We need help, somebody like you who's local and can connect us to resources and information."

"So, what are you, some kind of vigilante justice group?"

Quentin paused. He hadn't thought about how to classify himself, and now that he was on the spot, there didn't seem to be a great way to paint it. They weren't part of an organized rebellion fighting against the Empire. They weren't victims of oppression revolting against the oppressor. They were barely even a group, at four people.

"I hate to say it, because it sounds like it isn't really anything, but yeah, I guess we're a small vigilante group."

"Where is your funding coming from?"

Quentin grinned. "DimCorp is funding us. They don't know it, but they're paying for us to take them apart piece by piece."

Jake thought for a moment. "Okay, what else have you done to them? What's something I would have heard about on the news?"

This was it. In order to convince Jake that they were legit, they were going to have to show him the DimGate. It wasn't as big of a risk now, as he was clearly not going to side with DimRec, but they were still going to blow his mind, and there was no guarantee that he could handle finding out about the existence of other dimensions.

"We haven't done anything in this dimension," Quentin said, glancing at Eissa. "In order to tell you what we've done, we have to show you the DimGate. It's going to screw up your head for a few days, but there's no other way for you to understand or believe me."

"What do you mean by 'this dimension'?" Jake asked. "Do you mean in this country? And what's a DimGate?"

Quentin shook his head. "This dimension of reality, this whole world, is just one of a lot of dimensions. We're from a different one, which is why we don't know that much about this one, but we speak the same language. I know it sounds ridiculous, so that's why we're going to show you our DimGate. It's the portal we use to travel between dimensions."

"Alright, I'm calling it quits," Jake said, standing up. "I heard you out, but you're obviously either crackpots, or you're putting me on."

"I get it," Quentin said. "Look, I need a good GPS, something that will be accurate within three feet, give or take a foot. I won't try to convince you of anything else until you see the DimGate, but I need the coordinates to bring it here."

Jake sighed. "I really ought to get back to work. I've got shit to do."

"This is work," Eissa said. "We're buying a GPS, the best one you've got."

Jake walked around the end of the counter and led them up the aisle. "Alright, I'll show you the GPS section, but I don't know what a foot is. Are you talking about your feet?"

It took Quentin a moment to understand what Jake was talking about. "It's a unit of measurement in our dimension. It's about a third of a meter. What's the metric equivalent? Decimeters? Three decimeters? Anyway, a meter of accuracy, is that possible?"

Jake paused in front of a glass case and stared at Quentin for a long moment. He shook his head and opened the case, pulling out a couple of boxes. "This is the top of the line GPS, accurate to a decimeter anywhere on the globe."

Quentin blushed. "Alright, that's pretty accurate. Way better than anything we have. How does it work?"

Jake opened the box, setting aside the instruction booklet and packing material. He installed the batteries and turned it on, handing it to Quentin. "It's really easy. The top readout is your current location. Press the blue button to save it. You can store a couple thousand waypoints. The menu button will bring them up, and you can label each one."

"Perfect. Let me pay for this and the new vest." He grabbed the instructions and tucked them in his pocket. Jake led them back to the counter and rang up the purchases. While he was running the card, Quentin switched vests. He was much faster at it now, and he had his shirt buttoned before the receipt printed. "We'll be back in half an hour. Is there a spot behind the store that's safe for us to use, something out of sight of people, traffic, cameras, that sort of thing?"

Jake handed the card back to Quentin and studied him. "You're serious about this quix. I can't figure you out, dude. You seem like a smart guy, and you look like you ought to work in an office somewhere, not running an underground movement to take down some big company." He rubbed his face with his fingertips, massaging his temples briefly before dropping his hands with a deep sigh. "Alright, come on. I don't know why I'm even entertaining you on this. I must be losing my grip."

He led them to the back aisle and through a door into a large storage room filled with pallets and cardboard boxes. They turned a corner and went down a short hallway, and Jake used his key to open a door leading outside. He put a small block of wood in the doorway to keep it from latching behind them.

"There's a dead spot behind the dumpsters. Some of the guys use it as a place to smoke cigarettes while they're taking out the trash at the end of the day, so they don't get caught smoking on camera when it ain't break time." He walked around the corner and pointed. "That's about the best I can do."

Quentin walked around the dumpsters. There was an open space between them and the back of the building about fifteen feet deep. A stack of pallets sat on one end, blocking them from view of the loading dock. He moved to the center of the space, held up the GPS, and pushed the blue button.

"This will work. We have to run across town. Can you make sure there's no one back here thirty minutes from now?"

Jake nodded. "I'll be out here. What am I watching for? Lightning bolts, smoke, that sort of stuff?"

"Nothing so dramatic," Quentin said with a grin. "Just a big door suddenly appearing out of nowhere." He turned to face Jake squarely. "Once you see this, you can't unsee it. There's no going back to what you used to know about the world. Are you okay with that?"

Jake shrugged. "I'll be fine."

"Famous last words," Eissa said. "It took me a month to come to terms with it."

Quentin put the GPS in the cargo pocket of his pants and glanced at his watch. "Alright, see you in thirty minutes." He turned away and headed to the taxi stand at the front of the store. "Make sure you have a good hour to get your shit together afterwards," he called over his shoulder. "You won't be able to think very well right away."

"Yean, yeah," Jake said, giving them a little wave. "I hear you."

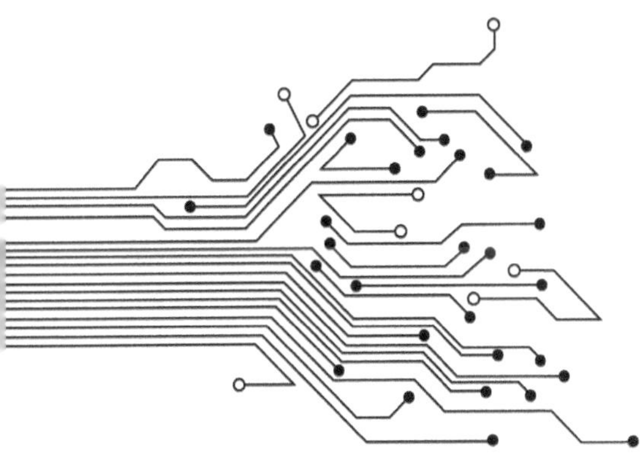

CHAPTER 7

Carl Holt read the email for the third time, trying to find some nuance, some little crumb of a clue that would help him connect the dots. Not even all the dots, connecting one dot to another dot would be a good start.

The email was from his contact in Dimension 165, a private detective who had put together the dossier on Quentin James. Holt had sent him the pictures of the mysterious woman James had with him when he snuck into IBZ and used the DimGate. It was definitely the same woman who had been at the spaceport in Dimension 443, and now he had a name to go with the face.

Name: Eissa Amor
Age: 41
Occupation: Unknown
Military veteran? Yes

There was enough information in the report to believe that it was her real identity, but it was also vague enough that it could be a very good fake. There was no work history aside from ten years in the military, she had one credit card and a shitty credit score, and no police record at all. Holt printed the report and tacked it on the bulletin board beside her picture. At least it was something.

He had a decent composite of Quentin James, since James was an IBZ employee. He also had James's laptop, which told them a fair bit about him. They had his resume, his driver's license, his emergency contacts, his discipline records… Holt smiled as his eyes drifted past that line item. What he didn't have was a known connection between James and Eissa Amor, other than they lived in the same town in the same dimension. James had never been in the military, so that possibility was out, and Amor had never worked at IBZ. Maybe they were dating?

He hadn't pushed the initial investigation on James very hard, as there were a lot of other things happening at the time that were much more critical. It was possible that the investigator assigned to him hadn't probed very deep. There was nothing in his file about social media activity, frequent purchases or activities, or any of that stuff. Now that he had surfaced with Spartacus, the situation was different, and he needed to know every detail about James they could find.

He punched the intercom button on his phone. "Sergeant Treijo, you awake out there?"

She responded immediately. "Yes, sir."

"Find out who the investigator was on James, Quentin 165. Tell them to reopen it, top priority. I want to know everything there is about James, and I want it ASAP."

"Yes, sir. Anything else?"

Holt thought for a moment. It was important to keep the big picture in mind. While he wanted to pull the Special Ops team in and have them standing by at the spaceport in 443, that would mean aborting the mission they were currently on and disrupting the schedule for the next few missions that were already lined up. He couldn't justify that at this point, with no evidence other than four people riding a tour bus. The security team at the spaceport would have to do the job themselves.

"No, that's it for now." He glanced at his watch. "When's the last time I ate?"

"If you have to ask, it's been too long. Do you want me to order you something?"

"Yeah, if you would. Gotta feed the machine if we're going to keep this circus performing."

He walked back over to the bulletin board and stared at the pictures of James, Amor, and Spartacus. What brought them together? Why were they touring the spaceport in 443? Where had James and Amor been for the last four months? Who was Eissa Amor, and was it safe to neutralize her? So many questions, so few answers.

Holt stood behind his desk with the phone in one hand, talking to Captain Mathers, his Special Ops commander. He rotated a pencil between his fingers on the other hand, a nervous tic he'd had since he was a kid. His stomach rumbled, reminding him that lunch had been hours ago. Setting the pencil down for a moment, he bent over the desk and refreshed his email inbox.

"It's not here yet. Just give me a synopsis of the situation, I don't have time to wait on it."

The voice on the other end was delayed several seconds. Interdimensional cellphone calls were tough because of the lag and the static, but they were a hell of a lot better than the old days when there was no way to communicate at all. The wired systems between offices worked just fine, but patching cell systems together between different dimensions for field agents was a whole different beast.

"Anderson found the recon team. They're holed up in a cave, and the locals have them under siege. He used his drone to fly them in a fresh battery for the radio, so they've got comms. Three dead, three wounded, one fit to fight. We'd need the wet team to get them out, and maybe more."

Holt rubbed his free hand over the stubble on his bald head, letting out a sigh. "What's the opposition size and tech?"

Static crackled on the line like distant lightning strikes. "Size unknown. The drone counted fifty on a single pass, so more than one hundred for sure. Could be a lot more. They shot arrows at the drone, so he didn't make a second pass, but there was no gunfire. Heavy foliage in the jungle, so visibility is low. If they had something explosive, they would have used it on the cave by now."

"Roger that. Stand by." Holt sat down at his desk and pulled up the up the unit allocation chart on his computer. The Special Ops team, or wet team, as the guys liked to call it, wasn't big enough to take on more than one hundred armed men in a jungle environment. This force could easily be that big if Anderson had counted fifty with the drone. He had a company of guards that had just rotated back from a diamond mine in Dimension 16. They weren't really trained for jungle warfare, but they could bolster the firepower for the wet team.

On the other hand, that was a lot of people to risk. There were only four men alive in that cave, and three of them were wounded. If he sent a company of regular troops with the Special Ops team, they were likely to lose more than four people in a direct engagement with an armed enemy. The statistics chart showed three dead and ten wounded for every hundred men deployed. One hundred and twenty troops plus the twenty on the wet team put them at risk of losing more than they would be saving, and that was assuming there weren't actually a thousand men waiting in the jungle.

Rescue missions were the worst part of decision-making in leadership. If he could give a speech to the graduating class of officers at the DimCorp Academy, he would give them this exact situation. *Alright, fearless leaders of tomorrow. Here's the information. Does anyone want to tell me what the fuck you do with that? Because, this is the stuff they don't teach you how to handle. They don't explain that you're the one who gets to decide which part of your team lives, and which part dies.*

Holt closed his eyes as he picked up the phone. "Mathers, tell Anderson to pack it up and come home."

The silence was worse than the static. He knew Mathers would never challenge his decision, but that didn't make him feel any better as he waited for confirmation. Abandoning his people made him feel like shit, no matter how logical the decision was. The second phone line began to ring, which meant that Sergeant Treijo was already gone for the day. At last, the static broke and the voice came through.

"Roger that, boss. Mathers out."

He punched the blinking red button on the phone. "Holt."

"It's Beck. I've got a connection between James and Amor."

He opened his eyes, trying to shift mental gears. "What've you got?" He picked up the coffee cup from amid the stacks of paper on his desk and took a sip. It was cold.

"I was able to use James's computer to access his cell-phone account. They have thousands of text messages to each other going back years, over twenty phone calls in the

Recently Dialed list. We've got a ton of activity as Facebook friends, which is social media in 165, just like MyPage here. They're best friends, from what I can see, and have been for at least ten years."

Holt grunted. "So, you're sure she's not working for us?"

Beck hesitated. "Well, if she is, she's using a false identity on one side or the other. I can't be positive, but I don't think she is."

"Alright. Send me a report with all the details. I'm still trying to connect them with Spartacus."

"Roger that."

Holt hung up the phone and leaned back, stretching his arms overhead. He wanted nothing more than to go home and take a long hot shower, and then sleep for a week. His dreams would be tormented by guilt over the recon team, though. They would follow along behind the long line of other people he'd killed over the years, whether directly or by his decisions. They didn't plague him as often these days, but every time a new name got added to the list, they all came out on parade. He grabbed his coffee cup and headed out to Treijo's office to make a fresh pot. If sleep wasn't an option, he might as well get some work done.

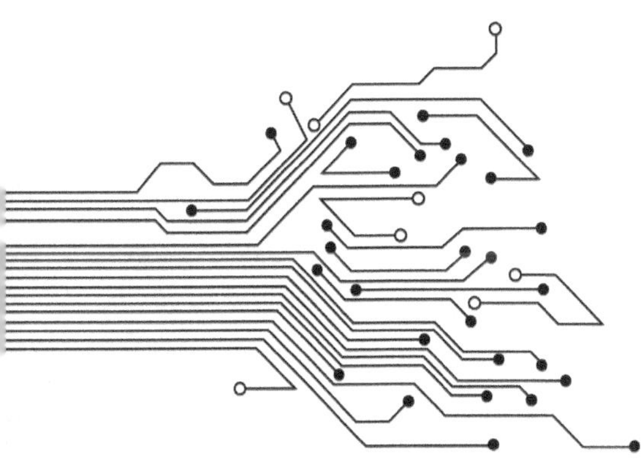

CHAPTER 8

When Quentin and Eissa got back to the Diablo Tower, the airlift shot them up to the roof. Quentin opened the panel and put the fuse back in place and powered up the DimGate. Eissa held the panel door steady to keep the wind from slamming it on him as he entered the destination information into the screen.

"It seems kind of silly that you can't move from one spot to another spot inside a dimension," Eissa said. "I can't believe they didn't come up with a way to do that."

Quentin activated the door and stepped back. "Well, if you think about it, the DimGate is opening up a portal between two different dimensions of space time. That's a completely different thing than teleporting within the same dimension. That's why they can do time travel, but not intra-dimensional travel. That's like asking a lightbulb to also dispense running water."

Eissa rolled her eyes and walked over in front of the door. "Whatever, Einstein. I assume you set it to go back to the island?"

"Yeah, it seemed like the way to do it. We'll jump to 107, and then back to 443 at Prepper's Paradise."

Eissa opened the door and peeked through. She waved her arm for him to follow as she stepped through, and he closed the panel and followed her. On the island side of the DimGate, a light rain was falling. Quentin pulled the GPS from his pocket as he opened the panel and hurried to input the coordinates.

"I'm all set. I hope he doesn't totally lose his mind."

Eissa smiled grimly. "Yeah, well, there's no way to prepare him for it, really. You did the best you could." She stepped in front of the door. "I hope that GPS is as good as he says it is. If we're inside the dumpster, I'm going to be pissed."

She moved slightly to the left of the frame and eased the door open a crack. Quentin kept his hand on the emergency kill switch and leaned over to watch as she opened the door wider. He could see the blue dumpster beyond Eissa's head, and a glowing beam of sunshine cut through the misty rain as it came through the door. She waved him on and disappeared through the gap. He quickly closed the panel and followed, leaving the door open so that Jake could see through to the island side.

Jake stood beside the dumpster, one hand holding onto it for support. The other hand raised to point at them for a moment but dropped limply back to his side as his mouth moved silently. Quentin chuckled.

"I tried to warn you, man. You're going to be brain-fried for a while. It's unavoidable." He opened the door up wide so Jake could see the jungle beyond. "You want to check out the island? Sorry about the rain, that happens a lot in the South Pacific."

Jake took a shaky step forward but seemed to think better of it and retreated to the safety of the dumpster, shaking his head. "It's… no, it can't be real. How can it be real?"

"It's a total mindfuck, man," Eissa said. She patted his arm, leaving a wet handprint on his skin. He stared at it, then back at the door.

"Come on over," Quentin said. "You don't have to cross over to that dimension, but you need to verify for yourself that it's not an illusion. Trust me, proof is good, because tonight when you're lying in bed, you're going to be trying to explain to yourself why it wasn't real, after all."

Jake slowly touched the water on his arm. "It's wet. You're wet."

He took a step forward, and Eissa grabbed his hand and held it tightly in her own. "I got you, buddy. Just take it easy. We're going to do this as a team. You'll be fine, it just takes some time."

They tiptoed to the DimGate. The rain was coming down a bit harder now, and some blew through the door, hissing as it turned to steam on the hot concrete. Jake sat down abruptly, still holding on to Eissa, and reached forward with his free hand and touched the wet dirt on the other side. He grabbed a few leaves and pulled them back through and stared at them wonderingly.

"That's a great idea," Quentin said. "Get yourself some evidence."

Jake sat in silence for a few minutes, sometimes looking through the door, sometimes at the dirt and leaves in his palm. At last he cleared his throat and let go of Eissa's hand. "I, uh…" He cleared his throat again. "I wasn't expecting this. I don't know what to say. Where is that?"

"Well, in our home dimension, which is a different one, we would call it Fiji, or the Marshall Islands, something like that. It's a deserted island somewhere out in the South Pacific. And that's Dimension 107. You live in Dimension 443." Steam was coming off Quentin's shirt, and he turned his back to the sun so it could dry. "Don't try to understand everything at once, it's too much. Just go with little pieces."

After a few more minutes of silence, Quentin shut the door and deactivated the DimGate. "Let's get you inside. You're going to need some time to let this gel." He reached down and grasped Jake's outstretched hand and pulled him to his feet. They walked slowly back around the corner, and Eissa opened the back door of the store and kicked the wood block inside.

"Is anyone going to come out here?" she asked. "I'm not sure we should leave the DimGate just sitting there."

"Nobody takes the trash out before closing time." Jake stopped inside the storeroom and licked his lips. "I don't think I can go back to work." He looked at each of them, his eyes questioning. "There's so many things I need to ask you, but I don't know where to start. Like before, when I asked you who you are? It's the same words, but the question is way bigger now, like, quix, man, who the hell are you people, you know?"

"We'll get through all of that, I promise. On the bright side, at least you've got us to help you through this. When we went through our first DimGate, we were all alone for the first day, with nobody to explain what was happening. That was a tough day." Quentin reached out and grabbed Jake's shoulder and squeezed it for a moment. "Let's go back up front. Familiar surroundings will help ground you. Besides, we've got some more shopping to do."

Jake nodded dumbly. "Okay, sure." He shuffled forward and led them back to the counter by the bulletproof vests. He took a seat on the tall stool behind the register. The store was still largely deserted, and Quentin's old vest still lay on the counter where he had left it.

"Okay, let me give you the two-minute version, and we can fill in the blanks later," Quentin said. "Sound fair?"

"Sure." Jake pulled his water bottle from beneath the counter and took a drink.

"Alright. The way I understand it, there are a lot of dimensions. They all share a history up to a certain point, but when something big happens that changes the course of the world, a new dimension is formed. For example, I assume Columbus discovered North America for the Europeans in this dimension, right?"

Jake nodded. "Yeah, in 1492, Columbus sailed the ocean blue."

"Well, that happened in our dimension, too. But in other dimensions, he didn't get a warm welcome. Instead, they killed him and his whole party, burned their ships, and pretty much changed the course of history for a lot of the world. In the first dimension we went to outside of our own, the Native Alliance controlled everything west of the Mississippi River. The US was tiny and primitive, didn't even have electricity. But that's just some dimensions. They're all different, depending on where they split off in history."

Jake shook his head. "How did you end up there? Where does this door come into things?"

"There's a company called DimCorp. They have these DimGates, or portals that they use to go to other dimensions. They enslave people and use them to work mines for resources, drill oil wells, clear-cut forests for lumber, grow crops, that kind of stuff. They take all that and sell it in other dimensions. They own lots of companies, such as DimRec, but they also own banks, oil companies, all kinds of things. And they're as unscrupulous and cruel as they get." Quentin paused, and took a breath. "I used to work for them as an IT tech, although I had no idea they did all that. I didn't know there was such thing as another dimension until we stumbled across a DimGate in the CEO's office. We were trying to get some evidence to take to the FBI about a murder, but we got caught, and we had to run through the DimGate to escape."

"So now you're trying to take them down? All alone?"

"Not completely alone," Eissa said. "We found a couple of old guys who've been fighting them for a long time, and they really saved our bacon. That's how we got a DimGate."

It seemed strange to be the subject-matter experts on alternate dimensions. It hadn't even been four months since the day Quentin found the pictures of Carl Holt and the pipeline protesters that he had shot, but they had come a long way in a short amount of time.

"So that brings us to DimRec, out at the spaceport." Quentin leaned forward, putting his elbows on the counter. "We saw a guy named Carl Holt out there the other day. He's the guy that killed some people in our dimension and got us started on this whole thing, initially. He's listed as the Director of Security for DimCorp, but he's also basically a hitman for them. He's bad news, and now he's popped up again, and we want to try to do something about him. That's why we need your help. We want to scope out the spaceport, see what we can figure out for a way to get him. The fact that you worked out there is a huge bonus that we weren't expecting."

"I think I get it," Jake said. "I only worked out there for about a year, though, and I never heard of Carl Holt."

Quentin pulled out his notebook and pen. "Well, let's start with what you know about that place. Any important details that might help us out."

Jake thought for a moment. "Well, first off, you ain't gonna just walk in there and look around. They take security serious."

"Are some places more secure than others? Where do they focus their attention?"

Jake reached under the counter and pulled out his holo-link and typed on the screen for a moment. He laid it on the counter, and a large 3D hologram map popped up. He manipulated the map in the air with his fingers, rotating it to the northwest and zooming in on the spaceport. When he was satisfied with the location, he shifted the view from overhead to just above ground level.

"That's awesome," Quentin said. "Way better than I'd hoped for!"

The spaceport was a huge complex. Quentin could tell from a glance at the map that while they had seen a lot of things on the tour, there was a lot that they didn't see. Jake zoomed in closer, raising the perspective a bit higher so they could see several buildings at once.

"These are the administrative offices over here, these four buildings. I never had to mess with them." He moved the map to the right. "That area is all vehicle assembly and repair stuff. That's super-secure. You can see the guard shacks all around the buildings here, see? Checkpoints everywhere."

"Jesus," Eissa muttered.

"Now these buildings over here are warehouses," Jake said, moving the map down. "That's where they store the metal they bring down from space before it ships out. They're guarded too, but not like the vehicle buildings. Well, except for this one." He pointed to a building in the middle of the warehouses. It was smaller than the other buildings, perhaps half their size.

"What's that?" Quentin asked.

Jake shrugged. "That's the mystery building." He pointed to a black line going from the road out front up to the building. "Nobody ever goes inside. This is a conveyor belt. The auto-forklifts bring pallets of metal ingots over here and put them on the conveyor. They go inside, forklift drives away. Pallets go in, nothing comes out. I think it must be an underground storage silo or something."

Quentin and Eissa glanced at one another, their eyebrows raised. "DimGate," they said in unison.

Jake looked at them quizzically. "DimGate?"

Quentin nodded, glancing around to make sure no customers had wandered up. Now that they were getting somewhere, it was easy to forget they were in a public place. "That's how DimCorp does it. That conveyor belt probably goes through a DimGate inside the building. There's some guy on a forklift in another dimension that unloads pallets of ingots coming out of a building that no one ever goes in."

Realization dawned on Jake's face, and his eyes lit up for a moment. "No shit… I can see how that would work. Well, except for the whole 'other dimension' thing. I can't really think about that part too much."

"Yep, that part takes a month or two to get used to," Quentin agreed. "But this changes things. I wonder where they're sending pallets of metal?"

Eissa shook her head. "There's no way to know."

"Unless we got on the conveyor belt and went through the DimGate." Quentin grinned as Eissa and Jake both spun to stare at him.

"Are you crazy?" Eissa shook her head. "He just got done telling us how this place is locked up tighter than Dick's hatband. Besides, what does it matter where it's going?"

Quentin stood up straight. "It's clearly a big deal to them, so that makes it a big deal to us. Maybe we can't get in there, but I think we should at least talk about it. This is what we do now, remember?"

They stood in silence for a moment. If Carl Holt was involved, then it was probably a significant operation for DimCorp. Sure, their operations at the spaceport seemed to be above board, at least in terms of their labor force, but it might be a very different situation on the other side of that DimGate. Quentin had no idea how they would get to it, though, or how they would get back to a safe location, assuming they made it through alive, and without being caught by DimCorp security.

"I think we should go talk to Bob and Tocho about it. They've probably got some ideas on how to approach something like this. After all, they operated for years without their own DimGate." Quentin glanced at Jake. "Can you get me the exact coordinates for that building?"

Jake switched back to a 2D overhead view, zoomed in on the map as close as it would go and clicked on a point near the place where the conveyor belt entered the building. "About there?"

"That should work."

Jake wrote down the coordinates and handed them to Quentin. "Are you going to open your DimGate there and try to run inside or something?"

Quentin shrugged. "I don't know. Right now, I'm just gathering all the information I can get. We'll go back and see what Bob and Tocho think. While we do that, you just chill out and try to get your head screwed back on straight. You need some time to stew on everything."

"You can say that again." Jake turned off the holo-link. "What should I do? It seems like the whole world is a lie, now."

"You just do what you always do. The world is the same as it's always been, there's just a lot more of it than you knew about before, that's all. Don't panic." Quentin started to turn away but paused. "One thing special you can work on, if you're up for it, is communication. If we're going to be a team, we need a way to get ahold of each other. Do you have disposable cell phones here, or something off the radar?"

"Yeah, that's easy."

"Okay, great. You work on that. We'll be back tomorrow to check on you." Quentin stuck out his hand. "And welcome aboard. Your life just got wild and exciting."

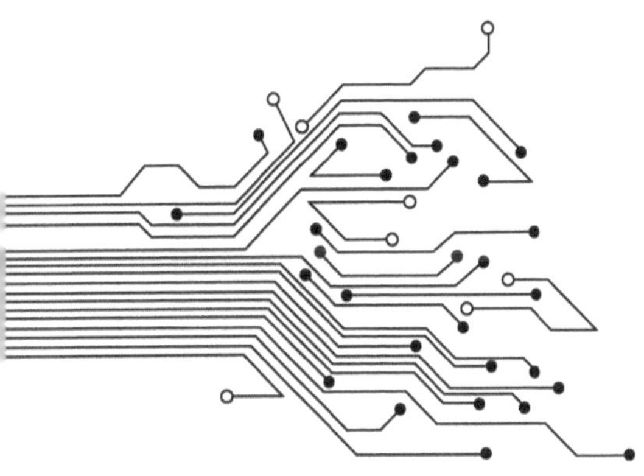

CHAPTER 9

Quentin leaned back in the new rocking chair and put his feet up on the rocking ottoman. The small porch was crowded with four rocking chairs, but they had all agreed that it was better than two of them sitting on the floor or carrying chairs back and forth from inside, as they had been doing. As usual, Bob was whittling on a stick as they mulled over the information Quentin had presented to them.

"It's just too risky to take the DimGate in there," Bob said at last, brushing the shavings off his lap. "We can't afford to risk losing it."

Quentin nodded. He had come to the same conclusion. Getting to the mystery building was easy, but they would either have to abandon the DimGate and go through the one in the building, which opened up a whole different set of challenges, or they had to try to see what was going on and get back through the DimGate before anyone got to them.

Eissa stopped rocking and leaned forward. "What if we took our DimGate to the spaceport, and as soon as me and Quentin run through and get on the conveyor belt, you guys close the DimGate and shut it down? Then we'd only be in 443 for a few seconds."

"Hhmmm," Quentin grunted. The idea had merit. "We're assuming the conveyor belt goes into an empty building in whatever dimension it's crossing over to. As long as that's the case, we could at least get there without anyone knowing, and then figure out what lies beyond and what to do."

"What if you go through the DimGate and it dumps you out on a factory floor in front of a guard with a machine gun?" Tocho asked. "That's happened to us more than once."

"Well, yeah, that would be bad." Quentin scratched his head. "But you guys made it. We could just turn around and run back through the DimGate, right?"

"To where?" Eissa asked. "The mystery building in the middle of the spaceport? Our DimGate will be long gone, Einstein. That's a one-way door as far as we're concerned."

Quentin's face turned red, more from the blatant oversight than the rebuke. "Yeah, fair point. I was thinking we could reprogram the DimGate on the other side, but that only works if we can do it without getting shot at. Going in blind suddenly doesn't seem like a great plan."

They sat in silence. A light breeze stirred the tree limbs at the edge of the woods, carrying the faint sound of waves crashing on the beach.

"I made a blind jump once," Bob said. "Well, I made a lot of blind jumps, but this one in particular stands out." He wiped the blade of his knife against his pants leg and folded it up. "Dimension 66. Similar situation, going back through wasn't an option. Most places I'd been, security wasn't very serious at the DimGate itself, it's usually further out. This one, though, they were waiting for me. Looking back, I think that whole thing was a trap. The second I went through the Gate, a team of DimCorp guards surrounded me. There wasn't anything I could do."

"What happened?" Eissa asked. "How did you get away?"

Bob chuckled wryly. "I didn't. Not then. They were all wearing these backpack rigs. One of them wrapped me up in a bear hug, and the next thing I know we're all in the security headquarters in the Genesis Dimension. Same place Quentin and I ended up a few months ago. I sat in there for a few days before Tocho managed to get me out."

"Wait a minute," Quentin said. "How did you get there? Did they take you through a DimGate straight inside the security building?"

Bob shook his head. "Nope. It was the backpacks. They're some kind of portable DimGate. When we got to the security building, they handcuffed me to a chair while they got them shut down and turned in to the armorer. I remember, because he was making a big deal about them clearing out the coordinates from their jump before they could turn them in."

Quentin's mind was churning through possibilities. Having a mobile DimGate like that would make an incursion like this much safer. If there was a security team waiting on the other side, all they would have to do is push the button and return to the island.

"How do we get one of those?" Quentin leaned forward, swinging his feet to the floor. "That's exactly what we need."

Bob glanced over at him, his bushy white eyebrows drawing together. "The point of the story was that I got caught the second I crossed over to that dimension, and I couldn't do anything about it."

"Right, I get that. But think about it. If we could get some of those backpack DimGates, we could travel way faster, and it would reduce the risk of getting caught to almost nothing. It's the perfect tool for the job."

Bob clearly wanted to argue; it was written all over his face. He continued to frown for a minute before leaning back in his chair, blowing air out his nose like an angry bull. "I'll concede that it would be a useful tool, but it's a pointless argument. There's no way to get one. It's a moot point."

Bob was right. If the backpack units were locked up in the arms room in the DimCorp security headquarters building in the Genesis Dimension, getting to them would be nearly impossible. Perhaps, if they knew the exact coordinates, they could open their DimGate up inside the arms room, but it would have to be an incredibly precise move. The only way they could get coordinates that precise would be to go there and take a reading with a GPS from that dimension, which wasn't a real possibility.

"I'm just brainstorming, so hear me out," Eissa said. "When we went to the Genesis Dimension before, we were posing as auditors, or inspectors. Nobody in the security department ever questioned that, right?"

Quentin snorted. "Sergeant Wilson questioned it, and took us to jail, if you'll recall."

"No, he wasn't questioning whether you were an auditor. You just didn't have credentials, and he thought you were auditing him on following the rules. That's why you went to jail."

He couldn't argue with her on that point. "Okay, so what? Are you suggesting that we go audit the arms room and steal a backpack unit while we're in there?" He couldn't help but laugh.

"That's exactly what I'm suggesting," Eissa shot back. "We get some badges made, we get the right clothes, we go in there like a couple of fucking bosses and tell them we're doing a surprise inspection on their arms room."

Quentin stopped laughing when he saw how serious she was. The idea sounded ludicrous, especially considering he had just been imprisoned there a few months before, even if it had only been for a few hours. "How would we get out of there with them? We might be able to bully our way in, but I don't see them letting us leave with any of their stuff."

Eissa rolled her eyes. "They're fucking DimGates, Quentin. Stay with me on this. We make them show us that they're in good working condition. They turn them on, we inspect them, program them to come here to the island, push the button, and *poof.* Bob's your uncle."

A new silence descended over the porch. Quentin glanced at Eissa. Bob and Tocho were staring at her, and she was grinning like an idiot. It was a pretty good idea, and no one was punching any holes in it. But still, there was no way they were walking back into DimCorp headquarters after so narrowly escaping there the last time. Were they?

"Just playing Devil's Advocate here," Quentin said slowly. "What happens if the armorer's not there, and they can't open the room?"

Eissa shrugged. "Then we go back to the DimGate room and come back here. Bob and Tocho can man the DimGate, in case we need to come back that way. And if something goes terribly wrong and we don't come back after an hour, they come looking for us. We'll get them badges made, too."

Quentin was impressed. Eissa was becoming quite the tactician all the sudden. The more he thought about it, the more the idea appealed to him. Perhaps they were going back to the Genesis Dimension, after all. No one seemed to be saying no. He leaned back in the rocking chair and put his feet up again. Excitement raced through his veins, riding on the undercurrent of fear that never quite seemed to go away. Somehow, they had managed to go from investigating

Carl Holt to breaking into the heart of the enemy. Again. It was becoming a recurring theme.

Quentin slid the list across the counter to Jake. "I'm guessing there's a website where you can order official-looking badges. Or there's probably a high-end costume place in Hollywood that can make stuff like this, right? Do they make the movies in Hollywood in this dimension?"

Jake looked at the list, then looked back up at Quentin with a twinkle in his eye. "Well, you could go to Hollywood, if you wanted to do it the hard way."

Quentin arched his left eyebrow. "Or..."

"Or, you could walk across the store with your trusted go-to guy and make them in about ten minutes."

"You make badges here?"

Jake laughed. "Quix, man. We supply the Vegas area law enforcement community with almost everything. Badges, uniforms, boots, weapons, you name it. Hell, half the preppers around here are cops." He walked around the end of the counter. "Come on, I'll show you what we've got."

He led them across the store to the clothing department. There were racks of camouflage coveralls, as well as prison guard uniforms, police and fire department uniforms, and regular street clothing.

"I've got a question," Eissa said. "What the hell is 'quix'? I've heard you say it a few times now."

"Quix? It means a lot of things. It's a swear word, so it depends on how you're using it."

"Gotcha. Question two. Why do you guys have all this

camo stuff? Isn't this the desert? It seems like it should be sand-colored instead of green."

"It's not about being invisible," Jake said. He walked behind a counter near the wall. "It's a style, like jeans with rhinestones on the back pockets, or football jerseys. It's tribal, right? It's how you know who your people are."

"Huh," Eissa grunted. "I guess that makes sense."

"Here we go." Jake cleared a stack of folded shirts off the counter. Inside the display case, a variety of badges lay on a black velvet cloth, the gold gleaming in the jewelry case lighting.

"I didn't know there were so many different kinds of badges," Quentin said.

"Oh, sure," Jake replied. "You've got the five and six-point stars for the sheriff's departments, a couple of different shields for the city cops, depending on what department they're in, the fire department shield, private investigator shield, building inspector shield, all kinds of stuff."

Quentin looked at the display doubtfully. He had no way of knowing if DimCorp Security had one standard badge or not. If they showed up with something different, would they still be able to pull it off? Maybe the whole badge thing was a bad idea. The stars were out, obviously, as were the fire department shields. Most of the police shields had their city name or initials on them, as well as some wording variation on the *Officer* theme, so those were out, too.

"I don't know if any of these will do it," Quentin said. "Do you have any that are a little more generic?"

Jake rummaged around under the counter and came out with a box and opened it up. "We've still got some of the older styles. I don't know what all's in here."

Eissa reached in and pulled out a tarnished gold shield. It had an eagle in the center of a circle, surrounded by elaborate scrollwork. The upper large scroll bore the legend *Inspector* in bold type. The lower scroll was blank.

"That's perfect," Quentin said. "Are there three more in there?"

Jake spread a shirt on the counter to protect the glass and dumped the box out. They dug through the pile and found three more, although one said *Chief Inspector.*

"I guess we'll make that one Bob's," Quentin said. "Does it come with an ID card or something?"

"Oh yeah," Jake said. "It's the whole thing, leather wallet, badge, ID card. Do you have a picture of your other two guys? We'll upload a photo of each of you and print you an ID card."

Quentin shook his head. "No, we've got nothing. Do you have a camera? I can go take one quick."

Jake looked up at Quentin with a hopeful look on his face. "We can take pictures with my holo-link. Can I go with you? I- I'd like to go to another dimension. I think."

Quentin was amused by the shift of power in their relationship. Before they had shown Jake the DimGate, he had been a tough guy, courteous, but slightly belligerent. Now he was anything but. "I think we can manage that. It's a safe location, which is more than we can say for most of them. Can you leave work for half an hour?"

A huge grin broke across Jake's face, a splash of white teeth against his enormous dark beard. "Sure. I'm the day manager, so I have a lot more freedom than most of the other guys here."

He swept the other badges back into the box and led them back across the store. Eissa was almost running to keep up, and even Quentin had to lengthen his stride. Jake was excited about his first trip to another dimension, which was understandable, but he had no way to appreciate how good he had it. When Quentin and Eissa had made their first visit to another dimension, it had been at gunpoint, and altogether stressful and unpleasant.

Jake grabbed his holo-link off the counter and slid it into a backpack. He dug under the counter and came up with two small cardboard boxes. "By the way, I got you each a phone. My number is programmed into them. I didn't know what other numbers you might want."

"Oh, that's great," Quentin said. "We need to get you some money to manage all this for us. How do we do that here, if all we have is a card?"

Jake pulled one of the phones out of the box and powered it up. "Super easy, man. We'll hook you up with Holo-Bank. I just so happen to have a couple of clean ID's set up, so we can use one of those."

Quentin's eyebrows arched. "Clean ID's?"

"You know, a false identity. That's how you do stuff online anonymously. I'm assuming you don't want to leave a trail with your name on it, right?"

"Right."

Jake worked on the phone for a few minutes, referencing his own phone occasionally. "Card number."

Quentin read it off to him.

"Okay, you're all set." He leaned towards Quentin, twisting to the side so they could both see the screen. "If you want to send me money, you just tap this money icon. I'm the only entry in here, so you click on it, select the amount, and hit send. Too easy."

"Nice," Quentin said. "That will make life easier." He slid

the phone in his pocket. "We need to get Eissa a vest, and a few other things, but we'll do that when we come back. Let's go introduce you to Bob and Tocho."

They stood together at the dumpster behind Prepper's Paradise. Quentin felt strange being the one running the DimGate and giving the safety instructions. Just a few months ago, he and Eissa had been the new kids, scared to death and excited about all the possibilities. Now that the Gate was functioning properly, they didn't have to worry too much about it opening in the wrong place, but it didn't hurt to be careful.

Quentin set the panel for the usual spot on the island. "Okay, listen up. When you cross over, you need to keep your fists clenched, and try not to let your ears stick out too much. Small appendages can get sheared off in the portal, especially if you go too fast."

Jake blanched, and moved back just a bit, his fingers curling. "Really?"

Quentin mimed pulling a gun out of his holster and pointed his finger at Jake, thumb raised. "Just messing with you, man." He burst into laughter. "You'll be fine."

Jake eyed him warily, but finally shook his head with a grin. "Alright man, you owed me that one. That was good."

Eissa looked back and forth between them, confused. "What the fuck are you two talking about?"

Quentin shook his head. "Nothing important. Now then, Jake, you stand over here with me. Eissa's going to open the door and make sure everything's safe, and then we'll follow her over."

Eissa cracked the door open and poked her head through. "All clear."

Quentin closed the panel and gestured to Jake. "After you. Just walk right through like any other door."

Jake stepped up to the door and paused. His fingers curled in, and he let out a deep sigh. "I can't believe I'm being such a chickenshit. This shouldn't be scary, right?"

Quentin clapped him on the back. "Hey man, you don't have to act tough with us, we're not impressed by manly-man bullshit. You're leaving your whole world. It's like going to another planet. Of course, it's scary."

Jake took a shaky step forward, crouching a bit as he entered the doorway. The sun was shining on the other side, the rain from the day before dried and gone, and humidity rolled through the open door from the jungle like steam. Jake placed one foot on the dirt and leaned slowly through to the other side, looking around uneasily. Eissa stood a few feet away on the trail, waiting.

"What do you think?" Quentin asked. "So far, so good?"

Jake nodded and shuffled over to Eissa. Quentin followed him through, closing the door behind him, and opened the panel and disabled the Gate.

"How does that work?" Jake asked. "Is the door still by the dumpster behind the store?"

Quentin shook his head. "No, the DimGate stays on whatever side you shut it down from. If you guys had come through and I stayed on the other side and shut it down from there, it would stay at the store with me." He opened the door, exposing the jungle on the other side. "See, since the Gate isn't active, it's just a door, doesn't go anywhere."

Jake's eyes took on a glassy sheen. "Dude, I don't know, man…"

"Don't try to understand it," Eissa said. "Quentin doesn't even understand it, and he's a fucking prodigy. Just think of it as a door that goes where you need to go, nothing more, nothing less. It's way easier that way."

Jake nodded. "Okay, sure."

Quentin led them down the short trail to the cabin. When they came to the clearing, Bob and Tocho were just walking out of the jungle on the beach trail, carrying fishing poles and the tackle box. Quentin waved.

"Perfect timing," he called out. "We brought Jake with us to meet you and see the island."

They met at the porch, and Quentin introduced everyone. "Jake's making us some official DimCorp Inspector badges and ID cards. They've got all the stuff to do it right at the store, he just needs a picture of each of us."

Tocho set his pole down and shook Jake's hand. "It sounds like you're the man for the job."

Jake grinned, his head swiveling around as he tried to look at everything at once. "I don't know, sir. I hope so. Right now, I'm still trying to grasp all of this."

Tocho grinned back at him. "Don't rush it. It's only new and amazing for so long. Then it's just amazing."

Quentin grabbed the tackle box from Bob and slid it under the porch. "Let's get the pictures done, and then we can show you the beach. It's pretty spectacular."

"Yes, yes," Tocho said. "Work first, play later."

Having a task seemed to help Jake get it together, and he soon had them lined up beside the cabin. Quentin caught Bob nodding in approval as Jake guided their posture and expression for the pictures and smiled to himself. Bringing a stranger into their trust was a huge gamble, and while Quentin's gut told him Jake was okay, getting Bob's approval still meant a lot to him. Bob might claim that he was retired, but he was still the head honcho.

Half an hour later, they stood in front of the DimGate. Jake shirt was soaked with sweat from the hike to the beach and back, and he mopped his forehead with a handkerchief. "Man, the humidity here is a bitch. I don't know how you do it."

"Ah, you get used to it." Quentin activated the DimGate, and Eissa cracked it open. "You got everything you need, right?"

Jake nodded. "I've got the list and the pictures. I'll have everything ready in two hours. We can do a quick handoff right here at the door if you want."

"Perfect." Quentin stuck out his hand. "Congratulations, man. You survived your first dimension change. That ought to keep you up tonight."

Jake shook his hand. "You can say that again. I'll probably never sleep again, too busy wondering what else is out there that I don't know about." He stepped through the DimGate back into Dimension 443 and turned around. "See you in two hours."

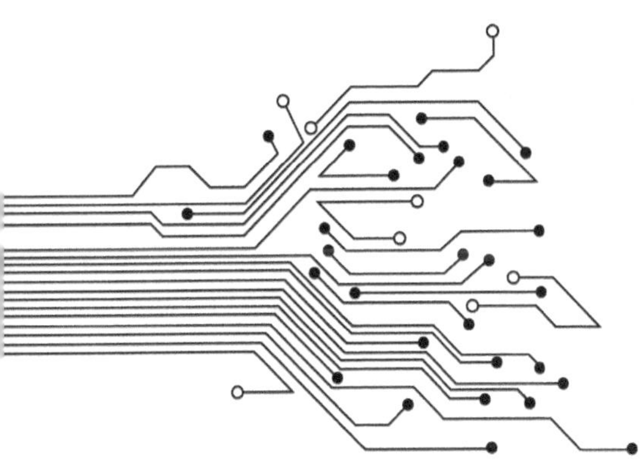

CHAPTER 10

Eissa fumbled with the Velcro straps on her vest, and Jake stepped over to help her. "This is a female cut, so it should give you enough space where you need it. It has a few adjustment points that the men's style doesn't have. Once we get it set right, you won't have to mess with that part again."

Quentin looked up from the bag of goodies Jake brought with him. "What's the range on these headset radios?" The entire radio fit inside the ear canal like a hearing aid, virtually unnoticeable unless someone looked directly at it.

"It all depends," Jake said. "Here in the jungle, you'd probably be lucky to get a hundred meters. Out in the desert, you might get a kilometer. Trees soak up the radio waves like a sponge."

Quentin grunted and turned back to the bag. He had no plans to get more than a hundred meters away from Eissa, so it probably wouldn't matter, but it was best to know what they had to work with in case of an emergency. He pulled a second set of micro-movers out of the bag with a grin and tossed them to Eissa. "You're going to need to practice with these, trust me."

Eissa laughed. "What, you don't think I can rip the door off a cab if I need to?"

"I was thinking of more refined movements, like catching a pencil as it falls off a desk so it doesn't hit the floor and make noise, but we can start big. The car door thing will leave scars on your wrists, though."

Jake stared at him in surprise. "You ripped a car door off with micro-movers?"

Quentin looked away uncomfortably. "It was sort of an emergency," he mumbled. "It happened about ten minutes after I bought them from you, so I wasn't very good with them yet."

Jake whistled. "Dude, that shouldn't even be possible. How did you do it?"

Quentin stood up and stretched, flexing his knees a few times. "Well, the cab locked us in and called the cops, so first I tried to open the door with the outside handle. That didn't work, and the cops were coming, so I imagined pulling the door away from the car at the top and bottom. I was pretty freaked out, but it finally broke the latch. I think the hinges went because I was trying so hard and I didn't back off fast enough. Anyway, the door came off the cab and we left. It burned the shit out of my wrists, though."

"That's incredible, man." Jake looked at Quentin with wondering eyes. "You must have some crazy-strong brain waves."

Quentin blushed, and squatted back down, shoving everything back in the bag. "I don't know about that. It was probably more that I was scared to death of getting arrested in this dimension. Anyway, thanks for bringing all this. You did great."

He hadn't seen his therapist in six months, but he could hear her correcting him as if she were standing there with them. *Quentin, you have to learn how to accept a compliment. When you deflect a compliment and turn it into a self-deprecating remark, you rob the person who is trying to say something nice to you. Just smile and say thank you.* Oops.

"Hey, no problem, man. Just make sure you get the right badges. I engraved your last names on them, so they look legit, except for Tocho. Does he really not have a last name?"

"They don't do last names in his dimension," Eissa said. "Lots of native cultures are like that." She raised and lowered her arms experimentally a few times. "This is a nice vest, way more comfortable than anything I ever wore in the Army."

Jake laughed abruptly and shook his head. "You guys are full of surprises. I never would have pegged you for a soldier."

Eissa stood up a bit straighter. "I was flight medic for ten years. I spent two years in Iraq pulling casualties out of the hot zone."

"Iraq? I'm not sure what that is."

Eissa rolled her eyes. "It's a country in the middle east, borders Iran and Saudi Arabia. It's between Africa and Asia."

Jake shook his head. "The only thing between Africa and Asia is the Ottoman Empire."

"That's it," Quentin said. "In our dimension, that empire fell apart in World War I. I guess that didn't happen here, huh?"

Jake shrugged. "I don't know, man, history's not really my thing. We can look it up on the holo-link sometime. But anyway, a flight medic? I'm impressed. You've got more-" He faltered for a moment. "I was going to say 'balls', but that doesn't seem right."

Eissa laughed. "I've got more balls than a lot of guys, you can say that."

"In our dimension, we have a saying," Quentin said. He stood up with the bag of stuff. "Don't judge a book by its cover."

Jake blushed. "Yeah, we have that one, too. I guess I'm guilty there."

"Alright, we need to get a move on, and you need to get back to work. We can't have you getting fired." Quentin stepped over to the DimGate and activated the door.

"Alright, good luck on your mission. Call me if you need anything." Jake crossed back over to Dimension 443 with a wave and closed the door.

Quentin powered it back down and closed the panel. "Alright, let's go get some rest. I want to hit the Genesis Dimension at nine pm sharp, and we need to be on our A game. If everything goes well, we should be back here by ten."

Eissa nodded. "That sounds good to me. Now that I have a great bed again, I'd like to spend as much time in it as possible."

They headed back up the trail to the cabin. Quentin went over the plan silently as they walked, trying to prepare himself for everything that might go wrong. There was risk involved, that couldn't be avoided, and despite the butterflies in his stomach, he felt pretty good about things. The biggest problem he could foresee was in the transition dimension.

The armorer, or whoever had the key to the arms room at night, would know what dimension they went to in order to test the units. If they didn't come right back, he would probably grab another unit and come find them, assuming something went wrong with one of them. That meant they couldn't come straight to the island. They would have to go somewhere else first, then reprogram both backpacks for the island, and get here before the DimCorp guard got concerned and came to find them. Hopefully the process for programming the backpacks was more or less the same as programming the DimGate. The only training they would get would be watching the armorer set them up, and that wasn't a lot to go on.

Quentin woke with a start, unsure of where he was, or what the shrill beeping sound was that woke him up. The dreams from his nap hung on him, fogging his mind. Finally, he realized the noise was coming from the phone Jake had given him, and he remembered setting an alarm for 7:00 pm. He fumbled with it for a moment and dropped back to his pillow once it was off.

There was a light knock at his door. "You awake in there?" Eissa's voice cut through the cobwebs, and he swung his feet to the floor and sat up, staring out the open window at the late-afternoon sun.

"Yeah, yeah, I'm up."

Eissa opened the door and stepped in. She was already dressed in a smart black pantsuit, the bulletproof vest invisible under her dark pink shirt and black jacket. Her hair was up in a tight bun, and the badge on her hip flashed with the movement of the jacket.

"Damn, you look like a cop," Quentin said, yawning around the words. "I guess I better get my ass in gear."

Eissa smiled. "Thanks. Now go take a thirty-second cold shower, it'll be good for you."

After a quick shower, Quentin got into his own costume. He put the micro-movers and his new bulletproof vest on, with a thick black t-shirt over them, and gray slacks and a jacket completed the look. He clipped the badge to his belt and slipped the leather wallet with his ID card into the breast pocket inside the jacket. The black dress shoes were a bit stiff, and he wished that he'd had time to break them in. He ran his fingers through his hair and headed out to the kitchen.

"Wow," Tocho said, his deep voice echoing off the walls. "You clean up pretty good for a white guy."

Quentin grinned, his face heating up. "Aw, shucks. 'Taint nothing." He pretended to fan his face, turning his head up and to the right to strike a diva pose.

Tocho and Bob roared with laughter, and Eissa joined from across the room. She tossed him an energy bar. "Here, eat this. We can't have you getting hangry in the middle of the mission."

Bob wiped his eyes as the giggles tapered off, and blew his nose on a handkerchief. "I wish we were going with you. I'm not saying you can't do this on your own, but I'd feel a lot better if I was there, anyway." He chuckled. "Being retired is harder than I expected."

Quentin opened the wrapper and took a bite of the bar. "You just don't have much experience with it yet, that's all." He drew a glass of water from the tap. "This will be good practice for you. Who knows, maybe you'll have to come rescue us."

Tocho snorted. "No, thanks. I'll be quite happy if you two are back here in an hour telling us all about it."

"Me, too," Bob said. "I'm jealous, but a rescue mission isn't the kind of action I'm looking for." He paused for a moment, looking at Quentin and Eissa. "I'm damn proud of both of you. You've come a long way since you stumbled into this world."

Eissa walked over and gave him a hug. "That's because we had great instructors kicking our butts. You've done a good job getting us ready for this. Now let's get going, chop-chop."

Quentin shook his head with a smile, following them out the door and across the yard to the trail. Twilight was settling in, and a few faint stars were visible in the soft sky.

Quentin stepped carefully, trying to avoid getting his shoes dirty. He wasn't accustomed to dressing like this, and he was hyper-aware of every branch that touched his sleeve. Concerns about his clothing kept him from thinking about what they were about to do, and they arrived at the DimGate before he had even practiced his lines.

Bob opened the panel and began programming the DimGate. "Alright, here we go. We'll keep the Gate active for an hour, in case you have to come back this way. Make sure you adjust the coordinates on those backpacks by a second, so you don't show up on top of us."

Quentin patted his pocket. "I've got all the coordinates written down right here."

"Alright, then." Bob nodded to them and activated the door. "Here we go. Good luck."

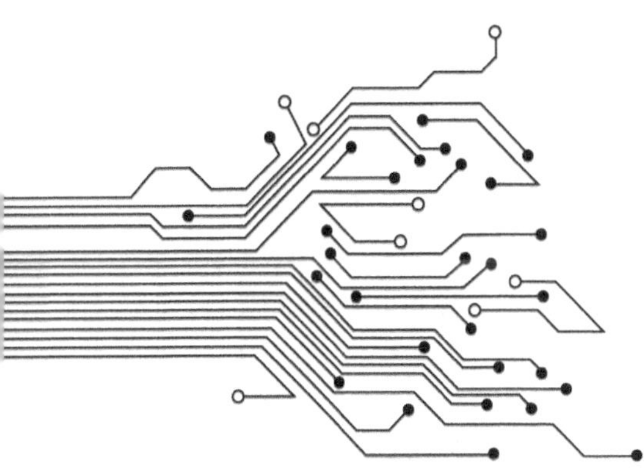

CHAPTER 11

Carl Holt finished off the cold remains of his coffee with a grimace as he waited for his computer to finish shutting down. Setting the cup on a stack of status reports, he dug around in the center drawer of his desk, searching for a roll of antacid tablets. Heartburn seemed to be a regular thing these days. That was probably a bad sign, but he didn't have time to worry about it.

He chewed two tablets, shoving the rest in his pocket. The monitor went dark, and he reached under his desk and turned the key sticking out of the computer tower, locking the power supply. He stood, sliding the key in his pocket with the antacids, and headed for the door.

Sergeant Treijo looked up as he walked out of his office. "You headed home, sir? You look like you could use a few days of regular hours for a change."

Holt laughed. "Home? Do I still have one of those? I can't remember."

She smiled sadly, shaking her head. "You work too hard, boss. I wish you'd listen to me and take a vacation. You're going to burn out if you keep this up."

It made him feel good that she was worried about him, even if her constant harping got on his nerves occasionally. If it wasn't for her, he probably wouldn't get half as many meals as he did. "I hear you, I promise I do. I've got to go to Dimension 443 to check out their physical security plan at the spaceport. I should be back in a few hours, and I promise I'll go home and sleep in my own bed as soon as I get here. How about that?"

Treijo looked at her watch. "It's already 20:00 hours now. I think you should put the inspection off until tomorrow, but if that's your best offer, I'll take it. It's better than sleeping on that cot you have in your office. That thing is going to wreck your back."

He gave her a mock salute. "Alright, I'm out of here. See you in the morning." He paused at the door and turned back to her. "Before I forget, get Anderson on my schedule for a debriefing as soon as he reports in. Bring Mathers in for it, too. We've got to put our report together for that clusterfuck."

"Yes, sir."

"And then get out of here. You should've left hours ago."

He gave her a wink as he walked briskly out the door and down the hall to the DimGate floor. Captain Young was a competent commander, and he had undoubtedly put together a solid plan to protect operations. Still, the ultimate responsibility rested on Holt's shoulders, and he wasn't leaving anything to chance.

When he reached the DimGate control room, he paused and stuck his head inside the door. Two techs sat at computer stations, and a security guard lounged in a chair at the back of the room.

"I need a Gate to the spaceport in 443, security office."

The tech nearest him looked up. "I'll need to see your ID, sir."

Holt stared at him, his eyes narrowing. "You've set me

up on four Gates in the last two days, Pierson. I think I'm cleared by now."

Pierson shook his head. "You said nobody goes anywhere without ID, and if we log it and say we checked and the camera shows we didn't check, we'll get transferred to someplace really bad."

Holt looked up at the ceiling and counted to ten. "Yes, I said that, but it doesn't apply to me."

"You said you don't care if the President walks in here, we'd better check his ID."

"Alright, alright, you're doing your job." Holt walked over, pulling his wallet out. The guard in the back snickered. "Keep laughing, and I'll have you standing your whole shift while I sit in the chair." He shoved his ID card at the tech.

"Thank you, Director Holt. Please sign the logbook, and make sure you put in your destination and expected return date and time. Please keep in mind that the DCC will shut down at 20:30 hours."

Holt gave him a long look before leaning over the desk and picking up the pen. Most of the time, the techs filled out the logbook for him as a courtesy. This was obviously a rebellion at the increased security measures he had imposed.

"I may be late. And, so help me God, if you shut the Gate down and lock me in Dimension 443 all night, a transfer is going to be the least of your concerns."

Pierson wilted. "Yes, sir. I'll leave your DimGate on Auto for you. Can you please make sure you shut it down when you get back, if we're gone already?"

Holt smiled grimly. "Yes, I'll shut it down. Which Gate am I using?"

"Number six, first row, last one on the left."

Holt walked out the door without another word. He stopped in front of the DimGate and checked himself. Weapon secured in holster, check. Pants bloused evenly over the boots, check. Fly buttoned, check. The DimGate hummed briefly, followed by a distinct click. He opened the door and crossed over to Dimension 443.

The DimGate opened in an empty room at the end of the hallway in the Spaceport Security building. This was a design that had been put in place long ago. It was mainly so that personnel could retreat if necessary and blockade the hallway to give them time to get the DimGate opened and everyone through it, or if there wasn't a DimGate on location, they could call and request an emergency evacuation. This rarely happened these days, which Holt took as a sign that his directorship of the security department was yielding positive results.

He opened the door to the hallway and stepped across to Captain Young's office, knocking on the open door. Captain Young looked up from his computer.

"Hey, come on in, sir." He gestured to the open chair. "What can I do for you?"

Holt stepped inside, but remained standing. "I'm glad you're still here. I thought we might do a surprise inspection on the guards and see how they're doing."

Young nodded vigorously. "Sure, we can do that. Let me just save this report I'm working on quick." He clicked his mouse a few times, then stood and grabbed his hat and keys off the file cabinet behind him.

"Let's take a cart, instead of your truck," Holt said. "That way they won't know who's coming. I want to get a feel for their readiness."

"Whatever you want to do, sir." Young set his keys back on the file cabinet.

They walked down the hall to a large room filled with desks. Young led them across the room, nodding at the few remaining people they passed, and out the door on the far side. He stopped at a window in the far wall of the waiting room. "I need the keys to a cart."

Holt stayed back a few steps, waiting. Through the glass doors leading outside, the sky lit up as a shuttle began its descent, and he walked over to get a better view. No matter how many times he saw a spaceship land, it never lost its magic. The blue flame from the thrusters threw shadows behind everything in sight. He squinted, trying to make out the ship, but it was too bright.

Captain Young stepped up beside him. "Ready when you are, sir."

They pushed through the double doors and walked down the sidewalk. The bass rumble of the shuttle shook the leaves of the small trees on the lawn, and he could feel it in the seat of the cart as he slid into it. The shadows returned to normal as the ship slid behind the buildings and out of view.

"Let's start at the guard towers in the warehouse district," Holt said. "We'll work our way around to some of the perimeter stations, and then come back."

Young nodded. "Sounds like a plan." He put the cart in gear and pulled out of the parking lot.

"What all have you put in place besides the additional guards in the towers?"

"We've got images of all four of the suspects in our facial recognition software, so if a camera picks them up, we'll know right away. There are paper pictures hanging at the monorail station in Vegas, so even if they beat the cameras with a disguise or something, the guards might recognize them." He turned right at the intersection and drove toward the warehouse complex a few blocks away. "We practiced take-down drills this morning, both in a civilian crowd and in a tactical situation. Everyone knows they're coming here to attack us."

Holt nodded. "Have the non-security personnel been briefed?"

"Some of them. We have photos at the ticket counter for the monorail and the museum, but I haven't put it out to the rest of the workforce."

He turned left at the next intersection. Half a block down, a large two-story guard tower sat in the middle of the street, and a series of speed bumps led to a boom barrier on either side of the tower. On the second-floor balcony, a guard with a rifle stood in each corner, while two guards manned each boom on the ground.

"We'll stop here and ask a few questions," Holt said.

Young pulled the cart into the center of the road, parking it at the base of the tower. The guards stood up straighter as they recognized the visitors, and one of them dropped a cigarette to the ground, crushing it beneath his boot heel.

"Well, quix," Young muttered. "We're off to a good start, eh?"

Holt grunted. "Go ahead. I'll wait for you."

Captain Young walked briskly to the boom barrier on the left. The two guards saluted him smartly, and he returned it. "Which one of you was smoking?"

One of the guards stepped forward. "That was me, sir."

"Get down. We're going to be here for a while. You will not stop pushing until I tell you to, is that clear?"

"Yes, sir." The guard slung his rifle across his back and dropped to the ground. "Do you want me to sound off with the number of pushups, sir?"

"No, because when you get tired and stop, it'll just piss me off even more. You've already made us look bad enough in front of the Director. I don't want you embarrassing your team even more."

"Yes, sir. Thank you, sir."

Captain Young returned to the cart as the guard began doing pushups. "I apologize, sir."

"We'll hope that the rest of them do a better job of following the rules." Holt walked over to the guards at the other side of the tower, with Young a step behind him.

"Good evening, sirs." The two guards saluted in unison.

"Good evening, men." Holt returned the salute. "Who are you on the lookout for?"

"We have four perps on the hot sheet," the older guard said. "Quentin James, white male, 1.8 meters tall, 90 kilos, round face, brown buzz cut hair. Looks like a nerd but may be dangerous. Eissa Amor-"

"That's good," Holt said, cutting him off. "Very good. What if someone comes up here matching that description, but they've got paperwork giving them clearance to go into restricted areas, or a badge?"

"Sir, my orders are to detain anyone who even remotely matches the physical description or pictures of any of these four individuals. If Captain Young wants to release them, that's up to him, sir. I'm taking them to the Top."

Holt allowed a small smile to brush his lips. "Very good, soldier. As you were."

He turned and started up the steps to the balcony. The guard at the top of the stairs kept her back to him, watching the area, and he stepped up to the rail beside her.

"Corporal, what are your engagement orders if Quentin James comes into your area?"

"Sir, my orders are to assist the ground team in capturing by providing a sniper threat. If James can't be taken into custody, or if he escapes, my orders are to shoot to wound."

"How good are you at wounding suspects in a situation like this?"

The corporal looked him in the eye, her gaze confident. "Sir, I've had three suspects flee in similar situations, and I shot all three of them in the calf. I'd say I'm as good as anyone you've got."

Holt surprised everyone with a deep belly laugh. "I can't argue with that, Corporal. I'm just glad you're on our team. If you ever decide to put in for Special Ops, come see me."

She smiled grimly, glancing at him out of the corner of her eye. "Thank you, sir. I'll let my section chief know you said that. He doesn't think women should apply."

Holt started to turn away, but paused, looking straight at Captain Young. "That matter will be looked into. If there's someone who's keeping the best from rising to the top, I'll deal with them personally."

The corporal and the captain answered in unison. "Yes, sir."

Holt marched back down the stairs to the cart. Captain Young followed him, pausing at the bottom of the stairs as he looked over at the guard on the other side, who was still in the pushup position.

"Alright, soldier, you can recover. If you're caught smoking again, it's going on paper."

He slid into the driver's seat and put the cart in gear. "What do you want me to do with her section chief? He's a good leader."

"Let's go to a perimeter guard tower, one of the remote points." Once they were out of earshot of the guard tower, he let out a deep sigh. "Bill, if he's holding his star performers back, then he has an inferiority complex, low self-confidence. That means he's probably holding everyone back. He might know his stuff, but if he's afraid of being out-performed by his people, then he's not a good leader, he's an anchor. And anchors belong at the bottom of the ocean."

Captain Young remained silent, turning right at the next intersection. They drove through the warehouse section, dodging occasional trucks and forklifts. The flashing yellow light on top of the cart splashed across the walls around them with increasing intensity as the sun set over the horizon.

Holt had dealt with every kind of leadership problem there was over the last twenty years. There were people who didn't know how to handle positional power and spent all their time trying to dominate their subordinates just to show them who was in charge. There were the scumbags who slept with their subordinates, which was a real morale killer for a team. There were cruel people who just liked to punish, sadistic people who liked killing, soft people who couldn't stomach killing, and crazy people who thought they would love it but had never had the chance to find out.

The problem with turning people into leaders was that you could never really know who they were until you put them in the position. All the training in the world wouldn't keep it from happening. The best thing you could do was deal with them harshly when they showed their true colors.

"We'll transfer him to the Gulag in Dimension 101. He can watch prisoners break rocks in Siberia. It's a miserable place."

"Yes, sir," Young replied, his voice low. "What do you want me to tell the others?"

"Tell them exactly where he went, and why. This will teach them a better lesson than any class you send them to. They need to know what zero tolerance looks like. We've got too much to do, and not enough people as it is. There's no room for bullshit like that. Our security forces should be the best of the best, not a bunch of people who never got to grow into their potential."

They left the warehouses behind and came to another checkpoint. Beyond, a field separated them from the launch and landing pads. Warning signs lined the road, cautioning them of the danger ahead. The pulsing yellow lights indicated that it was currently safe to proceed. A hive of activity surrounded the recently-arrived shuttle as it was unloaded and made ready for launch.

"Do you want to inspect this checkpoint, sir?"

"No, let's keep moving. I want to hit one or two others and get back to the Genesis Dimension before it gets too late."

They showed their IDs to the guards and drove on. Twilight deepened the shadows, and Young turned on the headlights as they passed the launchpad area. Beyond that was another field, a safety buffer in the event that something went wrong with a launch or a landing. They passed a fenced-in lot filled with construction equipment, and another filled with old derelict forklifts. The guard tower loomed in front of them, and the huge double perimeter fence lay just beyond. Both the inner and outer fence were three meters of chain link topped with razor wire, with an electric wire on the outside edge at the top. The tower was three stories tall, with balconies on the second and third floors. Huge lights lit up the desert beyond the fence. Cameras on the roof did most of the watching, with the guards inside monitoring the video feeds. Young pulled up to the base of the tower and parked by the stairs.

Halfway to the second floor, Holt's cellphone rang. He glanced at the number. It was someone in the security office in the Genesis Dimension.

"Holt here." Static hissed on the line, and he continued climbing the stairs as he waited for the lag to catch up.

"Director, it's Lt. Baker. I've got a tentative face match on the camera system for Quentin James. He's flagged as a High Priority contact.

Holt froze on the landing at the second floor. "Where is he?"

"It was the front desk camera, sir."

"Front desk of what?" Holt shouted, cursing the delay. "Is he in the spaceport?"

The seconds ticked by with interminable slowness. "He's at the front desk of the Security Building, sir. Right here in the Genesis Dimension."

Holt was stunned. That didn't make any sense at all. Why would James barely escape them here at the spaceport in 443, then go right into the lion's den in the Genesis Dimension? What could he possibly be thinking?

"Who's on duty? Is James alone?"

Static hissed and popped on the line. "Corporal Fleming is manning the desk tonight. Lt. Chastain is the officer of the watch, but his status beacon shows that he's at the barracks. I'm the only other one here, as far as I know, except for the door guard across the street. The roving patrols won't be back for another hour. I- wait, it looks like James has a woman with him, but they just left the camera frame. I'm not sure where they're going."

Holt slapped the railing in frustration. They were at least twenty minutes from the DimGate room, and Baker was next to useless outside the video monitoring room. Fleming was new, and Holt didn't know him at all. Of all the times and all the places for James to show up, this was the absolute worst. He waved at Young and pointed downstairs.

"Stay on the cameras. I'm twenty minutes away. Call Chastain and get his ass in there, then call the DCC and tell them I'm on my way, but I'm the only one who comes in or out of a DimGate. Got it?"

A few seconds later, the response came back. "DCC staff is gone for the day, sir. Everything's on the auto-system."

"Shit!" Holt needed to punch something, anything. "I'm on my way. Just try to figure out where they are, and don't let them leave."

Captain Young was staring at him with wide eyes. "What's going on?" he mouthed.

Holt hung up the phone and charged down the stairs. "Let's go. James is inside the goddamn Genesis Dimension security building."

They jumped on the cart, and Holt cursed himself for not taking Young's SUV instead. The drive back to headquarters was going to take forever, and while they were tootling along at fifteen kilometers an hour, James and Amor were right where he wanted them to be, but there was no one there to do anything about it. He gritted his teeth, knowing that Young was driving as fast as the cart would go, and returned to the question: What in the hell was James doing?

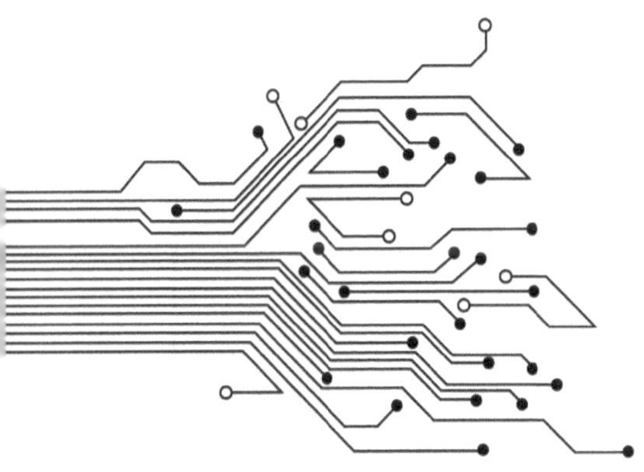

CHAPTER 12

Quentin tucked his clipboard under one arm and opened the DimGate. There was a row of DimGates across from him, which confirmed their location. To his left, the familiar white wall with the blue arrow showed the way to the DimGate control room and the exit. He nodded for Eissa to follow him and stepped across to the Genesis Dimension.

It had been months since he last stood in this room, but the feelings of fear and inadequacy that he had felt then came rushing back at him like it was yesterday. His failure to write a virus that would shut down the DimGate system flashed through his mind like a neon sign, ignoring the fact that had he succeeded, he would've been trapped on a deserted island forever. He shook off the negativity as Eissa closed the door behind them, and they walked down the aisle together.

Unlike their last visit, they weren't trying to avoid contact with other people, and being able to walk around the corner normally and head towards the big window of the control room created an odd sensation in his stomach. Stopping at corners and peeking around them came with its own stresses, but it also gave him time to work on stress management. Striding across the room like a boss meant they were up front in a matter of seconds.

The control room was empty, giving Quentin a rush of adrenaline as the first expected contact with the enemy failed to materialize, and they passed by it and into the adjacent hall. His fists were clenched, as was his jaw, which showed him how nervous he was. *Easy, Q. Don't get so wound up. Breathe. Be the character.* As they passed through the double doors, it occurred to Quentin that they wouldn't have to take the stairs this time. He pointed to the right. "The elevators should be working by now, right?"

Eissa nodded. "Good thinking."

A minute later they arrived in the main lobby, and the elevator doors opened with a soft whoosh. The overhead lights were dimmed, and the guard kiosks at the main doors were all empty save one. They crossed the open space together, the clack of their shoes echoing off the high marble walls.

Quentin was still nervous, but the idea that he was simply playing a role gave him courage in a way that nothing else could have. Eissa was a pillar of confidence beside him, exuding power and authority. He straightened his back as they approached the guard and pulled the edge of his jacket back to expose the badge on his belt.

"Good evening," Quentin boomed, deepening his voice. "DimCorp Special Investigators James and Amor. We're headed across the street to Security."

The guard stood up. Quentin didn't recognize him, and realized with a start that it was entirely possible that they could run into some of the same guards who were here last time. Would that be a problem? There was no way to know, but he couldn't believe he hadn't even thought about it until now.

"Yes, sir." The guard buzzed the door open. "Straight across the street, watch your step at the curb."

Quentin nodded curtly and held the door open for Eissa. She marched past the guard without so much as a glance, and they walked down the long sidewalk and across the street.

"So far, so good," Quentin murmured.

"Just remember that you're in charge," Eissa said. "That's the key to pulling off the role. You have to believe that you're the boss of everyone you're talking to."

He peered through the window as they approached the security office, trying to see inside. If Sergeant Wilson, the guy who had arrested him the last time he was here, was inside, this whole mission could be a bust. There was no way Wilson would believe that he had been an outside auditor a few months ago, and a special investigator now. There wasn't even a plausible explanation as to how that might have happened. He could feel the anxiety creeping from his gut up into his chest. They wouldn't be able to see who was inside until they got in there.

He paused when they reached the door, his hand resting on the handle. "Eissa, we may have a problem."

She glanced up at him. "What? Do you have to pee?"

He shook his head, choking down exasperation. "No, dammit. What if we run into the guys who arrested me and Bob? They won't believe for a second that I went from being an auditor to an investigator."

Eissa smirked. "The last time you were here you were an investigator, too. You were undercover, posing as an auditor. That's how you got out so fast. You have the same job today as you did then, just a different mission."

He shook his head with a grin. "You are a smooth-lying motherfucker, Eissa Amor. Remind me to never believe anything you say." She might be prone to anxiety attacks because of her PTSD, but as a general rule, Eissa was unflappable under pressure, and he envied her ability to stay calm and think clearly at times like this.

He pulled the door open. She elbowed him lightly in the ribs as she went by, but her face was a mask of seriousness. The entry room of the security building looked the same as the last time he was there. The magazines didn't even look like they had moved on the tiny table. The only person visible was the guard on the other side of the huge plexiglass window. The surface of the window was scuffed from years of cleaning solvents, but they could still clearly see the office beyond.

The guard behind the window looked up. He was young, maybe twenty, with acne all over his face. His hair was short, but still messed up, somehow. There was a tablet on the desk in front of him, and he fumbled to get it stuffed in a drawer as Eissa flashed her badge at him. He stood up, pushing the drawer closed with his leg, but the tablet was sticking out a few inches. Quentin flashed his badge as well and nodded at the tablet, his eyes hardening. "Looks like we interrupted you during movie time. DimCorp Special Investigators James and Amor. Who's in charge here tonight?"

The guard looked down at the tablet, his face scarlet. He jammed it into the drawer and slid it closed. The sound of the movie drifted out of the earbuds which still lay on the desk. "I'm in charge, sir. Corporal Fleming."

"Let's take a second and shut the movie off," Eissa said, cutting in. "We're not going to get anything done here with that happening."

It didn't seem possible, but Fleming's face turned an even deeper scarlet, nearing purple. He pulled the drawer open and tapped the screen a few times. At last, the screen froze, and the sound stopped.

"Thank you, that's much better." Eissa gave Fleming a tight smile, and Quentin cringed inadvertently. He had been on the receiving end of that display of scorn before, and knew the belittling feeling that came with it. "I'm surprised they allow you to watch movies here. Who's the officer on duty?"

Fleming shrank, clearly looking for a rock to hide under. "Lieutenant Chastain, ma'am. He's on call, though, he's not here."

Eissa leaned forward. "On call? They left a fucking corporal in charge of this place? Not even a responsible corporal, at that. Why the hell isn't the Lieutenant here?"

Quentin heaved an inward sigh of relief. If the corporal was in charge, then that meant Sergeant Wilson wasn't here. It was time to start playing good cop, bad cop. He put his hand on Eissa's arm. "Easy, Amor. We haven't even started the inspection yet, don't tear him to pieces before we get in the door."

Eissa glanced up at Quentin, heaved a theatrical sigh, and turned back to Fleming. "I'm doing my best. Now why did they leave you in charge?"

"It's a holiday weekend, ma'am. Everyone's off."

Eissa stared at Fleming, then turned to Quentin. "Did you hear that, Inspector James? It's a holiday. Apparently, the Genesis Dimension just shuts down when it's a holiday. Unbelievable. They're supposed to set the standard for the rest of us. Open the fucking door, Fleming. You better have the rest of your shit together better than you've had it so far."

Fleming hit a button on the wall, and the door to their left buzzed. Eissa stormed into the office like a tornado, and Quentin trailed after her trying desperately hard not to laugh.

Fleming stood behind his chair wringing his hands.

"I'm guessing this is your first CRS inspection," Eissa said.

Fleming nodded silently.

"Do you even know what CRS stands for?" Eissa asked. "I guess we shouldn't assume that you know your shit just because you work in the Genesis Dimension."

Fleming hesitated, taking a shaky breath. "I think, maybe…"

Eissa rolled her eyes, and Quentin stepped up next to her. "Well, let's hear it, Corporal. You gotta answer the questions, or she's going to chew you up."

"I'm pretty sure CRS stands for Can't Remember Shit," Fleming mumbled. "But that doesn't seem like what you're looking for."

Eissa's face turned purple, nearly as dark as Fleming's. "What the fuck did you just say?" she roared. "Get down on the floor, right now. Get down! We're going to conduct the rest of this interview from the front leaning rest position."

Fleming dropped to the pushup position. "I'm sorry, ma'am."

"You think this is a joke? Do you think Core Readiness Systems is a fucking joke, Corporal Fleming? Do you? You better start cranking out some pushups before I lose my shit."

Fleming started doing pushups. Quentin felt a little bit bad for him, and had to choke back another laugh when Eissa dropped down nose to nose with him and started doing push-ups, mirroring his efforts. "Come on, Corporal, tell me another joke. I can do this all day long. What does CRS stand for?"

"Core Readiness Systems, ma'am," he panted

"I can't hear you," Eissa said. "You better sound off like you mean it."

Fleming rested for a moment, sticking his butt up in the air. "Core Readiness Systems, ma'am," he shouted.

"Get on your feet," she growled, hopping up. "This is a fucking disgrace to DimCorp Security. We haven't even got started yet, and I've got three pages of failures to write down."

Corporal Fleming climbed slowly to his feet, gasping for breath. Eissa wasn't even winded, and she gave him a withering look. "I guess physical fitness isn't very important around here, either. Unbelievable." She turned away, shaking her head.

"Let's get going on the arms room," Quentin said. "Most of the CRS items are in there." He glanced at Fleming. "Or they better be, anyway. Get the key."

Fleming dashed over to the desk and rummaged in the top drawer, finally producing a small key. He turned back to them. "The key box is down the hall."

He led the way down the hall. They passed the holding cell where Quentin had spent some of the longest hours of his life. Quentin glanced through the window. The room looked exactly the same as he remembered it, dirty white concrete block walls, no mattresses on the bunk beds, toilet in the corner with a water fountain on top of the tank. He shuddered.

Corporal Fleming entered the office at the end of the hall and walked over to a steel box mounted on the wall behind the desk. He used the key to open the box and selected a heavy brass key from the rack inside. "Arms room is downstairs," he said, pointing out the office door. "Stairs are right across the hall."

He seemed eager to get back in their good graces, and Quentin winked at him. "Lead the way, Corporal."

At the base of the stairs, hallways branched off in every direction. The building was clearly much larger underground than it was on the surface. An idea popped into Quentin's head, and he asked the question before he even realized he was speaking.

"Carl Holt has an office around here somewhere, right?"

Fleming pointed down the hall to their left. "First door on the left. He's not there much, though."

Quentin nodded, and they turned right. They stopped at the first door on the left, which was wider than a standard doorway. A massive padlock hung from an oversized hasp, and Fleming grasped the lock and slid the key in. It open with an audible clunk. Quentin decided to see what else he could find out.

"What else is down here in the catacombs?"

Fleming pulled the lock off and released the hasp, hanging the lock back on the loop. "All kinds of stuff, sir. Firing range, offices, holding cells, the tunnel over to the DimGate floor, of course, squad training rooms, storage, that sort of stuff." He looked at Eissa. "I have to disable the alarm, ma'am, just so you know."

Eissa glared at him. "What are you trying to say, Fleming? Are you afraid I'm going to smoke you while the alarm is going off?"

"No, ma'am. Well, maybe a little, ma'am." Fleming shifted ed nervously, looking at his feet. "I just wanted to be clear about everything. Trying to do a better job representing the Genesis Dimension."

"Open the door, Fleming. You'll have plenty of opportunities to redeem your shitty start to this inspection."

Fleming opened the door and turned on the lights. A piercing alarm began whooping instantly, accompanied by a series of small strobe lights in the ceiling in the hallway and inside the room. Quentin was instantly grateful they hadn't tried to break in by brute force. A moment later the alarm fell silent, and the strobe lights turned off.

"Well, the alarm works," Quentin muttered, making a note on his clipboard. "That's a good start." He followed Eissa into the arms room.

Fleming's phone rang, and he answered it quickly. "Fleming here… Yes sir, I just entered the arms room. We're having a surprise inspection."

It had to be the officer of the watch, or maybe even someone higher up. It was pretty impressive response time to the alarm going off, less than a minute. Butterflies began swimming around Quentin's stomach.

Fleming glanced over at them. "The lieutenant wants you to hold your ID cards up to the camera." He pointed to the ceiling in the corner.

Quentin's stomach took a slow roll, but he was careful to keep his expression flat. He pulled the wallet out of his breast pocket and walked over to the corner. His hand was shaking a bit as he held it over his head, but maybe that would keep whoever reviewed the tape later from being able to read it clearly. Eissa held her wallet up as well, but even with her arm extended, it stopped several feet short of the camera. No one was going to be able to read hers, no matter how still she was.

"Yes, sir," Fleming said, hanging up the phone. He turned to them with an apologetic shrug, but his face shone with relief. "The LT's on his way."

"That's good," Eissa said. "I've got some stuff to talk to him about, too. In the meantime, let's get started. I don't want to be here all night."

Quentin looked around, trying to find the backpack units. He had no idea what they looked like, and the best that he could hope for was that there weren't any other backpack-mounted technologies in here that they could get confused with.

The left wall was covered in rifle racks. They were stacked three high and ran the length of the room. A thick cable was strung through the trigger guards, locking the weapons to the wall. Shelves in the center of the room held night vision goggles and gas masks. The wall to the right had ten big backpacks sitting on a counter. Each pack was plugged into an outlet on the wall behind it. *Jackpot.* Quentin walked over to them.

"Let's start over here. We'll save the weapons count for when the OIC gets here." He lifted the flap of a pack, exposing a tablet in a shockproof case. "Do you know anything about these, Fleming?"

Fleming walked over. "Mobile Gates? I've never used one, but everyone gets trained on them. What do you want to know?"

Quentin consulted his clipboard. "We need to verify that they all function, or that they're properly tagged out if they don't. Let's get them all turned on, and then we'll pick a few at random for a full function test."

Fleming nodded, and Quentin watched closely as he powered up the unit. "Talk me through what you're doing," Quentin said. "Your knowledge of the system as the arms room attendant is part of it."

"Okay, I'm powering up the unit while it's still plugged into wall power. Once the access screen comes up, I'll disconnect the power cable. At that point the unit will be ready for a self-test or destination programming. At all times, I make sure that I don't accidently press the red button on the shoulder strap."

"Sounds like you've read the book, Fleming," Eissa said. "I'm impressed. I didn't think you had it in you."

Quentin pointed down the row. "Alright, you know what you're doing. Get the rest of them powered up, and we'll start checking them out."

The access screen came up on the first one, and Quentin was elated to find that it was the exact same screen their DimGate used. Theoretically, they could probably jump straight to the island, provided Fleming didn't see what dimension he entered. It was risky, though, and wouldn't gain them much. *Stick with the plan, Q.* He pulled his notebook out and flipped to the page with their pre-planned dimension and coordinates info on it.

He had no way of knowing how long they had before the Lieutenant arrived, and that complicated things. He didn't want to alarm Fleming, but he didn't want to be standing here when Lieutenant Chastain came in. He might be easy to intimidate, like Fleming, but then again, he might not. They didn't want to find out the hard way that Chastain was a tough guy.

"When you get the last one powered up, start running the self-test on them," Quentin said. "You work your way back up here, and we'll meet in the middle."

"Yes, sir," Fleming said.

Eissa moved up beside him to the second unit. With Fleming at the other end, they had a minute of privacy, which would hopefully be all they needed. He laid the notebook on the counter between the two backpacks, and they started entering destination information into the screens.

As soon as they were done, he stuffed the notebook in his pocket and grabbed the chargers off the bench and slipped them in a side pocket on his backpack.

"Ready?"

Eissa nodded and slid her pack to the edge of the counter. He helped her get her arms through the straps, and she stood upright, hefting the pack into place.

"Are you testing them now?" Fleming asked.

Quentin nodded as he slid his pack to the edge of the counter and put it on. It was heavier than he expected. "We're checking these two out since they're ready to go," Quentin said. "We just have to make a quick test jump to another dimension. Do you have the coordinates for this room so we can come right back here?"

"Sure," Fleming said. "Let me show you." He hurried over and lifted the flap on Eissa's pack. "There's a card right here in this little pocket in the flap with all the details you need to come here or to the DimGate floor." His eyes lingered on the screen for a moment before he closed the flap. "Of course, you can input that data now into the second jump screen, and then all you have to do when you get to the other dimension is hit the button twice and it will bring you right back here. That way you don't have to take the units off and reprogram them."

Footsteps sounded in the hallway, and a moment later two men entered the door. One of them was young and unfamiliar, which Quentin assumed was Lieutenant Chastain. The other one was older and bald, and undoubtedly Carl Holt. Their eyes met across the room, and Holt reached for the pistol on his hip, his face hardening.

"Go, go, go," Quentin hissed at Eissa. Adrenaline surged through his body. He fumbled with the safety cover over the button on his shoulder strap, fighting to get it unclasped. From the corner of his eye he saw Eissa's arm move, and an instant later, she vanished.

"Freeze, motherfucker!" Holt screamed, charging across the room. His right arm swung upwards, bringing the pistol to bear on Quentin as he lunged forward.

Quentin's memory flashed back to Dimension 214, where Vincent Macalister had done the exact same thing. He had survived getting shot by Macalister, but he wasn't eager to do it again. Sure, he had the vest, but what if Holt shot him in the leg? Or the face? *Don't panic, Q.* Holt's lips peeled back in a snarl as he closed the gap, the tips of his knuckles shining white as his other hand swung up and wrapped around the base of the pistol grip. Quentin braced himself and pressed the button.

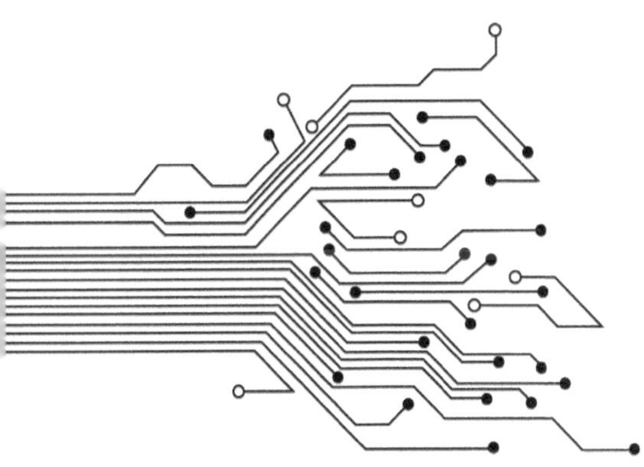

CHAPTER 13

Changing dimensions with the backpack unit was different than using a regular DimGate. With a DimGate, you could see the other side before you crossed over, which meant you could check for danger, obstacles, and so on. With the Mobile Gate, it was a lot like blinking. One second you were in one place, and the next second you were somewhere else.

Quentin's first dimension jump with a Mobile Gate was less than ideal. Everything went black for an instant, and then he was falling. It was a short fall, and he landed on his feet, his vision returning as he hit the ground, but he was disoriented for a moment, even though he was more or less where he expected to be.

"Come on, up you go." Eissa was standing above and in front of him, extending an arm down to help him up.

He recognized Tocho's A-frame cabin behind her in the dim twilight, which confirmed their location in Dimension 444. They had stopped here briefly on the way to the DimGate back when this whole adventure first got started. Tocho had buried a box of DimGate parts in his backyard years before, which they dug up on their way through. Somehow Quentin had managed to land in the hole they had left behind months ago.

"I guess we should have filled the hole up, huh?" Quentin grasped Eissa's outstretched hand and lurched up out of the hole. "I didn't think we'd ever be here again, not that that's a good excuse."

"Yeah, that was a shot in a million," Eissa said. "Now then, let's get the fuck out of here. Holt just keeps showing up, and we're only going to get away so many times."

Quentin nodded. "Turn around. I'll get yours programmed, and then you can do mine." Eissa turned around, and he quickly lifted the cover and activated the screen. The glare from it was blindingly bright in the near darkness. Fortunately, he had the coordinates for the Diablo Tower roof in Dimension 443 memorized. "Alright, got it."

Just as Eissa turned around, Carl Holt appeared beside her, his back to her. He was wearing a Mobile Gate and held his pistol out in front of him. He was turned to their right, facing away from the cabin, which gave Quentin an instant to grasp the fact that he was there before Holt sprang into action. How could he have followed them here? *Fleming.* He must have memorized the coordinates when he looked at Eissa's screen. That was impressive.

Holt's head swiveled around, and Quentin charged. The hole was right behind Holt, and Quentin slammed into him just as he turned to face them. Once again, Quentin was grateful for the bulletproof vest as it absorbed the impact. Holt staggered back under Quentin's weight, and they tumbled over as they reached the hole.

Quentin punched Holt in the face repeatedly as hard as he could, then pushed his forehead back and chopped him in the throat with his forearm. While Holt was gasping for air, Quentin held his arm on Holt's throat and used the micro-movers to wrench the pistol out of his grasp and toss it on the ground at Eissa's feet.

"Get out of the way," Eissa shouted. "Let me shoot him."

Holt was struggling against Quentin, swinging his fists wildly as he tried to twist out from under him. "No time," Quentin gasped. "Program my screen while I've got him pinned. Hurry up!"

"What?"

"My screen, fucking program it!" He punched Holt in the temple, trying to knock him out, but the struggling intensified.

Eissa leaned over and lifted the cover on his backpack. "Stop wiggling," she hissed. "I can't even hit the numbers."

Flashes of his fight with Macalister popped into Quentin's mind. He had gone into that confrontation convinced that he could end it with a peaceful solution, but he had ended up killing Macalister. His conscience wouldn't be able to carry the guilt of killing Carl Holt; there had to be another way out of this. With a roar, Quentin grabbed Holt into a bear hug. Ignoring the burning in is wrists, he threw every bit of energy he had at the micro-movers, willing them to crush Holt to stillness. Holt screamed, his arms slamming down to his sides as his bloody face pressed into Quentin's chest. They stood there, locked in a vicious embrace, as Eissa punched the coordinates into Quentin's screen. He could feel his energy draining like water from a tub, and he willed her to hurry before it ran out.

"Got it," she said at last. "Let's go." She stepped back from the hole, hit her button, and disappeared.

Quentin let go of Holt with one hand and flipped up the safety cover, jabbing at the button awkwardly. Holt's head swung up, crashing into his chin, and his vision swam. He could feel fists pounding his ribs, but the vest kept Holt from doing any serious damage there. He hooked his foot behind Holt's knee, using the micro-movers to shove him away and pin him against the side of the hole. He reached out and grabbed Holt by the throat with his left hand, locking his elbow. With his right hand, he reached over and hit the button on his shoulder.

He found himself falling again, as there was suddenly nothing behind Holt to hold them up. Quentin and Holt crashed to the roof of the Diablo Tower. The first thing Quentin became aware of was that Holt was still in his hands. How did Holt make the jump? Was it because he had been holding on to him? His focus slipped momentarily from the unexpectedness of it, and Holt punched him in the face. His head rocked back as pain exploded across his lips, his mouth filling with the taste of blood. The flashing lights from the massive billboards were blinding, and the sudden onslaught of noise pummeled his ears after the silence of Tocho's back yard.

Eissa appeared from the darkness on his left and kicked Holt in the head. He dropped back with a hoarse cry, and Quentin renewed his focus on the micro-movers. He turned his head to the side and spat a mouthful of blood, trying to figure out a way out of this. He didn't think he could get Holt to the edge of the roof and throw him off, but that wasn't something he wanted to do, anyway. What he really wanted to do was go home and never see Holt again.

All you have to do is hit the button twice, and it will bring you back.

He glanced up at Eissa. "I'm going to take him back to Tocho's and leave him there. I need you to hit my button twice."

Eissa reached for him, but hesitated. "Wait a minute. I'm going too, just in case something goes wrong."

Quentin nodded tightly, afraid to take more than a fraction of his attention off Holt. "Alright. Just make sure you're not touching him when you come back. Apparently, that's important."

Eissa nodded. "Here we go." She placed one hand on Quentin's button and the other hand on her own. "Ready?"

Quentin nodded, and trained his focus on holding Holt still with the micro-movers. "When we get there, I'm going to shove him away, and we'll come right back here, okay?"

"Got it."

An instant later, Quentin was falling again. The Mobile Gate had put him right back over the hole in Tocho's yard. *You gotta be shitting me.* This was his third fall in five minutes, so he was able to maintain his focus on holding on to Holt. They were both in the hole, which kiboshed his plan to just shove Holt away and jump back to the Diablo Tower. He struggled to his feet, keeping Holt wrapped in the bear hug.

It was almost impossible to tell what condition Holt was in. Whatever twilight that had been in the sky when they first arrived was rapidly waning, and Holt's blood-covered face was nearly invisible in the gloom.

"Eissa," Quentin grunted. "Are you here?" He was tired in a way that he'd never experienced before. His muscles were filled with lead, and even his bones felt heavy and unwieldy.

"Right here." She materialized beside him and snapped on a small flashlight, shining it in his eyes.

"Goddammit, don't blind me, I've got enough trouble."

"Sorry." She moved the light over to Holt.

Holt's eyes squeezed shut against the light. There was blood all over his face and bald head, but the strength he displayed by his struggle in Quentin's grip indicated that he still had a lot of fight left in him.

"Is that box still around here?" Quentin asked.

Eissa swung the light around the yard. "Yep, it's right over here. What do you want me to do with it?"

"Pick it up and smash it over his head, if you think you can do it without knocking me out, too."

Eissa turned the light off, and he heard her grunting in the darkness. Holt struggled harder in his grip, knowing what they were trying to do. Quentin focused all his mental energy on immobilizing him as he cautiously let go with one hand and repositioned it to Holt's wrist. Holt's eyes widened, the whites shining in the darkness. Quentin repeated the move with the other hand, the intensity of his mental effort causing him to quiver from head to toe. The burning sensation in his wrists had gone beyond pain, peaking in a thrumming agony that could no longer be ignored. Once he had both hands in front of him, he stopped, waiting for Eissa to reappear.

"Where are you?" he called out. He barely recognized the raspy voice as his own. Tears of pain and exhaustion streamed down his cheeks, and his entire body was shaking uncontrollably. He wasn't going to be able to keep it up for long.

Eissa set the box down beside them with a thump and flicked the light back on. "Right here. This thing weighs a fucking ton."

"Alright." Quentin stared at Holt, trying to maximize his focus on holding him still. "Stick the light in my mouth, and I'll keep it pointed at him. You pick the box up, and as soon as I lean back, whack him with it."

Eissa jammed the flashlight in his mouth, nearly gagging him with it. He tightened his grip on Holt's wrists and leaned back as far as he could. The flashlight bobbled wildly in his bloody, trembling mouth. A moment later the box crashed down, and Holt's wrists were ripped out of his hands. He scrambled up out of the hole, dragging his wooden legs to the surface.

"Ready?" Eissa asked.

"Go," Quentin gasped. He reached up and hit the button twice.

He staggered as his eyes and ears adjusted again to the cacophony of Vegas, trying to get his bearings. Eissa stood beside him. He turned and grabbed her shoulder. "Come on, we need to get back to the cabin. I can't take any chances on Holt showing back up, I'm dead on my feet."

She spun around and he began typing coordinates into her screen. His hands shook violently, and he couldn't remember ever being so tired. He double-checked each number as he typed it in, not trusting himself to get it right.

"Do you think his Mobile Gate will show that he came here?" Eissa asked. "He piggy-backed on yours, right? Do you think he can follow us here?"

Quentin finished programming her screen and spun around, dropping to one knee so she could reach his. "I don't know. Probably not, but I can't fight him anymore. I'm fucking fried."

She closed the flap and patted him on the shoulder. "Alright, let's go."

He stood up and grabbed her hand. Weariness was smothering him like a leaden blanket, and all he could think of was getting to bed. He wasn't even sure he could make it from the arrival point up to the cabin. If he had to sleep right there in the jungle under a tree, he was fine with it, as long as he didn't have to worry about Carl Holt showing up again. He turned his head to look at Eissa, every muscle in his neck protesting the movement. "On three?"

She nodded. "One, two, three."

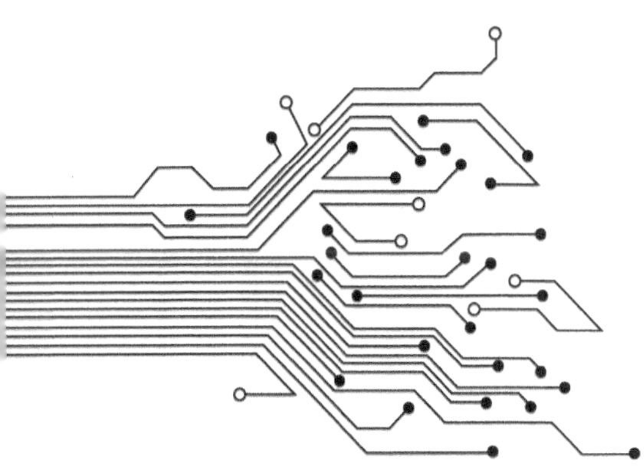

CHAPTER 14

Consciousness slowly returned, one excruciating heartbeat at a time. Holt's thoughts were hazy, shrouded by agonizing pain. He needed air, but each breath felt like someone was stabbing him in the back. Every part of his body hurt, though he couldn't remember why. He carefully opened his eyes. Nothing changed, and he blinked. Still dark. Darkness… he was outside, in the darkness. And he hurt like hell.

He tried to sit up, but something was holding him back. He felt around with his hands, trying to establish some understanding of where he was. The first thing he felt was dirt, which seemed familiar. He was lying on his back, his hips and legs hanging over the edge of a hole, but he couldn't sit up.

The pain was like a living beast, vicious and relentless as it attacked him. Holt cautiously lifted his hand to his face. It was wet, probably blood. He'd been in a terrible fight, a fight with…

As if a switch had been flipped, it all came back to him. Quentin James. Somehow, James had managed to squeeze him so hard he'd felt his ribs breaking. Then that Amor bitch had smashed him over the head with a wood box. He was hurt, and it was probably serious. He needed to get back to the Genesis Dimension ASAP.

The first thing he had to do was get the Mobile Gate off his back. He couldn't move with it strapped on, and he needed to program it. His ribs screamed in protest with every breath, and he could feel fresh blood running down his face as he rolled to one side, slowly sliding his arm out of the strap. Reversing his movements, he carefully turned the other way, easing the other arm out as gently as he could. His pulse pounded in his forehead, sending jagged spikes of light through his vision. Leaning back on the Mobile Gate, he rested for a moment. The pain was everywhere, consuming him.

"Don't pass out, hero." His voice came out in a weak croak, which scared him even more than the realization that he had almost blacked out. He definitely had a concussion to go along with everything else, and the disorientation that came along with it made it difficult to keep moving. That, and the excruciating pain.

The broken ribs wouldn't let him take a deep breath, but as he rolled on to his side, he gasped anyway. Lifting his leg up wasn't going to happen. He was going to have to do everything from the hole. It was pitch black, and that wasn't helping his disorientation. How long had he been out? He slowly pushed himself upright, tugging gently on the backpack to turn it around.

It took nearly five minutes for him to get the flap at the top facing him. With each pull, the backpack slid a few inches, but at the same time, his broken ribs ground against each other from the exertion. He had to wait for the pain to subside each time before he could do it again to avoid passing out. He was barely aware of the blood running down his neck, soaking his shirt. When it was finally close enough to reach, he opened the flap and touched the screen, activating it. His finger left a bloody smear on the screen, but he could still see what he needed to once his eyes adjusted to the blinding light.

He coughed, doubling over from the stabbing pain in both his chest and his throat. The continuing need to cough turned into a gagging retch as he tried to suppress it, and his gorge rose. Air wheezed in and out of his mangled nose with a whistling sound as he waited to see if he was going to puke or faint. He shivered, suddenly cold despite the warm, humid night air. How could James have hurt him so badly?

Once he was able to stand up, he pulled the card out of the flap. He could barely make out the writing on it, and he carefully typed the coordinates in, checking each number twice. The last thing he needed was to jump to the wrong spot. He might not be able to do this twice, so he had to get it right on the first try.

Putting the Mobile Gate back on was out of the question. As bad as it hurt to get turned over the first time, there was no way he could do that again. He hadn't used one very many times in the last few years, but he knew he had to get in contact with the sensors mounted on the front panel for it to work. If he was wearing the pack, they would be against his back, so if he could lean against it firmly, it should work. If he didn't have good enough contact, it would give him an error message, and he could reposition.

He took a few shallow breaths, preparing himself for the agony of exertion, and with a grimace, he pulled the backpack upright. The weight was almost too much, but he managed to lean back far enough to get it to stand up. His knees threatened to buckle, and blood ran down his face in alarming quantities as he waited for the pain to pass. When he was able to inhale again, he leaned forward, gingerly pressing his torso up against the backpack. He slid one arm around it, squeezing it against himself as tight as he could bear, and with the other hand he flipped the safety cover up. With gritted teeth, his trembling fingers brushed the edge of the button, then pushed it.

He saw a flash of light as he materialized in the arms room, but before his eyes could adjust enough to recognize the figures standing before him, the weight of the Mobile Gate, no longer sitting on the ground on the edge of the hole, pulled him to the floor with a crash. Sparks flew across his vision as broken ribs ripped into flesh, and he screamed until the darkness swallowed him.

When his eyes opened again, he was lying in a bed in a white room, and sunshine was pouring in the window. He recognized the cold tubes forcing oxygen up his nose from previous trips to the hospital, as well as the sluggish thoughts as painkillers did their job. He tried to turn his head slightly, but the muscles in his neck hurt too much to comply, and he relaxed back into the pillow. The television mounted on the wall was turned off, and he couldn't see anyone else in the room. The machine beside the bed beeped as it tracked his vitals, hypnotic in its regularity, and he drifted back to sleep.

His dreams were unusually agitated and distressing. He flashed from one murky scene to another, always being pursued, or searching for something he couldn't find. In each one, he would end up trapped in a corner, unable to move as Quentin James beat him mercilessly. Just as the crushing deathblow came, he would transition to the next dream. When he finally woke again, it was a relief.

"Hello, Director. How are you feeling?" A man in blue scrubs stood beside the bed, making notes on a chart.

Holt wiggled his fingers and his toes, trying to assess his condition. He was sore, but it seemed bearable. He licked his lips, but his tongue was too dry to moisten them. "I could use a drink." His voice was raspy, and his bruised throat contracted painfully at the effort.

The nurse filled a small cup from the pitcher on the table and put a straw in it. "Let's get you sitting up," he said, putting the cup back on the table. He pushed a button on the bed's railing, holding it until the bed was almost upright. He handed Holt the cup. "Can you manage it?"

Irritation flashed at the insinuation, but as soon as he reached for the cup, he understood the question. Every joint was stiff, and his hands were so swollen he could barely grasp the cup. He cradled it with both hands, just to be safe, and carefully raised it to his mouth. The straw was the next challenge, as his lips were swollen and sore, but he managed to create a seal, and soon drained the cup.

"That's better," he whispered. The water was cool and soothing, and he felt the flesh of his mouth and throat absorbing it like a sponge. Almost instantly he felt better, more alive. He licked his lips again, with more success this time. "How long have I been here?"

The nurse looked at the chart, then at his watch. "Almost 48 hours. You were pretty banged up when you arrived. Do you remember what happened? Nobody here knows."

Images of James blindsiding him flashed through his mind, James punching him in the throat, and somehow squeezing him so hard he couldn't breathe. "I had a disagreement with a guy."

The nurse's eyebrow arched. "Some disagreement." He turned as a tall woman walked in the door, her white coat blinding as she passed through a beam of sunshine. "Here's Dr. Hall. I'm sure she'd like to hear about it, too."

"Hello, Director." She stuck her hand out to shake his, but pulled it back as her eyes dropped to his hands. "Better not try that just yet. I'm Dr. Hall." Her blonde hair was pulled back in a tight bun, but her face was friendly, if a bit tired.

"Carl Holt." He nodded and wiggled his fingers in a small salute. His muscles were stiff, but not as sore as he expected. "How bad did I lose?"

She laughed, a bright, easy sound. "I guess that depends on how the other guy looks. You took a serious beating, though. Two broken ribs, one of which caused a pneumothorax, a minor endolaryngeal hematoma, concussion, thirteen stitches for the laceration on your scalp, six more in your cheek, a broken nose, and a pile of deep bruises. We got your lung re-inflated, so that's going to be fine, but you're going to be quite sore for a while."

Holt groped for the water cup, his mind reeling. The nurse grabbed the cup and filled it from the pitcher, then handed it to him. He took a mouthful, rolling it around his mouth before swallowing. "What's an endola- endo-"

"Endolaryngeal hematoma. Basically, it means that you took a hard hit to the throat, and you have significant internal bruising around your larynx. You're going to have a hard time swallowing for a week or two."

Dull rage began to warm Holt's skin. Quentin James had started out as a minor irritation. He then advanced to a minor problem. Now he was shooting up the charts to the top spot of Public Enemy Number One. It was embarrassing that a computer nerd had hurt him so badly, but it was also sobering. James clearly had some sort of highly advanced technology tool that had contributed to his current condition. That was something he had to find a way around, because the next time he saw James, he was going to tear James's arms off and beat him to death with them.

The vitals monitor beside the bed began to beep faster, and he took a few breaths to calm himself. "Okay, Doc. When can I get out of here? I've got a lot of work to do." He carefully brought the cup back up for another drink.

"You can leave this afternoon, but you're going to be on bed rest for a while. I don't want you working for at least a week."

Holt choked, painfully snorting water out his burning nose as he coughed. He dropped the cup, spilling water all over his lap as he tried to catch his breath. His ribs ached, the pain dulled slightly by the drugs, but his throat hurt like hell from the insult. He gingerly wiped his nose on a napkin.

"Easy there," the nurse said, picking up the cup. "You don't want to cough if you can avoid it."

Holt's eyes were watering from the pain. "No shit," he gasped. He cleared his throat as delicately as he could manage. "Sorry. A week? I don't have a week." His head fell back against the pillow.

"Well, you'd better come up with one," Dr. Hall said. "If you push it, you could end up in way worse shape than you're in now."

Holt shook his head. "I've got a catastrophe on my hands. I can't lie around waiting to feel better. Sitting at my desk won't hurt me, right?"

Dr. Hall took the clipboard from the nurse and scribbled some notes on it. "Look, Director. I'm sure you have pressing matters to attend to. I'm also sure you have a lot of capable people working for you. I suggest you learn how to delegate tasks and let them help you. I'll either see you back in a week for a check-up, or I'll see you back for another collapsed lung or a tracheotomy. It's up to you."

Holt closed his eyes as she left the room. There was just too much that he had to do himself. For starters, he had to figure out what James was going to do with the Mobile Gates. He also had to get security at the headquarters building ramped up. The fact that James and Amor had walked in there and stolen two Mobile Gates was beyond comprehension. That alone chilled him to the bone. While he wanted to publicly flog Corporal Fleming and Lieutenant Chastain, it was really his own arrogance that created the opportunity for this to happen. He never dreamed James would come back to the Genesis Dimension after escaping the first time, and he was wrong. Almost dead wrong.

There was time now to rest, so he tried to relax and let his thoughts drift freely. He ignored the throbbing burn in his throat and instead listened to the constant beep of the heart monitor. James had scoped out the spaceport in 443. He had then stolen two Mobile Gates from the Genesis Dimension. He had some sort of tech that allowed him to overpower people and prevent them from moving. For a second, Holt relived the claustrophobic squeeze, James screaming in his ear as he crushed the air out of him, the terrifying inability to take another breath or even move his arms or legs. With an effort, he returned his focus to the facts. James was clearly taking a series of steps towards a specific goal. What was the next logical step? What was his endgame? The questions remained unanswered as he drifted back off into a troubled sleep.

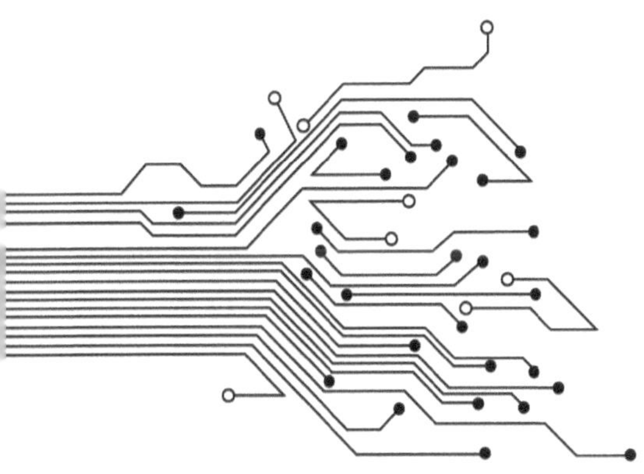

CHAPTER 15

"**H**ey, look who's back," Bob called out in a jovial voice. "What took you so long?"

Quentin turned to see Bob and Tocho over by the DimGate. The door was open, and there was a line of DimGates visible on the other side in the Genesis Dimension. "Close the door," he said. "Quick. We've got trouble."

Bob shut the door and disabled the DimGate. Tocho walked over to them, shining his flashlight across their backpacks. "What kind of trouble? It looks like you were successful, to me."

Panting, Quentin dropped to the ground, leaning back against the backpack. Gravity seemed to have doubled its powerful draw in the last few minutes. "We need to consider the Genesis Dimension a compromised location, at least at DimCorp headquarters. We ran into Carl Holt again."

Bob stepped over beside Tocho, his flashlight shining on the ground in front of them. "Did he recognize you?"

Quentin tried to laugh, but a tired wheeze was the best he could produce. "Yeah, he recognized me. There's not any doubt about that, trust me."

"We need to get him up to the cabin," Eissa said. "I need to see how bad he's hurt."

"Hurt?" Tocho exclaimed. "Why didn't you say so? Come on, let's get the backpack off of him. I'll carry it up. Can you walk, or do we need the litter?"

Quentin raised his hands in a weak protest. "It's not that bad. I'm mostly exhausted. Fighting with micro-movers really sucks the energy out of you." He let them take the Mobile Gate off and help him to his feet, but protested being helped up the trail. "I can walk to the cabin, I promise."

Once they arrived at the cabin, Eissa sat him down at the kitchen table. Bob turned all the lights on, and Tocho whistled as he got a good look at Quentin.

"Jeez Louise, what happened? Is that your blood?"

Quentin looked down. His black shirt was a sodden mess, but he really couldn't tell by looking at it. His light gray jacket, on the other hand, looked like evidence from a murder scene. It was covered in bloody handprints, blood spatters, mud, rips, and roofing tar. He grinned at Tocho. "Some of it's probably mine, but I think most of it belongs to Carl Holt. We had a bit of an altercation."

Eissa brought out her medical kit and began peeling his jacket off. "Yeah, you might want to avoid your house in Dimension 444," she said, handing the jacket to Tocho. "Can you toss that outside? We had to leave Carl Holt in your backyard. Bob, can you get me a bowl of water, please?"

Tocho had started for the door, but he stopped in his tracks and turned around. "Is he dead?"

Quentin and Eissa glanced at each other. "I'm not sure," Quentin said. "Probably not."

Bob carefully set a bowl of water and a few towels beside the medical kit and pulled a chair out from the table. "I think we're going to need to hear this story from the start.

There's a lot of missing pieces."

Eissa cut Quentin's shirt off with a pair of scissors, and Tocho put it on the porch with the jacket. When he was back in and seated, they took turns explaining the series of events. Eissa cleaned Quentin's face up as they talked, treating the cuts and scrapes, then treated the burns on his wrists. When they were wrapped in a dressing, she had him stand up so she could check him for any other injuries.

"Holy shit, look at this," she said, grabbing a small pair of pliers from her kit. "Hold still." She grabbed something that was stuck in the back of Quentin's bulletproof vest and wiggled, finally tugging it out. She laid it on the table so they could see.

"That's the tip of a knife blade," Bob said. "It's a good thing you got that vest, huh?"

The sight of the gleaming triangle made Quentin queasy. He tried to imagine what would have happened if he hadn't worn the vest. Holt would have turned his kidney into ground beef, and he would probably be dead by now. That made twice that he'd dodged the Grim Reaper. It was an unsettling realization.

"Yeah, I guess it's my lucky charm," Quentin said. Fatigue was dragging him down, making it hard to think. "The good news is that we got two Mobile Gates. I vote we go to bed and reconvene in a week, and then go from there."

Tocho laughed. "Good plan. And we need to find a way to keep you from killing yourself with those wrist bands. Too much power."

Quentin couldn't argue that the micro-movers were dangerous. They had nearly sucked him dry, but at the same time, they had saved his life. He was no match for Carl Holt without them. He needed to learn how to set some boundaries and figure out a way to know when he was approaching them. He also needed to learn how to fight. Those fourth-grade karate classes were a long time ago, and they weren't doing him much good at the moment. All problems for another day. He shuffled to his bed and collapsed and was asleep within seconds.

———o———

The afternoon sun was blazing behind Prepper's Paradise when Quentin and Eissa stepped through the DimGate from the island. No matter how many times they went back and forth between the desert and the jungle, the change in humidity always caught him by surprise. He opened the control panel but left the DimGate powered up as he pulled out his phone and called Jake.

"Hey, man, we're out back." He listened for a moment before closing the phone and sliding it back in his pocket. He turned to the screen in the DimGate control panel.

"Alright, let's see what we can figure out. We should be able to find the spaceport on the map, if we can find the monorail." He zoomed the map out a bit and followed the perimeter of the city until he located it. From the monorail station, it was just a matter of zooming the map out and sliding it northwest with the line of the track. Once he had the spaceport centered on the map, he zoomed back in.

"Dude, all these buildings look the same to me," Eissa said, shielding her eyes from the sun with one hand.

Quentin grunted in agreement. He moved the map around, trying to find the conveyor belt that Jake had showed them, but there was more than one, and he had no idea which building was the mystery building. A few minutes later the back door of the store opened, and Jake emerged, squinting in the bright sunshine.

"Sorry that took so long, had to finish up with a customer." He did a double take as he walked up to Quentin. "Quix, what happened to you?"

It had been three days since Quentin's fight with Carl Holt, but his jaw and left cheekbone were still deeply bruised, showing blue, purple, and yellow, and his lips were still swollen. "I slipped in the shower."

Jake barked out a surprised laugh. "Looks like the shower has a mean right hook."

Quentin grinned, wincing as it spread to his cheek. "You can say that again. I couldn't even get out of bed two days ago."

"Were you able to get whatever you went to get?"

Quentin nodded. "Yeah, we got them, but Carl Holt was there. It didn't go as planned, but we got out." He gingerly touched his chin.

"That's the guy you want to take down, right? The security guy at DimRec?"

"One and the same."

"So how did you take him down? Is it over?"

Quentin shrugged. "No, I don't think it's over. We had a nasty fight, but I ended up holding him still with the micro-movers while Eissa smashed a wooden box over his head so that we could get away from him and flip dimensions. It wasn't easy, though. I was barely able to hold him."

Jake shook his head. "Man, I don't think you understand the limits of those micro-movers. You aren't supposed to be able to do shit like that. They were made for changing the channel, or grabbing your water bottle off the coffee table, not ripping car doors off and subduing people."

"That doesn't really sound like a prepper thing," Eissa pointed out. "Why do you even sell them here?"

"Oh, they're great for preppers. If you've got a fortification with multiple mounted machine guns, you can use the micro-movers to fire two or three guns at once. You can't really aim them accurately, but it's a great way to lay down cover fire, or grab magazines for a quick reload. Didn't I give you the owner's manual?"

"No, you didn't." Quentin held up his bandaged wrists. "I'm learning where the line is, though. They let you know when you're crossing it. You lose your energy really quick when you're maxing them out. You start getting woozy."

"You could kill yourself taking it to that point," Jake said, his face growing pale. "You're so far past the recommended usage that I doubt anyone knows what it will do to you. I never should have told you about them."

"Whoa," Quentin said. "They saved my bacon several times already. We'd be dead or in jail if it wasn't for them. Same goes for the vest, by the way. Holt broke a knife blade off in this one."

Jake looked down with a bewildered chuckle, his head shaking back and forth. "Man, you are unbelievable. You're a straight-up computer nerd if I ever saw one, but since I met you, you've been shot, stabbed, burned, chased by the cops, chased by DimRec security, and God knows what else, and here you are, plotting your moves to break inside the machine. You're a fucking enigma, man. I just don't even know what to think about you."

And jumped out of a moving train, Quentin managed not to say, but he couldn't keep the smile off his face. It sounded so strange to hear someone lay it out like that. Those were things that happened to people in movies, or drug cartels in Thailand, but not to regular people. The idea that those things had happened to him was laughable, ridiculous.

"It sounds terrible when you say it like that," he said. "A lot of good stuff happened, too. But that's not what we came to talk about. We need some help getting the coordinates for the mystery building. I can't even tell which building it is on the map."

Jake stepped up to the map and looked closely. "May I?"

Quentin nodded. "Sure. You can drag it around with one finger and zoom with a two-finger spread. It's not near as high-tech as your holo-link, but you'll get the hang of it."

Jake zoomed out and found the right building, circling it with a finger. "So, what's the plan? Are you going to just open up the DimGate in front of that place, or what? How accurate do the coordinates need to be?"

"Pretty accurate. We just… appropriated some backpack units that do the same thing the DimGate does, except that they move with you. The plan is to program them to bring us into this dimension right beside the wall where the conveyor belt goes in. Then we're going to hop on the conveyor belt and see where it goes."

Jake nodded, thinking out loud. "Okay, okay, let's see. This map goes six decimal places on the coordinates." He pulled his holo-link out of the cargo pocket on his pants. "I just want to verify that we're all looking at the same numbers here."

"Seems like a good idea," Eissa said.

Jake worked on the holo-link, turning his back to the sun to shade the screen. After a minute he held it up beside the screen in the control panel. He shifted both maps around, zooming in and out until he was satisfied.

"Alright," he said, sliding the holo-link back in his pocket. "It all matches up. See this concrete square?"

Quentin stepped closer to the screen. The concrete had been poured in squares about fifteen feet by fifteen feet. "Yep."

"I can get you inside that square, but it's going to leave you a few steps away from where you're trying to go. The next number up on the GPS could put you inside or outside, it's too close to tell. You don't want to land inside the building without knowing what's there, right? Could be an acid bath, for all we know. This here's your number."

Quentin wrote the coordinates carefully in his notebook, double checking to make sure he got all the digits right.

"Next problem I can see is height." Jake pointed at the conveyor belt. "Those things are like a meter-thirty high. You're not going to just hop up on it. Especially not her. You'll need a stepstool or something. How heavy are these backpack things? Can you climb with them?"

That was something that Quentin hadn't thought about. He was learning to be grateful when people pointed out things like this, instead of beating himself up for missing it, and he forced a grin. "Damn, that's a good catch. They're not too bad, I think we'll be able to climb a ladder."

"What are you going to do once you get in there? How does all this tie into taking that Holt guy out?"

"I don't know," Quentin admitted. "This is a recon trip. I'm hoping we can see what we need to see without anyone knowing we were there. Then we can flip back to the island and decide what to do. I don't know what to do with Holt. We'll figure that out as we go."

Jake clapped him on the back. "Well, you're the pro,

man. I gotta get back to work. Let me know if you need anything."

"Will do."

Jake walked back inside, and Quentin opened the DimGate, gesturing for Eissa to lead the way. "Come on, kid. Let's go get ready to do this thing."

Her eyebrows shot up, then turned down in the center as she squinted her eyes in a mock glare. "A kid is a baby goat. If you're going to call me anything, it should be 'Teacher,' instead of 'kid,' because I school your ass in everything we do."

"Yeah, yeah. Sounds to me like I got your goat."

"No, I've got *your* goat, right here," she said, pointing to her fist. "And I'm going to shove it where the sun doesn't shine if you don't watch it."

"Promises, promises."

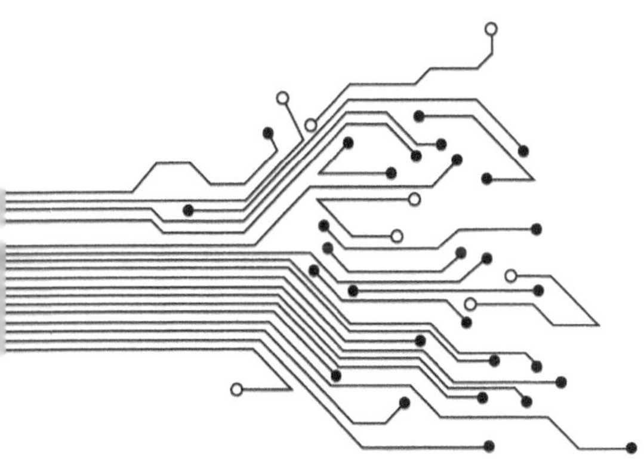

CHAPTER 16

"**T**esting, one, two." Eissa's voice blasted Quentin's eardrum, and he let out a shriek of pain as he clawed the radio out of his ear.

"Holy shit, why would these things even have the capacity to get that loud?" He rubbed his ear as he looked over the instruction booklet. "Okay, I need a paperclip or something. These have micro-buttons for controlling everything."

Eissa handed him a toothpick. "Will this work? I don't know if there's a paperclip anywhere on the island."

"Probably." Quentin took the toothpick and inserted it into the tiny indent, pressing down three times. "Okay, let's try it again. This time, just say 'test' so you don't rupture my eardrum if it's still too loud."

He slipped the radio back into his ear, but kept his fingers on it, just in case.

"Test."

He nodded. "Perfect. Now put yours in."

Eissa slid the radio into her ear. "Can you hear me now?" Her voice was faint and far away.

"Barely. Maybe that's why it was up so high. I guess we should have tried this first." He pulled the radio out of his ear and turned the volume back up. "Let's try again."

"I can hear you just fine."

Quentin nodded. "That's pretty good. Why don't you go outside and we'll test the range?"

Eissa slipped out the front door. "Picard to bridge, I'm going down the steps, over."

"Roger that."

"Ground Control, this is Major Tom. I'm entering the jungle on the DimGate trail, over."

"Still good," Quentin said. "Any static on your end?"

"Nope, it's like you're in my head, which is a terrifying thought."

Quentin chuckled. He had never used a radio before, other than toy walkie talkies when he was a kid, so he didn't have much to compare these to, but he was impressed with the audio quality.

"I'm at the DimGate," Eissa said. "How does it sound?"

"Crystal clear." He dropped his voice to a whisper. "Okay, let's try it at a whisper, like someone was in the room. Can you still hear me?"

"Perfect," Eissa whispered back. "These things are amazing."

"Okay, come on back. Let's get suited up."

They were wearing gray coveralls for this trip. The idea was that they would be nondescript, hopefully blending in to just about any environment they were likely to encounter, and if they were seen, they would look like they belonged there. The Mobile Gates were in large black backpacks, but they had cut the arms and legs off another pair of coveralls and fashioned an effective cover for each of the packs.

With the loose sleeves of the coveralls, Quentin was able to strap the micro-movers around his forearms. His wrists would need weeks to heal, but this way he could still use them if necessary. He had his vest on by the time Eissa got back to the cabin, and he helped her get into hers. Bob and Tocho helped them get the Mobile Gates programmed, double checking that the second screen would take them to Tocho's backyard in Dimension 444. After the fiasco with Holt, none of them wanted to risk jumping straight back to the island. If this location got compromised, they would have to start all over on setting up a new safe haven, and that was a daunting task.

Bob grabbed the folding stepstool that was leaning against the wall and handed it to Quentin. "Well, I think you're ready to go. It feels strange to send you off from right here in the house, but I guess there's no reason to go outside, huh?"

Quentin laughed. "I know, it seems like we should walk down to the DimGate or something."

"You'll be coming back to the DimGate, so at least there's that." Tocho adjusted the cover on Eissa's backpack. "Maybe Bob and I will get on the DimGate map and see if we can figure out the coordinates for the front yard, save you some walking."

"Remember your mission imperatives," Bob said. "Find a safe place to access your screen and get your current location. Dimension number and coordinates, both. Write it down if you have time, just in case something happens to the computer."

"I've got it," Quentin said, opening his notebook. "LOPES. I made up an acronym so I wouldn't forget anything. We need to know location, type of operation, number of people, equipment, and security. Then we jump to 444, then back here, and hopefully no one will be any the wiser."

"It's called a SALUTE report, jackass," Eissa said. "We did those in the army all the time. Size, activity, location, unit, time, equipment. You're reinventing the wheel."

Quentin blushed, turning his head away as he tried to think of something clever to say. "Well, I like mine better. It's only five things instead of six, so it's more streamlined."

Bob nodded. "Alright, you've got the gist of it, let's not get hung up on unimportant things." His eyebrows furrowed as he glared at each of them. "That's Plan A. What's Plan B, Eissa?"

"Pretty much the same as A, except that if we make contact with someone, we pull out our badges and explain that we are conducting a top-secret investigation. If they don't buy it, we bug out. No physical engagement, but no going to jail, either. Keep it as low-key as possible."

"And no dumping people in my backyard," Tocho said. "I may want to go back there some day, and I don't want some displaced DimCorp guard sleeping in my bed."

"Right," Eissa said with a wink. "No dirtying up Tocho's place."

Quentin picked up the stepstool and held it tight against his chest with one arm, flipping up the safety cover on the actuation button with the other hand. "Alright, let's do this." He shuffled around beside Eissa so that they were both facing north. "Ready?"

"Ready."

"Three, two, one, go."

The gloom of the cabin was replaced by the bright Nevada sunshine reflecting off the white concrete. The mystery building was on their left, and the big industrial conveyor belt sat a few feet in front of them, empty but running. Quentin looked around quickly, but there was no one in sight.

"Let's go," he whispered. He stepped over to the rumbling belt and opened the step stool. Eissa climbed the three steps, holding his outstretched hand for balance, and rolled onto the empty belt. Quentin followed her, awkwardly dragging the stool up with him as the belt slowly moved them inside the building.

He folded the stool and rolled over, clambering to his knees as they approached the flaps where the belt went into the building. The weight of the Mobile Gate made his movements jerky and uncoordinated. Eissa was a few yards ahead of him, and already on her hands and knees, ready to jump off the belt as soon as she found a suitable exit point. She disappeared through the flaps into the mystery building. Quentin's pulse was pounding in his temple, and he forced out the breath he had been holding. *Stay calm, Q. You got this.*

He glanced around one more time as he neared the building. They were out of the line of sight of the guard towers, and the only movement he could see was an orange fuel truck a quarter of a mile away. He turned back to the belt just as the hanging flaps brushed over the ladder, and a moment later he was inside.

The mystery building was dark, with no interior lighting and no windows, but there was no need for it. The conveyor belt went through a DimGate about fifteen feet inside the building, and there was plenty of light coming through it. He crawled forward, trying to get as close to Eissa as he could as they neared the Gate.

"I think we're clear to hop off on the left," Eissa whispered.

Quentin flinched, his heart pounding against his ribs. He had totally forgotten about the radio in his ear. "You scared the shit out of me."

Eissa didn't respond. She pushed herself up into a crouch. As soon as she was through the DimGate, she stepped off the belt to her left.

"There's a platform," she whispered.

Quentin used the stool to push himself up, crouching as he passed through the DimGate. They were in a massive warehouse, and the conveyor belt was the same height as the floor on this side. A line of automated forklifts sat ready, bristling with lasers and sensors. He prayed that the lifts wouldn't sense them and try to pick them up. Pallets of metal sat in neat rows behind them, separated by wide stripes of yellow paint on the floor. Quentin and Eissa hurried past the lifts and took cover between the pallets and the wall.

"Stay in the yellow areas," Quentin whispered. "These are probably the designated walkways. We don't want to get run over by a robot forklift."

"Right."

The building seemed to stretch out to infinity before them. There were pockets of activity here and there, and the noise of machinery was a steady roar, but nothing was moving nearby. Quentin relaxed slightly, leaning the stepstool against the pallet in front of them. They hadn't crossed into a swarm of DimCorp guards, so they were off to a good start.

"Turn around," Quentin said. "Let's go ahead and figure out where we are."

Eissa turned her back to him, and he pulled the cover away from the top of her backpack. The screen turned on at his touch, and he navigated to the *Present Location* tab. The page loaded instantly, and he recoiled in surprise, his stomach plummeting. "What the fuck?"

Eissa shifted, trying to see over her shoulder. "What? What does it say?"

"It says 01. We're in the Genesis Dimension."

"Are you shitting me?" Eissa hissed.

"I wouldn't shit you," Quentin said. "You're my favorite turd."

Eissa groaned at their childhood joke. "Seriously, Q. I know you make jokes when you're nervous, but this isn't the time. Write down the coordinates, and let's see if we can figure out where we're at on the map."

Quentin pulled his notebook out and jotted down the coordinates. He flipped back to the front cover to his list of repeated destinations and ran his finger down to the Genesis Dimension.

"I don't know how far it is in miles, but we're at 33.87 and the DimGate control room is at 33.61. That's pretty fucking close, probably less than ten miles. It might even be in the same complex for all we know."

He put the notebook back in his pocket. "Alright, so we've got our location. Now we need to figure out what they're doing here."

There were six rows of pallets in the staging area beside the conveyor belt, with ten pallets in a row. Each row was a different kind of metal, based on appearances, but Quentin couldn't tell what they were, other than that some were rods, some were plates, and some were ingots. An automated forklift appeared on their left, yellow and white strobe lights flashing on top of it. It drove on a blue stripe down the center of the wide throughway and pulled smoothly up to the furthest row. It picked up a pallet and went back the way it came.

"Should we try to follow that thing, see where it goes?"

Quentin shrugged. "Sounds like a plan to me. Everything seems to be automated so far, so that's something. If there aren't very many people here, maybe we can pull this off."

A floor-to-ceiling divider extended out from the wall after the last row of pallets, separating the receiving area from the next bay. They stayed against the wall as they made their way from one row to the next. It was impossible to tell if there were surveillance cameras in the high ceiling, but with the level of dust accumulated on everything, they probably wouldn't be seen even if there were.

To their right, on the other side of the travel lanes in the center of the vast space, a two-story concrete block structure stood, surrounded by a bright yellow catwalk. Doors and windows dotted the otherwise plain wall at irregular intervals.

"I'm guessing that's where the people work," Quentin whispered, pointing. "They probably monitor everything from in there, and the machines do the stuff out here."

"Sounds like a terrible job." Eissa pointed at an oncoming forklift, and they ducked down behind the pallet and waited for it to pass by.

They reached the divider and worked their way up to the edge of it, staying back against the last row of pallets. It was dim near the wall, but Quentin was still nervous about being out in the open. If someone happened to come out of their office and look around, the whole mission could be compromised.

From their vantage point behind the front pallet, they could see into the next bay. A robot was feeding sheets of steel into one end of a huge machine, and another robot was taking finished parts out of the machine on the other end and stacking them on a pallet. An automated forklift trundled the pallets of finished pieces up to a red square next to the travel lane and stacked them.

"What in the hell are they making?" Quentin asked. "Those look like gears or something."

"I don't know," Eissa said. "That second pallet looks like sprockets for a bicycle, except they're huge."

Quentin pointed down the row. "I think we can go straight down this line of pallets and get almost to the next bay under cover."

"Okay, let's move."

They crossed the bay in a crouching scuttle. Quentin kept his hand poised, ready to hit the escape button at the first sign of trouble, but they made it to the other side without incident. The next bay was a similar layout, but instead of one large machine, there was a line of drill presses. In front of each one, a robotic arm pulled blank steel plates off a pallet and slipped them into a jig. The press drilled a series of holes in the plates, and the arm stacked them on a different pallet. The red square was filled with finished plates.

"Whatever it is they're building, it takes a lot of heavy-duty parts," Quentin said.

They slowly crept across the bay, stopping twice to avoid forklifts. With all the sensors on the lifts, it was impossible to know if some of them were cameras that someone might be watching, or if the computer might register their presence and report it. Until they knew more, it was best to err on the side of caution.

The next bay ended in a wall. Across from it, the travel lane turned right and paralleled a line of bays down the side of the building. From their vantage point, they could see into the first huge bay across from them. It was filled with a variety of machines, some large, some small, some enclosed, some open.

"What are those things?" Eissa asked. "That one looks like a sewing machine, or something."

"3D printers," Quentin said. "I watched a documentary on these things last year. Some of those are way bigger than anything we have in our dimension, though. This is a serious operation. I'm dying to know what they're building."

Eissa elbowed him in the ribs and pointed to the far end of the building. "My guess would be that."

Quentin followed her finger. The control building in the center ended a few hundred yards down. Behind it, he could just see a line of pipes poking out, but it wasn't enough to recognize what he was looking at without moving to a better vantage point.

"I can't tell what those are," he whispered. "We need to get over to the wall so we can see."

"I can tell you exactly what they are," Eissa whispered. "Tanks."

Quentin gave her a puzzled look. "Tanks? Tanks of what?"

Eissa gave him an irritated sigh. "Tanks, Quentin. Battle tanks. Think army. M1 Abrams."

"Oh." Dawning realization settled on Quentin, and he recognized the pipes as a line of barrels. A long line. "Oh. We have to check that out."

"Agreed. Do you think we should take another GPS reading in this corner? It might not hurt to have some options, and there's some space back there that's out of the way."

Quentin nodded. "Good idea. I have a feeling we'll be coming back here."

They moved to the back wall behind a row of steel wheels.

The machine in this bay was coating them with a rubberized rim. "Road wheels," Eissa said. "Now that I know what they're making, this all makes sense."

In the dim corner of the building, there was a large open area that didn't seem to get used. Quentin paced it out and stood in the center of the square. "We'll take the reading here." He opened her backpack and turned the screen on. "I thought you were a medic. What do you know about tanks?"

"I know a lot about tanks," Eissa said. "I was attached to a mechanized infantry unit for a while. I even got to ride in a tank a couple of times. They're not very comfortable."

Quentin wrote down the coordinates in his notebook. "Okay, I think this will be a good alternate entry point. Let's try to get down to the tanks and see what we can see."

They stayed against the wall as much as possible, using the 3D printers as cover. The noise from the multitude of machines was deafening. Thick cables descended from the overhead cable trays to each printer, keeping the floor clear for the lifts to maneuver through the area. They also blocked the overhead lights, casting the whole section in a deep shadow.

By the time they reached the end of the bay, they were almost directly across from the tanks. He counted at least twelve tanks in the first row, but he couldn't be sure without getting closer. There were automated lifts moving around between him and the walkway, bringing raw materials to various machines and collecting finished products, and he was nervous about getting too close to them. On the far wall behind the tanks, he could see the flash of welders lighting up the ceiling like lightning.

"We need to get over there where the tanks are parked.

We'll be able to see the rest of the building from the center, and that will save us a lot of time."

Eissa hitched the Mobile Gate up and adjusted the hip belt. "Saving time sounds good. This thing is getting heavier by the minute."

They carefully worked their way out to the travel lane and stopped beside a steel support column. Two automated forklifts were coming towards them, one from each direction. Quentin glanced up at the control building. The mirrored surface of the windows reflected the dim walls behind them, making it impossible to see inside. The yellow catwalk was empty. Strobing yellow lights reflected off the dirty white walls as the forklifts passed.

"Okay," Quentin whispered. "Let's go."

They hurried across the wide expanse of the travel lane. Quentin's skin crawled with the sensation of being watched, and his stomach rolled at the vulnerability of being exposed like this. He had to resist the urge to run, which would look very suspicious if they were being observed. After a seeming eternity, they reached the other side and melted into the shadows between two rows of battle tanks.

"Hold up," Eissa said softly. "Did you see these labels?"

Quentin turned back to see what she was talking about. There was a piece of paper taped to the side of the tank, covered in production information.

Customer Name: Democratic People's Republic of Korea
Customer Dimension: 165
Project #: 2015165
Unit: 24 of 1,000
Delivery Date: 24 August

Eissa walked back to the first tank in the row. "This is unit 25 of 1,000. Now we know that there's twenty-five tanks per row."

Quentin tapped the paper with a finger as she walked back up to him. "I think you missed out on the wildly more important part. These things are being built for our dimension. See there? Customer Dimension 165."

"Oh shit, I didn't even catch that." She peered at the paper. "What the hell is the Democratic People's Republic of Korea? Is that North Korea or South Korea?"

"North."

Eissa slowly turned to stare at Quentin. "Wait a minute. Wait a minute." She raised her hands and massaged her temples for a moment. "So, DimCorp is building a thousand tanks for North Korea in our dimension? Is that what that says?"

"That's what I got out of it," Quentin said. "And the delivery date is a week away."

"But why? That's crazy. Do you know huge that is?"

Quentin shrugged. "It sounds like a lot."

"It's probably more tanks than the US and South Korea have."

Quentin's breath caught in his throat. If that was true, then North Korea was probably about to double its firepower. There was only one reason they would spend that kind of money. "Holy shit, they're about to start a war."

Eissa nodded. "Yeah, and if they attack South Korea, then the US is going to get involved."

"And then China, and Russia, and the UK, and the next thing you know, it's World War 3," Quentin said. "This is fucking huge."

"Right. And it's probably not just tanks. There're a lot of other vehicles that go along with them. You need ammo carriers, fuel trucks, armored personnel carriers, all of that."

"Which means this is just one factory," Quentin said. "How the hell is North Korea paying for all this?"

"Who knows?" Eissa said. "They're probably letting DimCorp pull oil out of there or something."

"Or maybe DimCorp gets to come in after it's over and set up operations." Quentin imagined Vincent Macalister running a farming operation in Gainesville and shuddered. It was one thing when it was somewhere else, but when it was your hometown being exploited, and the people you know working as slaves, it became a lot more personal.

This was a major game-changer. They had to come up with a way to stop these tanks from being delivered, as well as any other equipment that was being manufactured for North Korea, and they only had a week to do it. Quentin felt like an ant trying to stop a herd of elephants. He let out a deep sigh.

"Alright, let's try to look around a little more and see what we can see, then we'll go back and talk this out with Bob and Tocho. We've stumbled onto some major doings here."

They walked down to the far end of the row of tanks. The smell of fresh paint was sickly sweet, and as they approached the other end of the line, the tangy, biting smell of welding began to mix in with it. He tried to breathe as shallowly as possible to avoid inhaling the odors. "This place reeks. I'm probably going to have cancer by the time we get out of here."

Eissa snorted. "The way we're going, we won't live long enough to worry about cancer."

After listening to Jake's depiction of his recent near-death experiences, Quentin found it difficult to argue with her about that. It was better to not even think about that kind of thing, especially right now. He crouched down beside the massive track of the last tank and leaned forward, casting a quick glance in both directions.

The bay across the travel lane on this side of the building was very different than the ones they had seen so far. For one thing, the robots were mobile, rather than stationary. Overhead hoists lifted big sheets of metal up in the air while wheeled robots moved around on the ground, holding them in place while other robots welded them together to form a hull. The hull was then placed on a wheeled cradle, and the robots bolted suspension parts into place. Small carts carrying boxes of parts and bolts zipped in and out of the work area, delivering each piece just as it was needed and then backing out of the way. Quentin watched in amazement as the rough outline of a tank took shape in minutes before the cradle was towed to the next station.

"Look at that," Quentin whispered. "This makes our automated factories seem primitive by comparison.

"It's pretty impressive," Eissa agreed. "Those things are like a toolbox with arms."

The design of the wheeled robots made perfect sense. They had five multi-jointed legs, making them spider-like on the lower half as they adjusted their height to do various tasks. It was hard to tell how many arms they had, as many of them retracted when not in use. One hand-like appendage had a variety of sockets for fingers, while another was a welder, and another a grinder. They moved with fluid precision and surprising speed, especially the hands inserting bolts through holes and starting nuts. Having put his share of furniture together, Quentin was impressed that everything aligned perfectly on the first try, and they didn't cross-thread the nuts.

"Let's back up," Quentin said. "These things are parked bumper to bumper, but I think we can crawl across the rows right under the front end without getting the backpacks hung up. I want to see what's further down."

Eissa sighed in his ear. "What is it with you always trying to get me on my knees?"

Quentin groaned. "Now who's making inappropriate jokes?"

"What do you mean?" Eissa asked with exaggerated innocence. "I'm just saying that crawling across this concrete floor with a hundred-pound backpack is going to be hard on the knees. Get your mind out of the gutter."

"Uh huh. Let's go, Sister Chastity. Take it easy so I can see how much clearance you've got. We can't risk breaking anything on the DimGates and getting stuck here."

Eissa backed up to the front of the tank and gripped a tie-down eyelet as she carefully lowered down to her knees. The front of the tank was a narrow wedge shape, terminating a good four feet above the floor, but the back of the tank facing it was a much steeper angle. She slowly crawled between them, and Quentin squatted down and watched carefully.

"As long as we stay to the right, we'll be fine," he said. "Let's go, I'm right behind you."

They crossed row after row of tanks, and Quentin lost count after a while as his knees began to ache from the beating. He was thinking about the knee pads he'd seen hanging on a rack at Prepper's Paradise when his face hit something soft but yielding.

"Get your face out of my ass," Eissa hissed. "Your nose just gave me a wedgie."

He scrambled back a foot, scrubbing his face with his sleeve. "What the hell are you doing?"

"Stopping, what does it look like? I gotta take a break, this is killing my knees and wrists."

Quentin tried to see behind him to gauge how far they'd come, but it was impossible to tell. "Alright, let's go take a look at the bay and get our bearings."

He waited as she got to her feet and moved into the aisle. He didn't want to admit it, but he was glad she had thrown in the towel. This way she couldn't give him grief about tapping out first. Once she was clear, he crept forward and grabbed the outer tread pad of the track in front of him, pulling himself to his feet and brushing his hands off on his pants legs.

"Remind me to add gloves to our shopping list. Exploring factories is dirty work." He motioned with his head. "Let's go take a look."

He could still see the previous bay where the hulls were constructed, and he guessed that they had come past about twenty rows of tanks. In the bay across from them, a different variation of the spider robots was installing wiring harnesses into the hulls. Their freakishly long arms reached inside the hulls, feeding wires along the walls and screwing clamps in at regular intervals. The arms on the outside of the hull held spools of wire, wrapping them together in a casing as they dispensed into the hull.

To their left, a series of turrets sat in cradles. Similar robots surrounded them, installing wiring inside and outside. They pulled back as a large flat box on wheels came down the travel lane, towing a turret in a cradle. It stopped just past their position and backed the cradle into an open slot. A moment later it drove back the way it had come, small yellow lights flashing on both ends.

"Did you hear that?" Eissa's voice was barely audible, despite the earpiece radio.

"Hear what?" He turned slightly to look at her. She was facing the other way, looking down the walkway behind them.

"Voices." She tugged at his sleeve, shuffling back to the other end of the tank. "Somebody's out here. We've got to get out of sight."

Quentin looked around in alarm. The only thing he could hear was Eissa's breath panting in his ear as she slid back under the tank. He followed as quick as he could, ignoring the instant flash of pain in his knees as he crawled into the darkness. A moment later he heard it, two men talking. The voices grew louder as they neared, and a minute later he could see two sets of legs at the other end of the tank they were hiding beneath.

"No way, man," one of them said. "If he rushed for fifteen hundred yards, he'd be in the Pro Bowl, no question."

"That's not a guarantee," the other voice argued. "There's a lot of factors."

Quentin heard the telltale sound of duct tape being pulled from a roll and relaxed slightly. These guys were probably just taping labels on the tanks. They weren't security guards looking for intruders. Suddenly a sheaf of papers hit the floor, scattering everywhere. Some of them went out in the travel lane, but some of them came under the tank.

"Aw, shit," the first voice said. "That's twice now. Do you need me to carry the damn signs?"

Quentin jerked back as he realized what was about to happen, hitting his head on the bottom of the tank above him.

He scrambled to shift his weight off his arm so he could get to the button on his shoulder. "Jump, jump," he hissed. His fingers found the safety cover and popped it out of the way. A knee came into view at the other end of the tank, followed by a hand. He couldn't see Eissa from this angle, and all he could do was hope she could get out before the inevitable head followed the hand into view. He held his breath and hit the button.

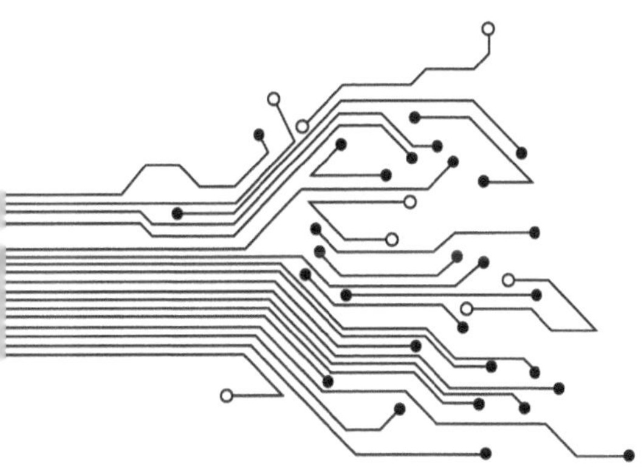

Carl Holt limped down the basement hallway, passing his office for the third time. The ever-present ache in his ribs reminded him why he was exercising so much. His next meeting with Quentin James could happen at any moment, and he wasn't going to be unprepared again.

Trekking up and down the hallway every two hours was serving other purposes, as well. The security staff here at DimCorp's headquarters had gotten lazy and complacent. He could easily see how they had slowly become that way. After all, who would be crazy enough to attack DimCorp right at the center of their operations? That would be like attacking the Kremlin, or the Pentagon. It was unthinkable, really, and if someone did it once, no one else would ever be brave enough to hit them again. No one until Quentin James, anyway. There were new failsafe policies in place now, and his continuous presence throughout the building ensured that they were being implemented.

He stopped at the IT room and opened the door. It was much smaller than the DimGate Control Center on the other end of the hallway, which housed most of the computing power for the entire complex. Lieutenant Baker sat in front of a bank of monitors, typing at a furious rate. Six other assistants were in the room, all absorbed in their screens. Baker glanced up as he entered the office and spun around in his chair to greet him.

"Hey, sir, how are you feeling?"

Holt shut the door behind him and nodded. "Not too bad. How are things going in here?"

Baker gestured toward the screen. "Doing pretty good. I'm writing a program that will allow the facial recognition software to operate in real time, or pretty close to it, in all the DimCorp systems in the Genesis Dimension."

"What do you mean?" Holt asked. He could tell that Baker was staring at his black eye but ignored it. "Don't we already have that?"

"No, not exactly. What we have is the ability to pull video from a hard drive at one of our factories, for example, and run it through our system. If there's anyone on there that we have flagged, the system will pick them up, assuming we have a decent shot of them on the video."

"Then how did it ping on James showing up here at the front desk last week?"

"That's different," Baker explained. "All the cameras here at Headquarters run through it automatically, since we're all on one network. Everyone else is on their own network, so their camera feeds don't come here, they go to their servers. This program I'm writing will create a duplicate feed at each DimCorp location and send it here. Once we get a dedicated server installed to handle the workload, we'll be able to monitor all the DimCorp locations here and get notifications if someone on the list shows up."

Holt shook his head. Technology wasn't his strong suit, and its shortcomings were baffling sometimes. It seemed like this sort of thing should have been overcome by now. For all their advancements, they were still only a stone's throw out of the caves in some ways.

"As long as it works." Holt reached for the door. "How long before we can have it running across all the dimensions?"

Baker looked at him uncertainly. "Sir?"

"I said, how long before we can have it running in the other dimensions? I want it running in 443 and 165 first. If James pops up somewhere, I want to know about it immediately."

"I- we don't have any way to do that," Baker said. "I'm taxing the system pretty radically just to make this work in our own dimension. We'd need a hundred people and two years to figure out how to make this function interdimensionally. And an unlimited budget."

Once again, the lack of resources was keeping him from protecting company assets. The irony was too much. DimCorp was *the* resource for resources, and yet, he couldn't protect their resources due to a lack of resources. Unbelievable. He opened the door.

"Well, do the best you can. I want someone monitoring this thing 24/7, and I will be notified instantly if James or Spartacus shows up. I don't care what time of day or night it is, understood?"

"Yes, sir."

"Get with the IT guys in 443 and 165. I want some sort of facial recognition running on their systems ASAP, and I want to know the second James shows up either place. This is a top priority for everyone."

"Yes, sir. Do you want me to pull people from the Dixon case for this? That's our current top priority."

Holt took a deep breath, welcoming the pain as his ribs expanded. He was tired of juggling things, tired of trying to perform miracles day in and day out. The Dixon case *was* a top priority. So was the James case. And ten other things. "Pull one person. Keep the rest on Dixon. We need to get that wrapped up."

Baker gave him a sad smile. "I'm sorry, boss. You know as well as I do, we could keep a hundred people busy if we had them."

"I know it." Holt's face hardened. "And make sure everyone knows that if someone gets James in custody and then releases him to anyone except me, and I mean me in the flesh, I will personally rip their fucking arms off and beat them to death with them."

Holt closed the door behind him and walked down the hall. This bullshit about James and Amor showing up with badges and bluffing their way around had to stop. It had already happened twice that he knew of, and that made him wonder how many other times they had done it that he didn't even know about. There were a hundred ongoing investigations at any given moment across the dimensions, and while most of them were fairly straightforward, there were several tough cases with no answers. Could James be involved in some of them? Was he failing to connect the dots on an even bigger picture than he realized? There were just so many unknowns.

Sergeant Treijo glanced up as he entered the outer office. Her desk was neat and tidy, as always, despite the workload he kept on her. "Good walk?"

He grunted. "It was alright. Any messages?"

She nodded. "Mr. Zimmerman called again. He said you missed your appointment with the FBI, and they're not too happy about it."

"Goddammit," Holt grumbled. "I forgot all about that. What else?"

"That was the only call," she said. "Captain Mathers is waiting for you in your office."

"Good." Holt walked across the room. "If Zimmerman calls back again, tell him I got hit by a bus and I'm in a coma."

Treijo chuckled as he closed the door.

"Mathers, tell me something good," Holt said, easing himself carefully into his chair with a grimace.

"Well, I think I know how James kicked your ass so bad," Mathers said with a grin.

Holt gave him a hard stare for a moment, but relaxed it into a weak grin of his own. Mathers was probably the only person alive who could say something like that to his face and get away with it, but with all the wet work they had done together over the years, he had earned the right to chide the boss now and then. "Let's hear it."

"I was trying to figure out how he could lock you down, what kind of technology exists that could do that. You said he was in 443, right? Well, they have a thing called a micro-mover. It's a device that picks up your brain waves and transfers the energy, lets you move stuff without touching it. They sell it as a luxury item, lets people change the channel, turn the lights on, pick the paper up off the porch without bending over, that sort of thing. It's not very strong though, definitely shouldn't be strong enough to pin your arms down."

"Huh," Holt grunted. "Is there a military version, something stronger?"

Mathers shook his head. "Not that I could find. There's a few different brands, but I didn't find anything else. Of course, if the Chinese military had them, we'd probably never know."

"How do we protect against it?"

Mathers shrugged. "I doubt that you can, really, other than keeping your distance. It won't have much of a range, so just don't get close to him. That's why God invented the rifle."

"Alright, moving on." Holt turned the computer on. "We need to brainstorm. I've got Baker working on facial recognition, so if they show up somewhere, we should know about it. That's reactionary, though. What can we do proactively? How can we find this fucker and take him down before he does something?"

Mathers leaned back in the chair, stretching his hands up over his head. "That's a tough one, boss. Are you still certain he's going to hit the spaceport in 443?"

"Pretty sure, yeah. I can't imagine why else he would've been there."

"Could have been a coincidence," Mathers said. "Just playing devil's advocate."

Holt didn't reply. What if it had been a coincidence? What would that change? The fact remained that James had fled instead of giving himself up, and then he'd stolen two Mobile Gates. The location of his next strike might not be 100% certain, but the fact that he was up to something sinister was beyond question.

"Anyway, if you want to find him, you've got to draw him out," Mathers said. "He's got wheels, so trying to find him will be worse than a needle in a haystack. You gotta make him come to you."

"I'm listening. How do we do that?"

Mathers grinned. "You gotta have something he wants, and let him know you have it. Something important."

Holt's eyes lit up as the idea took root. "Son of a bitch, you're right." He grabbed the mouse and clicked through the folders on his computer. "What was the sister's name? They lived together in 165. She ought to be a sufficient piece of bait, right?" He opened a document and scanned over it. "Here it is. Denise James."

"Want me to go get her?"

Holt smiled. "Yes, please."

How to let James know they had her was another question, but he could work on that while she was in route. He pulled up the list of duty assignments. He was going to need a team ready to capture James, and he wasn't going to underestimate him this time. When James showed up to either rescue his sister or negotiate for her release, they would take him into custody and make sure he never saw the sunshine again.

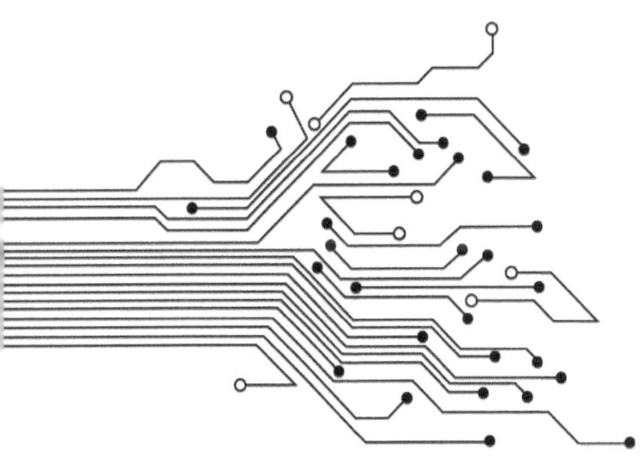

CHAPTER 18

The ground fell out from beneath Quentin for a long second, the fall completely disorienting him as his eyes adjusted to the light. It took him a second to identify the sudden assault on his face as rain, and his vision returned just as his face and arms hit the dirt. His feet continued down, splashing in the ankle-deep water as they plunged into the mud at the bottom of the hole. He spat out a mouthful of grass and dirt.

"Shit. I landed in the damn hole again." He looked around, his heart pounding. Eissa was behind him, laying on her back on the Mobile Gate like an upside-down turtle, her legs kicking futilely as she tried to flip over. He laughed at the spectacle. "I wish I could video this. You look ridiculous."

She paused in her struggles and lifted her head, glaring at him. "Keep laughing. Once I get up, I'm going to get the shovel and bury you in that damned hole."

"Alright, alright." He scrambled up to the surface and extended a muddy hand to her. "Let's get inside Tocho's cabin before the rain fries the Mobile Gates. I definitely don't want to get trapped in this dimension."

She reached up and grasped his forearm and made her way clumsily to her feet. "Thanks. These backpacks aren't too bad to walk around in, but they're a bitch when you're laying down."

They turned and jogged across the yard to the cabin. The door was unlocked, as Tocho had promised, and they quickly ducked inside out of the rain. Eissa opened the curtains on the front window to let in some light.

"We need to find a towel or something," Quentin said. "My hands are all muddy, and I'm afraid to touch the screen."

"It's nice to come here in the daylight and not have Carl Holt accompanying us," Eissa said. "At least we have a second to get our shit together this time."

The cabin was tiny but spacious. The A-frame was designed with one single room covering the ground floor with a small loft at each end. Most of the wall space was hidden by overflowing bookshelves, except for a small kitchen counter on the back wall. Quentin found a hand towel next to a large basin and a water bucket.

"This must be the sink," he said. "Do you want to wash your hands?"

"Yeah, for sure." She glanced over the books as she approached. "I thought Bob had an impressive library in his cabin, but I think Tocho could give him a run for his money."

Quentin chuckled. "Let's just be glad they haven't tried to move all these to the island. We'd have to build another extension on the cabin."

"Dude, no loud laughing. You're still in my ear, remember?"

"My bad." He wiped his face and dried his hands, stepping aside so she could wash up. "Did you get out before that guy saw you? I had my back to you, so I don't know who went first."

"I left before you did. The last thing I saw was his hand."

"Well, that's a relief. I can't believe how close it was, though. What are the odds?"

"Pretty good, from what the other guy said." She dried

her hands and hung the towel from the handle of the water bucket. "Let's get back to 107. My knees are fucking killing me."

Quentin programmed her screen, then knelt down so she could program his. As soon as his knees touched the hardwood floor, pain shot up and down his legs. Kneepads were definitely going on the shopping list. When she was done, he rose stiffly to his feet.

"Ready?" He flipped the safety cover up.

"Ready."

"See you on the other end." He pressed the button.

"North Korea?" Bob asked. "Are you sure?"

Quentin nodded gravely. "No question about it. A thousand tanks, and God knows what else, and the delivery date is a week away."

Bob grunted. "Ain't that a damn pickle." He absently brushed wood shavings out of his beard, his eyes fixed on the trees beyond the yard.

Quentin and Eissa sat side by side on the porch in the new rocking chairs, their legs propped up. Tocho had made a quick trip to Dimension 443 and procured some ice packs for their knees while they showered and changed.

"That's enough to start a war in any dimension," Tocho said. "But I think we have more than a week. It will take time for them to train an army to use them."

"True enough," Bob said. "But right now, they're all in one spot, and we know exactly where they are. Once they ship, it'll be impossible to track them all."

Tocho needed silently. The wind shifted, bringing the salty

smell of the ocean with it as it pushed fallen leaves across the yard to the porch.

"Did you know they have factories in the Genesis Dimension?" Quentin asked.

"Yeah, they're on one of the maps Rupert got us." Bob began whittling again. "The DimCorp headquarters building we went to is surrounded by factories and warehouses. You only saw a tiny piece of it, but it's huge, like a city."

The idea of being anywhere near the security building in the Genesis Dimension made Quentin uneasy. By now, every security guard would know who they were, and probably had orders to shoot on sight. Out of all the dimensions, why did this factory have to be there?

"How are we going to stop them from shipping?" Eissa asked. "It's not like we can just go slash the tires so they can't drive. Tanks are practically indestructible."

No one answered. They hadn't had much time to work on details like that while exploring the factory, and Quentin slowly realized how daunting the task was. Eissa was right, tanks were designed to be shot at by other tanks. There wasn't much they could do to disable them. Even if they managed to set the factory on fire, which wasn't very likely, since everything was metal and concrete, the tanks would probably escape with nothing worse than a singed paint job.

"Tell me some more about the factory," Bob said. He held the stick up to the light, critically inspecting his carving as he turned it back and forth.

"Everything is automated," Quentin said. "CNC machines, 3D printers, forklifts, assembly robots, welder robots, everything. If you take out the part about the tanks, it's actually really amazing."

"Mmmm," Bob grunted. "And it's all in a big rectangle, with the control building and the finished vehicles in the center?"

"Right." Quentin lifted the ice pack from his right leg and flexed his knee experimentally. It was stiff, but not as painful as it had been.

Tocho chuckled. "What was that grenade you had, Bob, the one that burned through the train tracks? You remember that?"

"Thermite."

"That's right!" Tocho laughed again. "We need a thousand thermite grenades. We can put one on top of the engine on each tank, and just go down the line. It would be a tremendous fireworks display."

Bob laughed heartily. "Yeah, that would do it, for sure. Can you imagine the smell in there after that?"

Quentin smiled faintly, not really seeing the relevance of the idea. The logistics of locating, getting, transporting, and using a thousand thermite grenades would be impossible. Even if they had a thousand of them sitting on the porch, they wouldn't be able to use them on more than about ten tanks. What they needed was something that would disable them all at once, permanently. Not fire, not a bomb, not a thousand grenades. What if…

"Hear me out." Quentin sat up, swinging his feet down. The ice packs dropped to the floor with a thump. "I'm thinking out loud, alright? What if, and I know this didn't work last time, but what if we used the robots?"

Eissa looked puzzled. "What the hell are you talking about, Q?"

"The robots," he repeated, excitement creeping into his

voice. "There're hundreds of robots running around there with welders and drills and grinders, right? They've got to be controlled by a central computer program. If we can get into the computer, we can reprogram them to start destroying the tanks."

Eissa scrunched her nose up. "How is the robot going to destroy a tank?"

"It wouldn't take much, really. They could use a torch or a welder to burn a hole in the hull, and then burn another hole through the engine block, maybe weld something together in the engine or the transmission. They could probably do that in two or three minutes, right? Then the tank can't be sold, and it would need major repairs. I don't even know if they could fix a hole in the hull, they might have to scrap the whole thing."

The other three were staring at him, sparks of interest glinting in their eyes as the idea began to sink in. It was impossible to know exactly how many robots were in the factory that could be used, but even if there were only a hundred, each robot would need to disable ten tanks. At five minutes each, just to be safe, the whole operation would be done in an hour.

"What about the people in the control room?" Bob asked. "They're sure to sound the alarm, even if you go in shooting, and knowing you, that's probably not going to happen. The cavalry won't be far away in the Genesis Dimension."

"That's a fair question," Quentin said. "We'll have to figure out how to deal with the people inside. But if we can make that work without setting off an alarm and bringing the death squad in, we could probably run around to some of the other factories and do the same thing. That would set them back a year or two, at least."

Bob chuckled as he resumed whittling. "You might be getting carried away, but I like your idea. Let's figure out how we get you inside the control room and then back out again."

The control room was the one thing they didn't know anything about, other than it was two stories tall, concrete block, and had a yellow catwalk around it. Quentin kicked himself for not paying more attention to it. Little details could be important later, like what kind of doors it had, where the windows were, was there roof access, that kind of stuff.

They had to plan for the worst-case scenario, so it was safe to assume the doors were steel, and locked at all times. What would it take to gain access? Would someone open the door if they knocked? Was anyone inside armed? And speaking of being armed, how would they handle it if Holt brought an army? They had bulletproof vests, but faced with the possibility of twenty people shooting at them, the vests seemed inadequate. He'd feel better in a fully armored vehicle.

He thought back to the exoskeletons Jake had showed them at Prepper's Paradise. They weren't enclosed, but what if they could be? If so, they would be very useful, assuming the Mobile Gate could move one between dimensions. He could open doors with it, run fast if necessary, and it had an onboard computer with a heads-up display in the helmet. Maybe he could load a map on it or something.

He reached over and poked Eissa in the ribs. "Hey, you remember the exoskeletons at Prepper's Paradise?"

"Yeah, what about them?"

Quentin rocked back and forth, the chair click-clacking as it moved across the floorboards. "What if we could come up with a way to add some armor to those things? That would protect us a lot more than the vests could, right?"

Eissa's brow furrowed. "I guess, but I don't really see how that would be practical. You have to sit at a computer, right? How would that work?"

"I don't know. We should go talk to Jake and see what he thinks. He seemed to have a plan for modifying them to add weapons back when he was trying to sell us one, so maybe there's an up-armor kit for them."

"What are you thinking?" Bob asked. "Use the armored suit to defend the control room while you work on the computers?"

Quentin nodded. "Yeah, exactly. Two of us in full armor, inside a concrete block room, we can probably hold off a serious attack for an hour or two. Even if we have to bug out early, the damage will be significant enough to do the job. We'll need guns to keep them from rushing us, and to make the employees comply, but I really don't think anyone needs to get hurt for us to accomplish this. Then we jump back here with the Mobile Gates. Job done."

Except it wasn't job done, not completely. Once again, something that had started out as a crusade to bring Carl Holt to justice had morphed into a whole different thing. He didn't even have a plan for Holt, or how to go about presenting him to the police, or even what dimension to do it in. All he'd managed to do in that regard was get in an ugly street fight that nearly got him killed.

"What about programming the robots?" Tocho asked. "How sure are you that you can do it?"

"Not very sure," Quentin said. "But I bet the people that work in there can do it. If we kick the doors in like Terminator and shoot up a filing cabinet or something, I think they'll be happy to do it."

Bob snorted, sending wood shavings flying out of his beard. "You sound awfully confident."

"They're computer geeks, like me. They're not going to sacrifice themselves to save DimCorp's tanks. Hell, they'll probably get a kick out of it, truth be told."

Silence settled over the porch. Even if they couldn't figure out how to add shielding to the exoskeletons, they could probably pull this off with a couple of pistols. It was hard to guess how many people would be in the control building, but it wasn't likely that very many of them would be cowboys, willing to duke it out on behalf of the company. A little bit of gentle persuasion would go a long way with most of them. For the few resistors, there was always the old axiom of speak softly and carry a big stick.

Quentin stood up slowly, stretching his hands up to the ceiling and then dropping them with a sigh. "Let's go see Jake and figure out what our equipment options are."

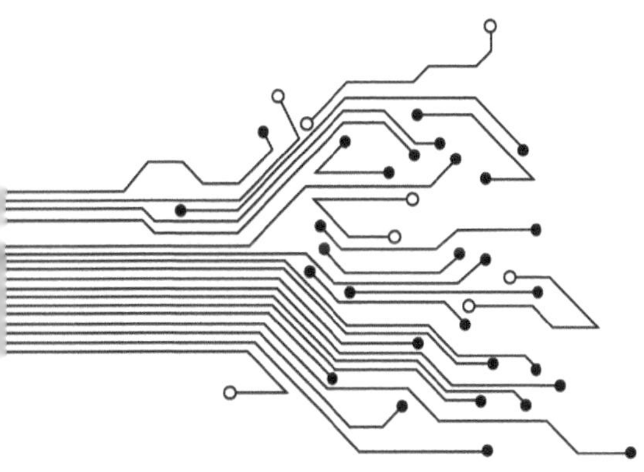

CHAPTER 19

The DimGate made its characteristic hum and engaged with a click. Quentin watched as Eissa poked her head through the door and glanced around. He was starting to get nervous about showing up behind Prepper's Paradise during business hours. Eventually, there would be someone standing there smoking a cigarette when they opened the Gate, and that wouldn't be good.

"Let's go," Eissa said over her shoulder.

Quentin followed her through to Dimension 443. As always, the sun reflected off the white concrete, blinding him with its intensity. Yet another reason to find a better spot to cross over. A nice cool spot inside the storeroom would be good, or maybe a dark corner in the basement. He made a mental note to ask Jake about it.

The back door to the store was locked, so he pulled his phone out and sent Jake a quick text. The reply came back a moment later.

It's Sunday, dude. Store's closed. What's up?

"Well, shit," Quentin said with a laugh. "I've been spoiled by the island life."

Eissa looked up at him, shading her eyes with her hand. "What are you talking about?"

Quentin held his phone out so she could read the message. "We may not operate by the calendar, but apparently the rest of the world still does."

It had been a long time since he'd thought about what day of the week it was, which was a bit startling. He would be hard-pressed to even say what month it was. Quentin had spent his entire life revolving around the calendar, dreading Mondays, anticipating Fridays, dating this form and that, punching the timeclock. Somehow all that had fallen by the wayside, and he hadn't really been conscious of it happening.

r u available for quick mtg? We can come to u if u have safe spot for Gate.

"Why would they be closed on Sunday?" Eissa asked. "Don't they know we have shit to do?"

Quentin's phone buzzed in his hand.

36.243746, -115.342877

"Alright, we're in business." He opened the panel on the DimGate and input the data to take them back to the island. "I do wish this thing could take you back to the previous location like the Mobile Gates do, that's a huge time saver."

Eissa huffed. "I still don't see why you can't go from one spot to another inside the same dimension. That's ridiculous."

Quentin didn't bother responding. Eissa tended to ridicule things she didn't understand, and he didn't want to get into an argument over science that he could barely grasp, himself. The Gate clicked, and they stepped back through the door to the island. He opened the panel and began inputting the coordinates Jake had sent him.

"Alright, we're going to an unknown spot." He peered closely at the map. "It looks like he's sending us to the open desert just outside of Vegas. Be super-cautious when you open the door, just in case."

"I know, I know." She put her hand on the knob. "I'm not five years old, I remember the rules from the last ten thousand times you told me."

Quentin activated the Gate, unperturbed. "Chance favors a prepared mind."

He kept his hand on the emergency shutdown button as she opened the door a crack. This part was always stressful, trying to be ready for anything, but praying that his hand didn't twitch and accidently shut down the DimGate while she had her head poked through to the other side. Finally, she gave him the all-clear.

Jake was sitting a few yards away on the tailgate of his truck cleaning a pistol when Quentin crossed over. A cardboard box with an orange target on it was wedged under some scrub brush nearby, and off in the distance a low mountain range shimmered in the heat. Las Vegas was off to their right, the first subdivision perhaps a mile away.

"Hey, you made it!" He laid the gun on a rag and hopped off the tailgate. "You guys want to burn up some ammo?"

"Sounds like fun," Eissa said. "What kind of hardware do you have?"

Jake handed her the pistol. "This is a .45, kicks a little harder than a nine, but way more knockdown power. You used one before?"

Eissa took it and ejected the magazine, then pulled the slide back and checked the chamber. "Yeah, it's been a bit, but I used to know my way around one."

Jake handed her a loaded clip, and she gave him the empty. She chambered a round, and before Quentin could plug his ears, she spread her legs in a wide shooter's stance and fired five shots in rapid succession. The box danced around under the bush as the center of the orange bullseye disappeared. Dropping to one knee, she fired five more times. The slide locked back, and she ejected the empty magazine and stood up.

"It's got a heavy trigger," she said, laying the gun back on the rag. "It's fine for target shooting, but if you were in a firefight, that would slow you down."

Jake nodded, a wide grin splitting his face. "Medic, huh? You really know your quix, lady."

Eissa shrugged. "Medics have to qualify at the firing range just like everybody else. I was attached to a lot of different units, so I've shot just about everything you can think of."

Quentin felt awkwardly out of place as he listened to Eissa and Jake talk guns. He had only fired a gun a few times in his life, and the last time was when he killed Vincent Macalister in Dimension 214. His stomach lurched at the thought, the image of Macalister splayed over his chair, blood pooling around him, burning in his mind as if it had happened minutes before, rather than months.

"So, what are you two up to today?" Jake's voice brought him back to the present, and he shook off the ill feeling in his gut.

"We're brainstorming," Quentin said, hopping up on the tailgate. He shifted to his right a bit, putting his back to the sun. If they were going to keep coming to the desert, he was going to have to get a pair of sunglasses. "I wanted to talk to you about those exoskeletons you showed us."

Jake laughed. "Those things are great fun. I'm guessing you're not looking to do the gaming thing with them though, huh?"

"Not exactly." Quentin pointed at the pistol beside him. "Didn't you say there was a way to modify them, some sort of weapons thing?"

Jake began disassembling the pistol, wiping each part down. "Yeah, it's possible. Tell me what you want, exactly."

"I don't know if it's possible, but I'd really like to weld some armor plating onto one and be able to shoot a gun of some kind. It would be even better if we could have something with a scope that would show up in the heads-up display."

Jake was silent. He scrubbed at a black smudge on the bolt, turning it back and forth as he inspected it. Quentin was starting to wonder if he had heard when he put the bolt down and looked over.

"You're going into DimRec, right? You think you're going to end up in a shootout with the security guards, and you want more protection than a vest can give you."

Quentin nodded. "In a nutshell, yes."

"What's your mission? What do you need to be able to do in the suit?"

"We're crossing into another dimension. All that metal from the spaceport is going to an automated factory where they make battle tanks. We're going to break into the control center, force the programmers to reconfigure the robots out on the floor to destroy the tanks, and then jump dimensions to escape. Resistance from the employees should be low, but I rather expect some soldiers to show up, and we need to be able to fend them off until the tanks are destroyed."

"Are you going to need to access a computer, or plug into the network?"

Quentin paused. "I don't know. Maybe."

Jake reassembled the pistol and shoved it in a black holster. "I'm going way out on a limb here, man. There's a possibility we can do something really cool, but I need to make a phone call. Just sit tight for a minute, okay?"

"Sure thing, man." Quentin watched as Jake walked away, pulling his phone out as he scrambled up on a low ridge nearby. The breeze whipped his words away with the occasional tumbleweed, but his body language indicated that he was having a serious discussion with the person on the other end of the phone. His free hand waved about as he stalked up and down the broken rocks. Two minutes passed, then three. The sun beating down Quentin's neck was starting to burn when Jake finally hung up the phone and trudged back to them.

"Alright, we're going to go see a friend of mine. He's got something that will work perfect for this." Jake pointed at the DimGate. "His place is out in the boondocks. Can we use that to get there?"

Quentin's breath caught in his chest. Taking the DimGate to an unknown place was risky all by itself, but showing strangers that it existed was a terrifying proposi-tion. "I don't think that's a good idea. You know what it was like when we showed you the DimGate, remember? We can't just let people know about this thing. Who are we going to see?"

Jake raised his hands. "This isn't just anybody, man. He goes by da Vinci. He's an off-grid Tech-Mod, probably one of the best."

"What's a Tech-Mod?" Eissa asked.

"Maybe you have another name for them," Jake said. "Tech-Mods build hi-tech stuff like robots, AI controllers, augmented-body tech, that kind of stuff. Some of them work for the government, or big companies, and some are off-grid, and only do black market stuff."

"Huh," Quentin said. "I don't think we have anything like that in our dimension. Of course, if it's a black-market thing, I probably wouldn't know about it, even if it was happening next door to me. So, what can this guy do for us? Da Vinci, was it?"

"Yeah. I doubt that anyone knows his real name except for his mother. These guys are nuts about security, and understandably so. He's going to hook us up with FAT suits. It won't be cheap, but it'll be worth every penny."

Eissa's nose wrinkled doubtfully. "Fat suits? Are we going to disguise ourselves as fat people? Because I just lost fifty pounds, and that really doesn't sound appealing to me. Or helpful, now that I think about it."

Jake chuckled. "FAT suits. Functional Armored Tech Suits. It's like a robot, or a cyborg, but you get inside of it. I don't know how to describe it, other than to say it's bulletproof and you can run through a concrete block wall with it. It'll have automated onboard weapons systems, infrared scanning, all kinds of neat quix. We had comic books about them when I was a kid. Do you have anything like that in your dimension?"

"It's an Iron Man suit." Quentin felt dizzy and put his hand on the tailgate to steady himself. "Are you shitting me? Does it fly?"

"No, it doesn't fly. It's complicated enough on the ground."

Quentin stifled his excitement and tried to focus on logistics. If these things were all that Jake was claiming, they would be a huge asset. And if da Vinci had that kind of tech, then taking the DimGate to his place was not only an acceptable risk, it was also necessary. They would need to see if the Mobile Gates could transport a FAT suit. That would be a very big deal.

"How do we pay for them?" Quentin asked. "If this guy is off the grid, do we need to have cash?"

Jake burst out laughing. "Cash? Like gold coins? Nobody has used that stuff in a hundred years." He shook his head. "You guys are something else. No, you'll pay me from your card, and I'll use one of my clean ID's to pay him. It's all anonymous."

"Okay, let's go back to the island," Quentin said. "We'll grab the Mobile Gates so we can test them out on the FAT suits. If something needs to be modified, maybe da Vinci can make it work. Do you have coordinates to his place?"

Jake patted his phone. "Right here. Let me lock my truck."

Quentin walked over to the DimGate and opened the panel. Jake was proving to be an excellent source of hi-tech toys. The orange target caught his eye as he waited for Jake and Eissa. She had obliterated the inner rings. Hopefully they wouldn't need her shooting skills, but it was comforting to know she had them.

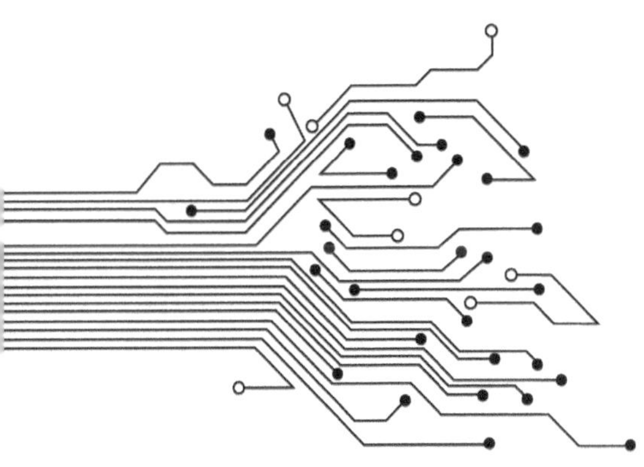

CHAPTER 20

Rain beat silently against the thick tinted windows of Zimmerman's office in Dimension 165. Carl Holt sat in Zimmerman's chair, his feet kicked up on the low bookcase in front of the window, staring out over Gainesville. The FBI investigator on the other end of the phone shifted through stacks of reports, the silence dragging on as he searched for some detail, some statement that someone had made. Zimmerman himself sat on the couch nearby, sighing audibly from time to time, as if that would speed the interview along. Holt pointedly ignored him.

"So, it looks like you told the US Marshal, let's see, what was his name-" papers rustled in the background. "Marshal Higgins. You told Marshal Higgins that Whitefoot screamed that he was going to kill the white devils, and then he charged you. Is that right, Mr. Holt?"

Holt pinched the bridge of his nose between his thumb and forefinger. "Yes, that's right, Larry."

Heavy breathing came over the line. "It's Special Agent Wood, Mr. Holt."

"It's Director Holt, Larry. And we've been over this, three times now. I know you don't have anything else to do, but I have a list a mile long, and every minute you waste confirming my previously confirmed answers, my list gets longer. Can we agree that you know everything that happened?"

"This is a potential murder investigation, Mr. Holt. I'd expect you to be more conscious of that when you talk to me, considering you're the one who shot the victims. I'm just trying to put all the pieces together so we can more fully understand what happened."

"Larry, I understand the situation. I also understand the judicial system. You aren't going to find anything that the people before you didn't find, because there's nothing there to find. The US Attorney isn't going to press charges against me, no matter how many times you ask me the same questions." Holt swung his feet to the floor, his face turning red. "Now, I've been very cooperative with you, Larry, but if you can't respect my time any better than this, then you can subpoena me. Until then, I'm through riding the merry go round."

Holt turned and slammed the phone down in the cradle. Zimmerman watched him from the couch, a slight smile on his face.

"How to win friends and influence people," Zimmerman drawled. "Textbook conversation closer. *Subpoena me.*" He laughed darkly.

Holt glared at him. "I don't have time to keep running in circles. I've got a dozen things to get done today." He stood, gesturing to the chair. "You can have your throne back. If that asshole calls back again, tell him to get lost."

"You're awfully angry, Carl. Are you sleeping okay?"

Holt bit his tongue. What he really wanted to do was flip Zimmerman's desk over and scream at him about how bad Quentin James was making things, which was all Zimmerman's fault. Maybe even break a few of Zimmerman's ribs, so he could appreciate what Holt was dealing with as a result of Zimmerman's piss-poor decision making. Fortunately, twenty-five years of training had taught him how to clamp down on those urges. That, and the broken ribs.

"I've got a lot of fires burning, and some of them are difficult to put out, that's all. These little trivial things are burning up my daylight hours and keeping me from getting things done."

Zimmerman nodded. "I understand. Well, thanks for coming over and talking to them. Maybe they'll leave us alone for a while."

"Let's hope so." Holt swiped his card and opened the door to the DimGate room. "See you later."

Zimmerman gave a little wave from the couch as Holt swung the door closed. The DimGate sat open and waiting, the glass wall of the DCC visible on the other side. He stepped through, closing the door behind him.

"Hey, boss, good timing."

Holt turned. Captain Mathers and Sergeant Grant from the Special Ops team stood on the yellow square near the wall, which was the designated landing point for Mobile Gates. Sergeant Grant had an unconscious woman draped over his shoulder, one arm and her hair reaching for the floor. Holt took a few steps towards them.

"Hey, Mathers, how did it go?"

"Piece of cake. Caught her at home, knocked her out. You want her upstairs or downstairs?"

"Downstairs." Upstairs, she would be visible to anyone who came through the security center. Downstairs was his domain, and few people ever ventured past his office to the dungeon, as the guards called it. She could sit in there for a week, if necessary. "Put her next to my office. We need to get some pictures, and maybe some video of her once she wakes up. How big of a dose did you give her?"

"Just a cc. She'll be coming out of it in ten minutes or so." Mathers trotted forward and held the door open. "Let's get her in a cell before that happens. I don't have a bump dose drawn up."

They moved down the long hallway at a fast walk. A dull pain radiated from Holt's ribs, but the satisfaction of successfully collecting Quentin James's sister kept his spirits up. It was about time something went right with the James case. Holt pulled his phone out and called the front desk.

"This is Director Holt. Send someone down with the keys for the cellblock. Don't fuck around, we'll be there in two minutes with a prisoner." He listened for a moment before sliding the phone back in his pocket.

Denise James stirred as Grant lowered her to the ground in Cell Three. Holt slipped out and walked next door to his office. Sergeant Treijo smiled as he came in.

"Hey, boss, how did it go in 165?"

"Like getting hit by a bus, which is pretty good for an FBI interview. I need the camera."

Treijo dug around in her desk drawer and came up with a small black case. "Do you need me to set it up for you?"

Holt gave her a tired smile. "I'll figure it out. You just be ready to get the pictures onto the computer. That's the hard part."

He walked back around the corner to the cell. Mathers was squatted next to Denise taking her pulse while Grant took notes. He lifted her eyelids and peered closely at her pupils before standing up. "Alright, she's coming around.

Everything looks normal."

Her head sagged against her chest, and she let out a low moan as a string of drool reached down to her shirt. "Whmmm."

Holt unzipped the case and pulled the camera out. Technically, it was inferior to the camera on his phone, but one of his big pet peeves was when someone took official pictures with their phone. Invariably, inappropriate pictures ended up on social media as a result of that. He strictly enforced the company camera rule, which meant that he had to follow it, too, especially in front of his subordinates.

"Whaaaa ha'ned?" Denise lifted her head with obvious difficulty, her eyes rolling wildly. "Whaaas ha'ning?"

"Sit still," Mathers said, squatting back down. "Don't try to move yet. Give it a minute or two." Her head lolled to the side as she tried to look at him. He gently pushed it back upright.

Holt sat down stiffly on the bunk, wincing as various bruises protested the movement. "Go ahead and handcuff her to the bunk. I don't want there to be any question as to what her situation is when he sees the pictures of her."

"Roger that." Mathers produced a set of handcuffs from his utility belt and snapped one around her wrist, reaching across her to attach the other end to the steel bed frame. Her eyes followed his movements, and her breath quickened. He checked her pulse one more time before stepping away from her.

Holt tried to size her up. Their file on her was minimal, consisting only of what data they had gathered from their interview with her right after Quentin had pulled his stunt with Zimmerman's DimGate. She'd claimed to know nothing about any of it, and there wasn't anything to suggest she'd been lying. The interviewing officer had written in his notes that she appeared to have an antagonistic relationship with Quentin, and he didn't doubt that they rarely talked except to fight about bills or food consumption from the shared refrigerator.

Her brown hair hung past her shoulders in limp curls, mussed by her recent inversion over Grant's shoulder. She was thin, and not particularly pretty. Her profile showed that she was 35 and worked part time as a store clerk. Had lived with Quentin off and on for years, bouncing from boyfriend to boyfriend and job to job. Not a model citizen.

Holt cleared his throat loudly and she looked up at him. "Can you hear me?"

Her eyes were bloodshot but looked more alert than they had a few minutes before. She nodded, and slowly licked her lips before speaking with an effort. "What's going on?"

"I'm going to ask you a few questions first. Do you know your name?"

"Den-Denise." She took a deep breath, her eyes widening momentarily. "Denise James. Was I in a car wreck?"

Holt pressed forward, ignoring her question. "What's your brother's name?"

A look of confusion crossed her face. "Quentin? What about him?"

Holt nodded, lifting the camera. "Alright, look right here, please. No need to smile." She flinched at the flash, and he snapped a series of pictures, careful to make sure the hand-cuff was visible. Her bewildered expression was perfect for his purposes. "Have you talked to Quentin recently, or seen him around?"

She shook her head. "Quentin's missing, been missing. Where am I? Who are you?"

Holt switched the camera to video mode. "I want you to beg Quentin to come rescue you. Tell him you're scared. Can you do that?"

"Wh-what?" A shudder ran through her body. "What do you mean?"

Holt nodded at Mathers and pressed the record button. "See this guy right here? He's going to start cutting your fingers off in 24 hours, one every hour until Quentin gets here. If you run out of fingers, he'll start removing toes."

Tears welled up in her eyes as she tried to comprehend what he was saying. "Quentin?" Her voice was tinged with rising panic. "Quentin, I don't know what's going on! These people are talking about cutting my fingers off. Quentin!" She ended in a mild shriek, and Holt stopped the recording.

"That was perfect, thank you." He stood up carefully. "Take the cuffs off, and let's go. Make sure she gets on the meal schedule."

They filed out of the cell.

"Wait," Denise called after them. "Wait, don't leave me in here! I don't understand what's happening."

Holt closed the cell door, locking it carefully. Mathers and Grant headed for the stairs as he turned into his office. He handed the camera to Treijo. "Here you go. I think the video will be perfect. Now we just have to figure out how Quentin James sees it."

"Okay. You just got an email from someone in Dimension 17. It says a group of guards killed the project supervisor, his number 2, and some of the other guards. It sounds like they're either staging a coup or revolting against the leadership."

Holt's heart hammered in his chest, and he swallowed the rage that threatened to take over him. There was no time for this shit, not now. "Who was the project supervisor? Who wrote the email? I don't even know what the fuck Dimension 17 does." He ripped the phone out of his pocket and hit the speed dial.

"Mathers here."

"Get back down here, we've got an emergency. Bring Grant."

"Yes, sir. Mathers out."

Treijo was rapidly clicking through screens on her computer. "Looks like we've got a coal mine operation in 17. Project Supervisor is Steven Horn. Email came from the clerk, Christoff Townsend."

Mathers jogged into the room, the phone still in his hand, with Grant right behind him. "What's up?"

"Give him what you've got," Holt said to Treijo. "I've got to think for a minute. Come in here when you're up to speed." He walked into his office and collapsed into his chair, turning on his computer before leaning back and rubbing his face.

There was just no time for something like this to happen. Everyone was already committed to something. He needed the Special Ops team to take Quentin down, but they were also the only ones he could send to 17. He might be able to send Sergeant Anderson over to assess the situation and buy some time, but there was no way to know how long it would take to get James in custody.

Mathers lead Treijo and Grant into his office, and they lined up in front of his desk. Holt ignored them for a moment and pulled up the information file on Dimension 17.

The coal mine in 17 supplied coal to three power plants in Dimension 443. It had three hundred workers and thirty guards, along with a small support staff. He opened up the email in a separate window and scanned it quickly, but there was no additional information to be gleaned from it.

"Have you replied to the email?" he asked, glancing up at Treijo.

"No, sir. I didn't want to endanger the clerk if the email was intercepted."

Holt nodded. "Okay. There are thirty guards assigned to Dimension 17. We don't know how many of them are in on this, or if they killed everyone who wasn't in on it. We don't have a motive, so we don't know if they're going to be hostile to us or not. We don't know anything. We're in a bad spot."

"I can take the wet team in, but it's hard to go on a mission when we don't know what the mission is." Mathers grinned sheepishly.

"Right," Holt said. "Let's talk this through. Why would a group of guards kill the leadership team?"

"Power struggle?" Treijo ventured. "Seems like a questionable way to get promoted, though."

Grant shook his head. "Yeah, there ain't no security guards trying to take over the project supervisor spot at a coal mine. Maybe a diamond or gold mine, if they wanted to steal some product, but not at a coal mine."

Holt picked up a pencil and rolled it between his knuckles from one finger to the next. "Keep going."

"Could have been a retaliation thing," Mathers said. "Maybe the PS was being an asshole and pushed them too far. It's happened before."

Holt wrote *retaliation* on a piece of paper. "What else?"

They all looked at each other. "I got nothing," Grant said. "What else could it be?"

Holt sighed. "If that's it, then they know they're fucked. DimCorp can't overlook it, even if it's justified. We have to assume that it will be a hostile engagement."

"We'll need the whole team if we're going to clean the jobsite," Mathers said.

"I know." Holt leaned back in his chair and folded his hands on his lap. "But I need the team to take down James, too. I can't do it without you."

Silence settled across the room, except for the buzzing of the broken light fixture. He stared at it, trying to find another option. He could just let them sit in Dimension 17 until the James case was wrapped up, but if they were still killing people, then he couldn't wait. He needed more information.

"Get ahold of Sergeant Anderson. Have him do a stealth assessment and get back to me in 24 hours. Maybe we can send a negotiator over to 17 and talk to them. We're going to proceed with James in the meantime. I'm not about to let him take out the spaceport. It's way more important than- wait a minute. The coal mine supplies fuel for power plants in 443. Does the spaceport run off one of those power plants? How do we find that out?"

Three blank faces stared back at him.

"I don't know how we'd find that out quickly," Treijo said. "What are you thinking?"

The pencil worked its way up his knuckles. "I'm probably being paranoid, but it occurred to me that James could be behind this. Maybe he's trying to disrupt the power at the spaceport."

"That's a pretty convoluted way to go about it," Mathers said doubtfully.

Holt sighed. "Yeah, you're probably right. Let's see what Anderson can find out and go from there."

They filed out of his office, leaving him to stare at the flickering light overhead. There were twenty better ways to shut the power off at the spaceport. He was jumping at shadows, and that was bad. There were just too many things going on at once, and not knowing what some of them were was making him paranoid. It was like juggling ten bowling balls, but he could only see seven of them. He might be lucky enough to keep them going for a bit, but at some point, one of them was going to fall, and that would probably bring the rest of them crashing down around him. He rolled the pencil between his knuckles, hoping that no one would add another bowling ball to the mix until he could get a few of them out of the rotation.

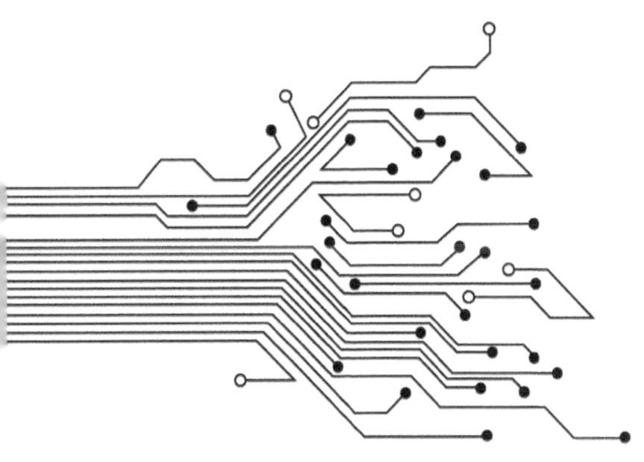

CHAPTER 21

"I can't believe how humid it is here." Jake sleeved the sweat off his forehead. "I've been here for thirty seconds and I'm already sweating my ass off."

Quentin laughed. "I have the opposite problem in Vegas. My skin feels like it's drying out and cracking apart. I even got a nosebleed a while back."

He double-checked the coordinates on the screen with Jake's phone. The map showed nothing but low mountains and open desert, no buildings, no roads. The nearest sign of life was a dot on the map ten miles away called Carp, and it only showed two buildings. Da Vinci was clearly the hermit-type. "I don't see anything on the map. Does he live in a tent or something?"

Jake stepped up next to him and looked at the screen. "Yeah, that's the place. What you can't see is an old gold mine that burrows into the mountain right around there. This whole thing is hollow. It's amazing."

Prickles of claustrophobic tension ran across Quentin's skin. "Oh boy."

Jake pointed to an area at the base of the mountain. "This is where helicopters land when someone comes to visit. We're going to cross over right in front of the mine up here. It's plenty big, they used to have the processing area set up there."

"Okay, then, I guess we're good." He switched back to the main screen. "We're going to follow our usual safety protocol. You'll stand over here by me while Eissa checks it out. Once we know for sure the Gate is in a good spot, we'll cross over."

Quentin hoisted the Mobile Gate up on his shoulder and engaged the DimGate. Eissa was carrying the other one and led them through after a quick check. Jake followed her and Quentin brought up the rear, closing the door behind him.

They were on a wide ledge facing away from the low mountain. Scrub brush poked up in the cracks among the broken rock, and the desert floor below them was spotted with Joshua trees. The flawless blue sky went on forever to the left and right, disappearing behind another low ridge across the wide valley floor. Quentin breathed in deeply, savoring the scent of sage, juniper, and piñon pine.

"This is nice," Eissa said. "It's a long way from the ocean, but it's still pretty good."

Quentin turned around and immediately saw why the map showed nothing here. The tunnel entrance leading into the mountain was covered by a huge tan camouflage net. There was nothing manmade outside the net, which came all the way to the ground everywhere except for a small walkway. It would be invisible from a satellite camera, and since no one drove a vehicle out here to see him, there were no tire tracks to lead curious eyes to his door.

"How does he go grocery shopping and stuff?" Eissa asked.

"Chopper," Jake said. "He calls a friend with a helicopter if he wants to go somewhere or needs something delivered."

Quentin was impressed. In a high-tech world, it was still possible to be invisible if you had the resources and the savvy. Jake led them under the netting and stopped in front of a steel door mounted to the surrounding rock. He tilted his head up and grinned, then stepped back. "Everybody step up and smile for the camera."

Quentin searched the face of the wall quizzically, not seeing a camera. At last he noticed a tiny lens less than half an inch across. It blended in with the dark rock that it was bored in to, making it nearly invisible.

The door opened a moment later, pushed wide by a huge hairy arm covered in tattoos. Jake began making introductions and Quentin tried not to stare at da Vinci. He was nothing like what Quentin had been expecting. Quentin's image of a hermit tech-mod was a skinny, pale, mousy-looking nerd. Da Vinci was a giant, at least eight inches taller than Quentin's six feet, and easily three hundred pounds, little of it fat. His long blond hair was pulled back in a ponytail, held tight by a beaded leather wrap.

"FreakMan!" Da Vinci pulled Jake into a crushing hug. "It's good to see you." He pushed Jake back to arm's length and stared into his face. "The man with one red shoe walked across the bridge at night. What day was it?"

"Every day is Friday when you're living the dream," Jake said.

Quentin realized they were exchanging coded messages at the same time as Eissa, and their eyes met. If Jake said something wrong, were they going to be zapped by some hidden laser beam, or fall through a trap door? He gave Eissa a tiny shrug. They were helpless, so there was nothing to do but wait.

Jake turned to Quentin, grabbing him by the shoulder. "Quentin, meet da Vinci. Da Vinci, this is my friend, Quentin. Don't underestimate him. He may look like a geek, but he lives a very interesting lifestyle."

Quentin stuck his hand out, and it was immediately lost in da Vinci's massive paw. Quentin hoped da Vinci wasn't one of those guys who tried to crush your hand to show you how tough they were. It wouldn't take much, of course, but da Vinci was evidently both secure in himself and conscientious of Quentin's comparative frailty, as he firmly but gently shook his hand. "Welcome, welcome. FreakMan doesn't trust anyone, so that fact that you're in his good graces says a lot."

Da Vinci turned to Eissa. Quentin watched in amusement as her hand reached out to shake his. His own hand had been dwarfed; hers was like a toddler's hand in his.

"This is Eissa," Jake said. "She'll surprise you, as well. She was a combat medic, but she's a better shot than me with a handgun."

Da Vinci's eyebrows shot up. "That's saying something. Welcome, welcome, please, come in."

He led them through the door. Quentin's chest tightened at the thought of walking inside an old mine. Every story he'd ever heard about cave-ins flashed through his mind in an instant, and he broke out in a cold sweat. Eissa followed da Vinci, and Quentin was right behind her. He was surprised to see a hallway behind the door rather than a tunnel. It had a tile floor, sheetrock walls, and tasteful LED lighting. If he hadn't just been standing outside, he wouldn't have known that he wasn't in an office building or a home somewhere.

Jake shut the door behind them, and Quentin turned back to him. "Why does he call you FreakMan?"

Jake chuckled. "It's a play on my last name, Freeman. That's been my nickname since high school."

"Gotcha. I just didn't know if we were supposed to have a codename or something."

"Nah, you're fine. You don't have a registered identity here, so you're basically invisible in this dimension anyway. It wouldn't matter if everyone knew your name and date of birth." He pointed down the hall. "We better catch up. This place is a maze."

Quentin turned and jogged down the hall. Da Vinci and Eissa were just turning a corner as he caught up to them. They stopped in front of a tall wide door.

"We're going to take the freight elevator down to the lab. It squeaks a bit, but it's sound, I promise." Da Vinci opened the door and lifted a gate, gesturing for them to enter. When everyone was in, he stepped in, pulled the gate back down and engaged a lever. "This thing is over a hundred years old, and still as reliable as the day it was made. I've seen a few marvels of engineering, but this lift is one of the finest." He pushed the lever back, bringing them to a stop. "If you'll turn around, we'll go out the back side." Jake lifted the gate on the back wall and opened the door.

A huge room lay before them. The high ceiling was natural stone, as was the floor, but the floor had been painted white, and the walls were white sheetrock and covered with lights. Workbenches and toolboxes divided the area into stations, and while the counters were cluttered with parts, the floor was clean, and the first workstation was brightly lit.

To the left, a long workbench held a series of computers, a pile of circuit boards and wiring separating one from the next. Pegboard stretched to the ceiling behind the counter, with hundreds of small items hanging from it. To the right, a variety of small and medium-sized drone helicopters sat on a wide bench. Da Vinci led them to the other end of the room. The lights came on as they moved forward, bringing one workstation after another into view. He stopped at the third space and turned to the left.

Quentin was briefly reminded of the display at the spaceport showing the evolution of spacesuits over the years, but it was much more like a display of movie characters over the years: Terminator, RoboCop, Cyborg, Iron Man. The suits stood along the wall, each plugged into a fat black cable. He hadn't known what to expect from a guy living in an abandoned mine, but it certainly wasn't anything this polished and professional-looking. Each suit was different in design, but they were all sleek with beautiful lines and shiny paint. The thought of wearing one was both exhilarating and terrifying.

"FreakMan tells me you're in need of a FAT suit," da Vinci said.

Quentin nodded dumbly, unable to tear his eyes away.

"I know we just met," Eissa said. "I don't want to be one of those people who are critical right off the bat, but can we talk about the name? Does it have to be FAT suit?"

Da Vinci let out a rolling laugh. "You don't like my joke?"

Eissa gave him a doubtful look. "It brings to mind a completely different image."

"Exactly! That's the joke." He laughed again.

Quentin took a step forward, entranced by the luminous deep blue suit on the left end. "Can you tell us a little about them? What all can they do?"

Da Vinci walked over to the suit on the left, nodding for them to follow. "This is the Foxtrot. It can run forty kilometers an hour and last twenty hours at max activity on a charge. Armor can deflect sustained small arms fire indefinitely. It can deflect a .50 if it comes in at an angle, but a square impact could penetrate. It has four onboard weapons which can automatically select targets, or you can assign targets or sectors for each weapon. It has a 3D heads up display which can show you a map of the area or building you're in, heat signatures of others in the area, source of incoming fire, and the interactive onboard computer can access internet, email, link audio and video with other FAT suits or outside observers, et cetera. All the controls operate on brainwaves, so you can do everything in real time just by thinking about it."

"Holy shit." Quentin was stunned. Up until five minutes ago, he thought the micro-movers were incredible technology. This made them seem like toys by comparison. He glanced down the line. "What makes the others different?"

"Mostly their weapons configuration. Some of them sacrifice armor or computing power to carry more ammo or additional weaponry. Some sacrifice weapons for more computing power or battery life." He shrugged. "It depends on what you're doing, as to which makes the most sense."

Eissa poked him in the arm, nodding pointedly at him and then his Mobile Gate. "Are you going to ask him about the, uh, backpacks?"

"Oh, yeah." He'd forgotten all about that in the awe of the FAT suits. He took his backpack off and set it on the ground. "We have a bit of technology here, and we need them to be able to work together."

Da Vinci pulled back the flap and glanced inside. "Mobile DimGate?"

Quentin's jaw dropped as his brain made a mad scramble to make sense of things. How could da Vinci know what it was? If he knew what it was, then he must know about the other dimensions, right? What did that mean? Da Vinci laughed, clasping Quentin on the shoulder. "I can see you weren't expecting me to know about any of that."

Quentin shook his head dumbly. "Well, no, not exactly."

"That's what got you in the door, my friend. I used to be a Tech-Mod for DimCorp. I know all about them, and I know all about these units. I designed the first version of the Mobile Gate. When FreakMan said you were trying to fight DimRec and needed a FAT suit to do it, I had a feeling I knew what the situation was. I'd love to hear how you got these, that's got to be a good story. And don't worry, I'll make sure the FAT suits are compatible with them."

Quentin sat down on a stool by the workbench, not trusting his legs to keep him standing. He'd been trying to figure out how to explain the Mobile Gates as minimally as possible, and here he was, talking to the guy who invented them. That changed the game in so many ways he couldn't even process it.

"You kinda blew my mind," he finally said. "I need a minute to get my shit back together."

Jake pointed at Quentin, then back at himself. "Right there with you, brother. Here I was, thinking that finally, I knew something that da Vinci didn't know. Wrong."

Da Vinci and Jake laughed. While Eissa explained their mission to steal the Mobile Gates, Quentin sat on the stool in silence, processing everything. Jake was a great resource, but having an ally in da Vinci was an incredible windfall. This was a relationship that needed to be fostered.

"Carl Holt?" da Vinci thundered. "I know that guy. He shot my partner when we quit DimCorp. Granted, we were trying to steal as much as we could carry out of there, but still.

I had to pull two bullets out of his ass once we finally got away."

"Quentin ended up fighting him across like three different dimensions," Eissa said. "They beat the hell out of each other. He finally got Holt in a mental bear hug with the micro-movers, and I smashed a big wooden box over his head so we could escape back to our dimension with the Mobile Gates."

Da Vinci glanced over at Quentin. "Micro-movers, huh? Have you tweaked them?"

Quentin shook his head. "No, they're stock."

"He's pushing them way too hard," Jake said. "Take a look at his wrists. He keeps burning the quix out of himself. He tore a car door off with them a while back."

Da Vinci whistled appreciatively. "Damn, man, you need a heat sink. Leave them with me, and I'll work out a sleeve of some kind to distribute the heat." He laughed, shaking his head. "You're packing some juice, I'll give you that. Now then, do you two want to try out a FAT suit? I've got a firing range downstairs where you can get the hang of things without tearing anything up."

Quentin's heart skipped a beat, and his mouth went dry. *Don't seize up now, Q. Every geek in the whole world would die to have this opportunity. You're going to do this, and you're going to do it big.* "Absolutely. Let's do it."

●────○

The FAT suit was harder to get into than Quentin expected, and he felt a moment of claustrophobia as the helmet locked in place. *Breathe, Q. You're okay. In through the nose, out through the mouth.* When the 3D screen came on, he forgot about all of that. He could see everything around him in a much wider periphery than he was used to, and Eissa had a soft blue aura around her suit, identifying her as a friendly unit.

Okay, Q, control your thoughts. This thing is monitoring them, waiting for commands. If you think about porn, or something ridiculous like that…

A window popped up on the left side of his viewing area, showing a list of search results for porn sites.

Shit. Close that window. The window vanished. *External audio.* "Hey, can you guys hear me?"

Speakers inside the suit relayed the sound of his voice as it blasted across the room. The only way he knew it was his voice was because the words were the same. The sound was something befitting a suit like this, very deep, commanding, and robotic. And very loud. He cringed as da Vinci and Jake clapped their hands over their ears.

"External speaker volume to 20%," da Vinci bellowed.

External speaker volume to 20%. "Okay, how about that?"

Jake gave him a thumbs-up. "Much better."

A soft tone sounded in his right ear, followed by a female computerized voice. "Commlink request from Darth Vader. Accept or deny?"

Accept. Show me as Captain Picard. Belay that. Show me as King Arthur.

"Dude, these things are fucking awesome!" Eissa said. A video window popped up in the lower right portion of his field of vision. Eissa's face was dark inside her helmet, lit erratically by the data from her screen. She was grinning, her eyes dancing around the visor.

"Darth Vader, huh?" He laughed. "I would have expected some lesbian icon, or an Indian name like Crazy Horse or something."

"Native American," she said. "Just like every other culture, all the heroes are fucking dudes. And I love Ellen DeGeneres, but it just didn't seem like an appropriate name for a battle suit. At least Darth Vader was gay. That's close enough."

Quentin burst out laughing. "What the hell are you talking about? Vader wasn't gay!"

"Sure, he was. Had a kid thirty years ago, never touched a woman again, hides his identity, hates everyone, acts tough, trying to destroy the world, it's all there. Don't argue with me, this is my territory."

"Oh my God," Quentin said. "Anyway, I'm going to try to move. Hopefully I won't break anything."

"I'll wait and see how you do, *King Arthur*. I'm assuming that's Monty Python."

"Of course. It's still the best movie of all time." *External speakers.* "Hey, you guys look out. I'm going to try to take a few steps. I don't want to run over you."

"Just think about what you want to do," da Vinci said. "If you get in trouble, just think about stopping. You'll get the hang of it in no time."

Quentin looked at the center aisle a few steps away, and instantly began walking to it. It was a strangle sensation. He couldn't tell whether he was walking, or if the suit was moving his arms and legs as it walked. Either way, he made it to the aisle and stopped, spinning back to look at the others. *Open comms to Darth Vader.* "So far, so good."

"Okay, I'm going to give it a shot," Eissa said. A moment later her mechanized female robot voice boomed across the room. "Attention, bad motherfucker on the move."

Quentin laughed as Jake and da Vinci jumped out of the way. "You sound cool as hell in that thing."

"Not bad for a displaced Chippewa, huh?" She walked across the room, turning to stop beside him. "That's weird, man. But I like it."

Map to firing range. A 3D map popped up, superimposed over his surroundings. A green arrow directed him to the elevator door, and the proposed route was a yellow line descending the elevator shaft to a huge room directly below them.

Inventory of weapons and ammo. A window popped up on the left listing each weapon and the number of rounds he had. In addition to the guns in each arm, there were two rear-facing guns mounted in the shoulders, and a high-voltage incapacitator in each palm. *Battery life.* A battery meter flashed up on the right, briefly showing 99% before fading away.

External speakers. "Okay, I think we're ready to go downstairs to the range."

"Go ahead," da Vinci said. "We'll stay up here where it's safe. If you need to talk to me, say 'Call the boss.' We'll watch on the monitors."

"Got it." Quentin turned and walked to the door. He could see on his screen, without turning his head, that Eissa was right behind him. The floorplan of this level expanded across his screen as they moved forward, but the only two heat signatures were Jake and da Vinci. He reached out and carefully opened the door and slowly lifted the gate. The last thing he wanted to do was accidently break the elevator with his new super-strength. Eissa followed him onto the lift, and the floor dipped noticeably under their weight.

The elevator controls were unfamiliar to Quentin, but as soon as he looked at them, the onboard computer began giving him verbal instructions. "Computer, can I ask you questions?"

"Yes, of course."

Quentin grinned. "Okay, thanks. How about audible commands? If I say something instead of thinking it, will it still work?"

"Your thoughts will be picked up before you speak, but if it makes you more comfortable to speak, I can delay reaction time to match your verbal commands."

"Oh no, don't do that," Quentin said. "I'm just trying to learn my way around. What do I call you?"

"My name is Foxtrot Artificial Intelligence Technology Hybrid. You can call me Faith. It's an acronym."

"Yes, I recognized that," Quentin said.

"I know. I was just trying to make you feel at ease. Please engage the lever on your left to descend."

A soft tone sounded. *Ping.* "What are you doing?" Eissa asked. "Are we going down, or what? You did figure out the map, right?"

"I was having a conversation with my FAT suit, if you don't mind," Quentin snapped. He grabbed the lever and lowered it. "And yes, I have the map up, and I've inventoried my arsenal."

A moment later he lifted the lever, bringing the car to a stop. Eissa raised the gate and opened the door, stepping out into total darkness. Quentin followed her. *Do we have night vision?* His screen turned green, showing the floor in front of them. A few feet away, a pile of sandbags formed an above-ground foxhole. He walked over beside it, and a hologram popped up, the neon green dazzling in the darkness.

"Please select course difficulty."

Quentin stuck his hand out and touched the box for Novice Training.

"Please select number of participants."

He touched the 2.

"Each participant will enter a separate foxhole. The course will begin in ten seconds."

"Oh shit," Eissa's voice came over the commlink. "You take that one, I'll use this one on the right."

"Okay." Quentin couldn't see anything on his screen that might be a target. The night vision only gave him a few feet of visibility, but it was better than nothing. He crouched behind the sandbags, scanning the darkness. Suddenly a series of strobing flashes came out of the distance. His screen dimmed instantly to keep him from being blinded, and Faith spoke in his ear.

"Incoming small arms fire."

Engage. Faster than he could have moved on his own, his left arm extended over the top of the sandbags, and the forearm section opened. A barrel rotated out, and his screen partitioned. On the left, the engaged weapon showed in green, with a countdown of remaining rounds. A small window beside that showed target status, which was currently active. In the right corner, a small notice advised him that Darth Vader was also engaging the target. He could feel a slight recoil from the gun, but it wasn't loud or jarring like he expected. A moment later the target status changed to inactive.

The hologram popped up in front of him. "Advance to the next firing position."

He stood up and moved out of the foxhole, the motions becoming more natural now. Eissa was right behind him, her blue status beacon showing on his map. The floor was littered with piles of rock, old trolley cars, and unidentifiable junk. Quentin maneuvered around it, trying to spot the next foxhole in the dark. Without warning, they began taking fire from three different places at once.

"Shit!" Quentin yelled. *Engage all targets.* Windows popped up all over his screen as three weapons deployed, and he ran forward, searching for the foxhole. Eissa's blue marker was moving further away to the right. The flashes were coming from all over the room, and the smoke from his guns was beginning to obscure his vision. "Faith, where's the damn firing position?"

A beacon popped up on his map. It was a few meters ahead, to the right of a mangled machine. "Okay, so next time we'll do that first, huh?"

"The object of this training is for you to learn how to work with me," Faith said. "Experience is the best teacher."

"Yeah, yeah. I don't have an owner's manual, so feel free to throw a tip out there once in a while."

Ping. "Hey dude, are you using the threat screen and assigning targets, or just letting the suit do everything?" Eissa asked.

Threat screen. Four small red boxes popped into his screen, along with several yellow boxes. *Faith, what do the colors mean?*

"Red squares are threats that have engaged us. Yellow squares are threats that have not engaged but have been identified. Blue squares are friendly units. White squares are threats that have been neutralized."

Open comms to Darth Vader. "Of course, I'm using the threat screen, it's a great resource."

He assigned two squares to his left gun and two squares to his right. *Okay Faith, we're going to jump up, engage, and drop back behind cover.* Quentin had intended to do a countdown first but the moment he thought it, the suit leaped into the air and blasted first one set of targets, then the other before dropping back behind the sandbags. The whole movement took less than two seconds. Three of the red squares turned white.

"What are you doing over there, anyway?" he asked. "We need to quit playing Lone Ranger and teamwork this thing."

"I'm working, motherfucker," Eissa retorted. "I've neutralized seven targets so far. It looks like you're up to four. You need to quit slacking."

The hologram popped up in front of him again. "Advance to the next firing position."

Where's the next firing position? A beacon popped up on the screen. *Best route?* A green line wound through the piles of debris.

"Moving out, Vader." He stepped out of the foxhole and ran to his left, following the map. The one remaining gun began shooting again and he engaged it on the run. He dodged around a column, and suddenly all the yellow squares on his screen turned red. *Oh, shit!* Flashes strobed all over the place as he rapidly assigned targets to guns. He leaped over a pile of concrete blocks and slid into the firing position on the other side. Eissa's blue square was still off to the right, zigzagging across the floor. "I'll take the ones on the left; you take the ones on the right."

"Roger that." Eissa's voice was calm.

He checked his ammo levels. The guns in his arms were down to 60% ammo remaining, and the shoulder guns were still near 100%. He took out two more targets, but the other three were obscured. *I need to see what's going on. Do we have exterior illumination, Faith?* His screen transitioned as the whole room lit up in front of him. It was filled with smoke from all the gunfire, but now he could see that the gun emplacements were up in low towers and surrounded by armor plating. Shooting at them was just a waste of ammo.

"Vader, I'm going to rush the towers."

"You know, when King Arthur rushed the castle in Monty Python, they flung a cow at him. You better watch out."

"Thanks," Quentin said. "I'll be ready to run away if necessary."

He sprinted towards the nearest tower, dodging around piles of rock. The towers themselves were just four pipes with a platform on top, maybe fifteen feet up. The armored enclosure was small, just big enough for a computer and the gun. Quentin rammed the base of the tower at full speed, leaning into it as the pipes buckled under the impact. A moment later the platform crashed into the floor, and the red square turned white.

He slowed, untangling the pipes from the suit. Suddenly all the squares on his screen turned white.

Ping. "Commlink request from The Boss. Accept or deny?"

"Accept." A video window opened, and da Vinci's face popped up, with Jake looking on from the side. They were both grinning like little kids. Eissa's video window appeared beside them.

"Hey, hotshot," da Vinci said. "Don't tear my range apart. Do you know how hard it is to build those towers by yourself?"

Quentin flushed. "Sorry, man. I got all wrapped up in the moment."

Eissa looked puzzled. "I missed it. What happened?"

Da Vinci leaned forward and typed something into the computer, and a moment later a third video screen popped up. It was an overhead shot from one side showing Quentin as a line of LED lights flashed on from the front of his suit, lighting up the room. A moment later he took off, and the camera followed as he crashed into the gun tower. It was hard to believe that he was inside the cyborg on the video. It looked totally badass, like he was a trained one-man army, or something.

"Ahh, I see." Eissa clucked her tongue, shaking her head. "You were supposed to stay in your firing position, Q. For shame, for shame."

"Oh, bullshit," Quentin laughed. "You're the last person who can call me out for breaking the rules."

"Fair enough." She grinned. "So, until Quentin tried to tear the house down, how'd we do?"

"You two are born naturals," da Vinci said. "Come on back upstairs, and I'll give you a few pointers."

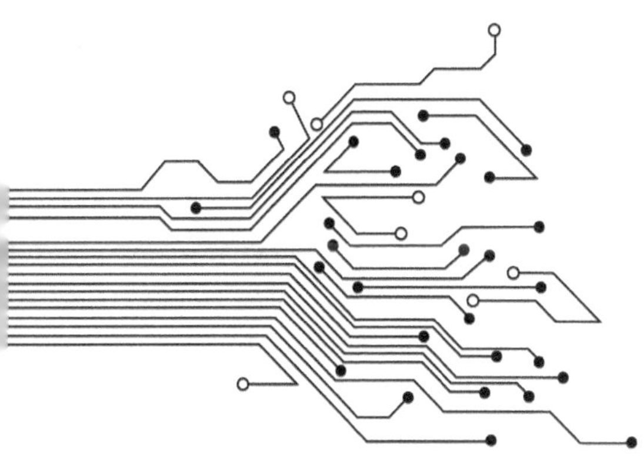

CHAPTER 22

Retract face shield. Fresh air washed across his face, and Quentin took a deep breath. The suit did a great job of keeping him cool and comfortable, but the fresh air made him notice how stale and metallic the recycled air in the suit was. Eissa stepped up beside him, her face shield sliding smoothly away.

Jake grinned at them in an unsuccessful attempt to hide the envy on his face. "How was it?"

"Fucking incredible." Quentin reached up to scratch his nose. A film of gunpowder residue covered his armored hands, and he glanced around for a towel. Seeing nothing nearby, he wiped a finger on Jake's shirt before gingerly touching his face. The metal was still hot from all the gunfire, but it didn't burn him. "A weakness of the cyborg suit is you can't scratch any itches. Otherwise, this thing is flawless."

Da Vinci laughed. "It's a bitch when you have to pee, too. I haven't got that part of things figured out yet. Hopefully you won't have to stay in it long enough for that to be an issue." He sat down on a stool at the workbench. "I'm loading an update into both suits right now. I just need to install a bit of hardware, which I can do while you're in the suit, and you'll have Mobile Gate tech onboard without having to carry the Mobile Gate with you."

"Oh, man, that's fantastic," Quentin said.

"I tried to incorporate the micro-mover tech into it as well, since it already runs on your brainwaves. The armor is going to limit the range, but you'll still be able to do some up-close stuff if you need to. The suit will disperse the heat." He donned a pair of glasses and turned Quentin around. The computer beside him opened a video window showing what the glasses were seeing. "Okay Faith, open access point 14A."

Quentin watched on the computer screen as a small panel opened in the back of his suit. Da Vinci clipped a wire and soldered a small circuit board in place. His huge hands looked out of place, but his touch was steady and precise, like a surgeon. It was done in a minute, and he waved Quentin out of the way. "Next."

When Eissa's was done, he took the glasses off and laid them on the counter. "Alright, here's the deal. The suits stay here until you're ready to launch your mission, and they come back here once this mission is over. The coordinates to this spot are programmed into the onboard Mobile Gate under *FAT Suit Home Station*. You can get me through the suit comms anytime, day or night. Questions?"

"Can we communicate with you if we're in a different dimension?" Quentin asked.

Da Vinci shook his head. "No, you'll be on your own there. The onboard computer can probably answer anything you want to know, though."

Quentin stuck his hand out to shake da Vinci's, forgetting for a moment that he was still wearing the FAT suit. Da Vinci grabbed his hand anyway, and Quentin was surprised to find that he could feel da Vinci's hand in his own, as if there wasn't a layer of metal between them. "That's crazy, man. I can feel your hand."

Da Vinci grinned. "It's a handy feature. It'll keep you from crushing things that you need to pick up." He let go of Quentin. "Okay, let's get you out of there, and then I'll take you back up top to your DimGate."

Quentin marveled at how much the FAT suits changed their situation. The day had started out with the hopes of a crude shield to protect them from the DimCorp guards that were sure to come to the tank factory. Now, just hours later, they were nearly invincible, had incredible firepower, and the thought of taking on twenty armed men was no longer terrifying. Once again, Jake had come through in a very unexpected way.

The other bonus to a computerized gun and a bulletproof suit was that they could probably pull this whole mission off without killing anyone, which he still believed was a big deal. Carl Holt might need killing, but most of the other guys were just regular people doing their jobs. If he and Eissa could pin them down with threatening fire, and intimidate the programmers into hacking the robots, then maybe they could save the world and not actually hurt anyone. Maybe. At least it was a possibility now.

"Wait a minute," Quentin said. The others looked at him expectantly. "Do we really need to wait? I mean, other than reloading ammo, we're basically ready to do this, right?" He looked at Eissa. "Am I forgetting anything?"

"Are you talking about going to the tank factory right now? I mean, like, doing this for real?"

Quentin nodded. "We don't need to get anything from the island. I guess we could go back there and tell Bob and Tocho that we're going, but that's all I can think of. With the FAT suits, we basically just need to program coordinates into the Mobile Gate to get us in and out. There's nothing else to do to prepare."

He looked around the group. It felt like he was rushing things, but by now he had done enough to know it always felt that way. Jake merely shrugged. Da Vinci stood up and pointed them to a fireproof cabinet in the corner.

"Well, if you're going now, let's get your ammo topped off. What's your power level?"

"96%."

"Okay, that's good. Stand in these yellow footprints on the floor and tell your onboard computer to reload."

Quentin stepped up to the cabinet. *Faith, reload our ammo.* His arms extended as the cabinet doors opened, and a metal sleeve extended from inside and connected to a port on each arm. There was a metallic shucking sound as rounds of ammo began pumping into the suit. When the sleeve retracted, he stepped back and Eissa reloaded.

It seemed rude to leave Bob and Tocho in the dark while they went on the mission, but he hated the idea of wasting an hour. Maybe they could go by the island afterwards and show them the FAT suits. Bob would probably be pissed, he decided. It was best to at least pop in and explain the situation. If the roles were reversed, that's what he'd want, right? Yes. *Look at you, being all selfless.* The ever-present voice of his therapist, but at least she was complimenting him for something. Maybe he was making progress.

Bring up the Mobile Gate command screen. "King Arthur, please close the visor to enable visual data display." Faith's voice rang out across the room, and da Vinci burst out laughing.

"I'm glad it's not just me that does that. Wait 'til you've been in the suit all day, and then you take it off. You'll spend the next two days trying to do everything by mental commands and wondering why nothing works."

Quentin laughed. "Yeah, I can see that happening. I was just going to enter all of our coordinates data while I can still get to my notebook."

Da Vinci nodded. "You can save up to fifty locations, so you don't have to keep reentering it. You can also share your saved locations with Eissa via datalink, so she won't have to manually enter them."

Quentin set to work entering data, and Jake turned the pages in the notebook for him. He saved the island on 107, Prepper's Paradise in 443, Tocho's cabin in 444, both locations inside the tank factory in the Genesis Dimension, and the roof of the Diablo Tower, just to give himself all the options available. When he was done, he transferred the data file to Eissa.

"Okay, what's the plan?" Eissa asked. "How do you want to do this?"

Quentin retracted his face shield again. "I think we need to go see Bob and Tocho, and explain all this. We owe them that much, and Bob will disown us if we don't. From there, I think we jump to the back corner of the factory in the second place we took a reading. Then we just walk up to the control room door and push everyone into the next room, and keep going until we clear the control building. We can ask for volunteers to reprogram the robots. Hopefully we can keep anyone from sounding the alarm, but if they do, then I'll fend off the cavalry while you work crowd control. We ought to be back here in an hour and a half, and home in time for lunch. What do you think?"

"Alright, let's do this. It probably won't be that easy, but let's do it anyway."

●———○

Retract face shield. "Hey, Bob," Quentin shouted. "Tocho. Anybody home?" They stood at the edge of the porch outside the cabin. Quentin was afraid of scaring them to death if they just barged in. He was also pretty sure the floor would collapse under the weight of the FAT suits.

A chair scraped across the floor inside. "What's all the yelling about?" Bob grumbled, his voice drifting through the open door. "You can just come in and talk like civilized people." He opened the door and stepped out onto the porch. "What's-"

His voice dropped off in mid-sentence, and Tocho stepped out the door behind him. As he moved over beside Bob to where he could see, he froze. They both stood with mouths hanging open, and Quentin burst into laughter.

"Surprise!" Eissa laughed. "What do you think?" She turned in a circle, then closed her face shield, leaped straight up in the air and dropped to a combat crouch upon landing, one arm pointing at Bob. "YOU WILL BE ASSIMILATED." The metallic robot voice echoed off the front of the house. She stood back up and retracted the face shield with a grin.

"Where in the world did you get those?" Bob asked, clearly flabbergasted.

"Let's just say we know a guy that knows a guy," Quentin said. "And the guy he knows has some really cool toys."

Tocho spoke up. "I hope you didn't steal these. Someone who has suits like this is not someone to steal suits like this from."

"Oh, no," Quentin said. "He was happy to loan them to us. This guy used to work for DimCorp."

"He helped design the Mobile Gates," Eissa added. "He's excited to let us use these to go kick DimCorp's ass."

Bob and Tocho looked at one another, eyebrows raised.

"When you said you were going to go see Jake about some equipment, I thought you might get a gun, or a Kevlar helmet or something. I wasn't expecting all this." Bob walked down the steps and ran a hand over Quentin's arm. "I didn't even know something like this existed."

"Me, either," Quentin said. "We got lucky. These things will take almost all the risk out of this mission. They're bulletproof, they've got computerized guns, and they have an onboard Mobile Gate, so if things go bad, we can just leave."

Bob nodded, stepping back. "When are you going to do it?"

"Right now. We came to let you know what's going on and see what you think."

Bob's face was unreadable behind his beard. He looked them up and down for a moment before glancing back at Tocho. "Kids. They get all the good stuff, eh?"

Tocho's eyes crinkled as he grinned. "Why, back in my day, we had to carry a shield in one hand, and a sword in the other, and that was just to walk to the outhouse."

"Which was uphill both ways," Eissa added.

"Through three feet of snow." Tocho shook his head with a chuckle. "I don't know how you pulled this off, but it seems to me that you've got this pretty well under control. I gotta say, you're a whole lot more resourceful than we ever were."

"Nah, we just happened to meet the right guy who

knew the right guy," Quentin said. "We struck gold, but it was all luck."

Tocho gave Quentin a sage look. "Someone I know is fond of saying that chance favors a prepared mind." He moved over as Bob stepped past him and sank into a rocking chair. "I know I've told you before, but I'm proud of you. You're doing good."

Quentin blushed, looking down for a moment. "Thanks, Tocho. Hopefully we'll be back in a few hours with a success story to tell you."

"Maybe when you get done, you can take us to meet your new friend," Bob said. "Tell him I'd like to try out one of his suits if he doesn't mind."

"Definitely."

He backed up a few steps. There was a sadness in Bob's eyes, and Quentin felt guilty for leaving them behind. *They chose to retire,* he reminded himself. *They might be regretting that decision right now, but I'm not exactly able to go back and ask da Vinci if they can use the other two suits, right?* It felt like selfish justification, rather than the truth. Was he afraid that Bob and Tocho might steal his thunder if they came along? The idea made him feel bad, but it didn't necessarily ring false. Maybe he was trying to prove to them that he could handle this. Or, maybe he was trying to prove that to himself. That felt like the right answer. *Compromise: I'll make sure to ask da Vinci if we can bring them out to his place afterwards.* It might have been a bullshit compromise, but it made him feel better. *And once I have a successful mission under my belt, maybe I won't need to prove anything to them anymore. Or to me.*

Eissa stood up and gave them a wave before turning to face him. "Alright," she said, her visor sliding into place. *Ping.* Her voice was in his ear. "You ready to do this?"

Okay, Faith. Deploy face shield. Give me the Mobile Gate screen. Keep commlink with Darth Vader open. "Yep. Here we go."

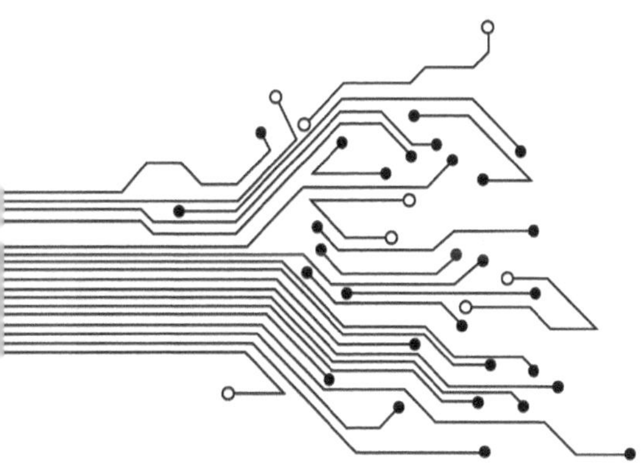

CHAPTER 23

The phone on the desk rang, startling Carl Holt out of a light doze. He grabbed it on the third ring.

"Holt here."

"Sir, this is Sergeant Wilson, upstairs at the front desk." There was a pause on the other end of the line. "There's something weird going on at one of the auto-factories."

Holt rubbed his face with one hand, trying to clear away the cobwebs of sleep. "What are you talking about?"

"I'm not sure. Somebody called in and said two cyborgs just showed up in the middle of the plant."

Holt sighed. "Did you confirm it? Send someone out there? See a video feed?"

"Not yet, sir."

Holt slammed his hand down on the desk. "Why are you calling me with this shit, Wilson? Follow the damned protocols, that's what they're for."

"I'm sorry, sir. It was a pretty convincing call. This sounds really unusual, and I didn't want to ignore something potentially important."

"Check it out. Call me back if it actually becomes important. I don't have time for maybe." Holt hung up the phone and massaged his temples. The lack of sleep was starting to kick his ass, but there was just too much happening to rest for very long.

He checked his email, hoping for a report from Sergeant Anderson on the situation in Dimension 17. There was a pile of new emails, but none were from Anderson. If he was going to have to pull the Special Ops team out of the spaceport in 443, that would cause major problems. Maybe it was time to put in a budget request for a second wet team. That would certainly make some of this easier, not that the Board would ever release the funds for it.

He got up and walked to the door. Sergeant Treijo was at her desk, typing away. He poked his head into her office, and she looked up.

"I'm going to lay down for fifteen minutes and try to shake this headache. Wake me up if something happens."

She waved one hand at him and resumed typing. "I'll hold the fort down, boss."

"And try to come up with a way to let James know we've got his sister," he added. "I'm still drawing a blank on that."

Closing the door, he retreated to the cot at the back wall and carefully stretched out. His ribs hurt, his head hurt, and his stress level was peaking at an all-time high. A few minutes of sleep wouldn't fix it all, but it would make him feel better about it.

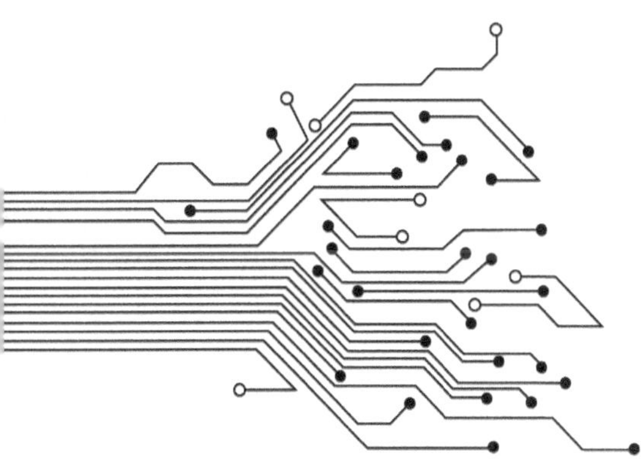

CHAPTER 24

Quentin's visor transparency adjusted to the dim lighting in the corner of the factory. Eissa was beside him, just behind the robot unloading road wheels from the coating machine.

"Welcome back to the Genesis Dimension," Quentin said. "We hope you'll enjoy your stay. Be sure to help yourself to a complimentary battle tank as you exit the gift shop."

Initiate Threat Screen.

A series of white boxes appeared on his visor as Faith identified robots throughout the area, then disappeared, leaving the screen blank. "No threats identified at this time."

Keep the scan active. That might change any second.

"Where do you want to go in?" Eissa asked. "It looks like we've got two downstairs doors and one upstairs."

"I would guess that the downstairs is offices, and the upstairs is probably computers." As he spoke, a 3D layout of the control building appeared on his screen. "Hang on, Faith is scanning it for me. This is such an awesome resource. It takes the guesswork out of everything. It looks like we have four rooms downstairs, and heat signatures show three occupants. There are no internal stairs, so let's get those three and herd them upstairs. There are three people up there, too, in one big room."

"Okay, I got the heat signatures."

They moved past the machine and out into the travel lane. Quentin pointed to the far end of the building. "Let's go in on that end and bring them out this end. Then we can just go right up the stairs."

"I don't think both of us need to go inside," Eissa said. "Why don't you go in and get them, and I'll wait out here to point them up the stairs. That way I can be on guard too, in case someone else shows up while you're in there."

"Okay, that makes sense." He walked down to the far end of the building, while Eissa turned and walked over near the stairs.

The door in front of him had shutters pulled on the window, and he caught a glimpse of his reflection. Knowing he was inside a badass FAT suit was one thing, but seeing himself in it made his chest swell. He couldn't keep the grin off his face. *Faith, can you apply a mirror tint to the face shield?* His face vanished in the reflection. Perfect. He stepped forward and grabbed the doorknob. *External speakers 30%.*

The heat signature overlay showed that there was one person in this room. He opened the door, ducking as he entered. A woman sat at the desk to his right, typing on a computer. She glanced up at him, a half-formed smile frozen on her lips.

"Stand up," Quentin ordered. "Follow my instructions and you will not be harmed."

The woman shot to her feet, her chair rolling back into the wall. She raised her hands hesitantly, as if she wasn't sure what to do with them. She was an attractive executive type, probably in her early fifties. Her smart gray business suit was set off by her short salt-and-pepper black hair, and it was an easy guess that she was the boss.

"What is your name and position?" Quentin asked. One of the other heat signatures was moving their way in the room next door.

"Sheila Parker, Site Supervisor."

Quentin pointed to the inner door leading to the next room. "Open the door. Tell your staff to remain calm and follow my instructions. We're going to the other end of the building. Do it now."

She reached the door just as the person on the other side opened it. "Bill, turn around and walk down to Art's office. We have a visitor."

Quentin ducked through the door and followed them through the room. It was filled with file cabinets running the length of the wall on his left, with a few desks down the wall on the right. A table stood in one corner, a box of donuts sitting next to the half-empty coffee pot.

Bill glanced back as they crossed the room and stumbled as he caught sight of Quentin behind them, his eyes growing impossibly wide. Sheila helped him to his feet. "Just walk," she murmured. "Everything's fine. Keep going."

Art met them at the door to his office. "What's going on?" He was bald on top, but the scruff around the sides and back of his head was wild and curly. His belly hung over his pants and was liberally sprinkled with crumbs from the donut in his hand.

"Do as you're told, and you will not be harmed," Quentin said. The robotic voice filled the room. "Walk outside and up the stairs. Do not attempt to run."

Sheila gave him a calculating look but said nothing. She led the way out the door, pausing briefly as she caught sight of Eissa beyond the stairs.

Ping. "Everything good?"

"So far, so good," Quentin said. "I just hope these stairs can support the FAT suits. And the floor up there, now that I think about it."

"I'll stay down here, just to be on the safe side."

Sheila reached the top of the stairs and walked directly to the wide steel door. She raised her fist and knocked an odd pattern on the door. *Three taps, pause, two taps, pause, three taps.* Two of the heat signatures in the upstairs room were running to the door. They reached it, then turned around and headed to the other end of the building.

"Shit," Quentin said. "She just gave them a panic code of some kind." He charged up the stairs, ignoring the vibration in the catwalk above. Art clung to the railing with both hands, his knees sagging.

External speakers 40%. "Open the door," Quentin said, pointing at Bill. "Now."

Bill grabbed the door and rattled the handle. "It's locked. I'm sorry, but it's locked."

"Move." Quentin stepped over in front of the door as Bill scrambled to the side and slammed both hands into it. The door flew into the room with a tremendous crash, taking the frame and a few concrete blocks with it. He stepped back and pointed through the cloud of dust. "Everyone inside."

They filed in, carefully moving around the rubble on the floor. Three young men stood huddled together in the middle of the room. Quentin did a quick scan of the area, looking for a safe place to stash them away from telephones and computers.

The front wall was a solid line of computer screens. Cables streaked across the ceiling to a bank of servers along the back wall. The windows overlooking the factory gave an impressive bird's-eye view of everything on the front wall, but the server racks obscured the windows on the back wall.

"Everyone to the far end of the room," Quentin ordered. "Now." They scurried to the back and huddled around the water cooler. Art's face was red, and he was panting, and Quentin was concerned that he might be having a heart attack.

Retract face shield. Quentin walked forward, allowing them to see him as a person. He stopped a few feet away.

"My name is Quentin James, and I'm here to talk to you about the tanks you're building." He looked at each of them. "Those tanks are supposed to go to my home dimension, and it's going to start World War 3. If we let this happen, millions of people will die. Hell, with all the nukes out there, this might even become the apocalypse. I don't want that to happen. Surely you don't want that to happen either, right?"

No one said anything.

"Sheila, do you want to give them the tanks that bring on the end of the world?"

She raised her shoulders in a helpless shrug. "We're just doing our jobs. We don't have any control over what people do with the products we manufacture."

"Hhmm," Quentin said. "It sounds like the company line for absolving yourself of any responsibility. That doesn't cut it for me, especially when you build tanks for a living."

"What do you want us to do?" she asked. "We don't have any control over where the tanks go."

Quentin smiled grimly. "We're going to make sure that they can't leave. Here's how we're going to do it."

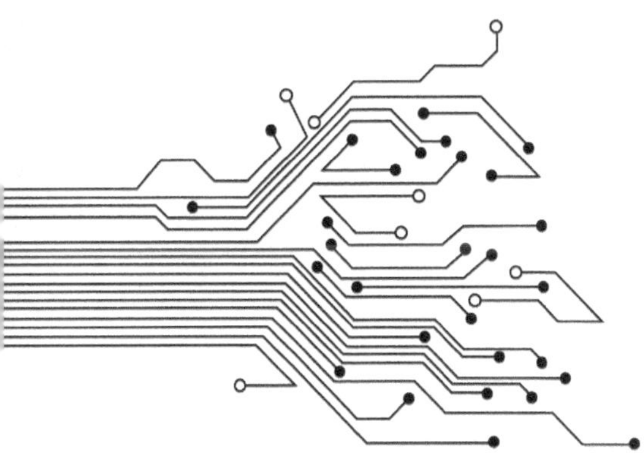

CHAPTER 25

The phone rang shrilly, and Carl Holt moaned in his sleep. It rang again, then a third time. "I'm coming, goddammit." He sat up stiffly and glanced at his watch. He'd only been asleep ten minutes. The phone continued to ring, and he slowly stood up and limped over to the desk.

"Holt here."

"It's Lieutenant Baker, sir. I've got a hit on the facial recognition software for Quentin James."

Holt stood upright, his brain locking into gear. "Where is he?"

"Building 23260. It's one of the factories."

"What dimension?" Holt asked, confused.

"Uh, this one, sir. Genesis Dimension."

Holt stared at the wall blankly. James was in the Genesis Dimension? In a factory? "What the fuck is he doing there?"

"He's got the staff held hostage in the control room. He appears to be wearing some kind of cyborg suit. We're lucky the camera got a decent look at his face."

"Can you bring the video up on my computer?" Holt asked, powering up the screen as he sat down. The cobwebs of sleep cleared rapidly as adrenaline coursed through his veins.

"Yes, sir, just a minute."

Holt put the phone on speaker and hung up the handset, grabbing his cell phone. Mathers picked up on the first ring.

"Yes, boss."

"Pull the Spec Ops team back from 443 right now. We've got Quentin James in a factory here in the Genesis Dimension. I want everyone at the DCC in two minutes."

"It's going to take longer than that, boss."

"Why are you still on the phone, Mathers?" Holt shouted. "Make it happen, now!"

"The video should be coming up any second now," Baker said.

Holt hung up the cellphone as the image popped up on his screen. The camera was ceiling-mounted in a corner of the room. Sure enough, there was a cyborg standing in the middle of the floor with James's head poking out the top. He appeared to be talking to the staff.

"I want every video camera in that factory up on your screens," Holt ordered. "You're going to be my eyes when we go in there." He glanced up at the closed door to his office. "Treijo," he shouted. "Get in here!"

"It looks like we only have a few cameras in the building," Baker said. "The dust out on the factory floor makes cameras out there useless."

Sergeant Treijo opened the door. "You called me?"

"I did." Holt said. "We've got James. Baker, what factory is that?"

The sound of Baker typing drifted out of the speaker as Treijo walked over. "Let's see, Building 23260 is… Auto-Factory 23. It's about five miles from here."

Holt looked at Treijo. "Find out what they're building. I want the number of staff, who's in charge, everything you can find in two minutes. Go." She spun around and jogged out of the room.

"Baker, I'm going mobile. I'll call you on my cell shortly." He hung up the phone, staring intently at the video feed. That suit James was wearing looked like something out of a movie. He didn't appear to have any guns, but if the suit was as hi-tech as it looked, it wasn't safe to assume it was unarmed. It was probably armored, too. That would add an element of difficulty to the operation, but the Special Ops team would be able to handle it. He would be there in person to be sure of it.

He got up and walked over to the closet, his aches and pains forgotten, and pulled out his body armor. He'd gone in cocky and underprepared last time, and James had gotten the best of him. This time he was ready. There would be no next time.

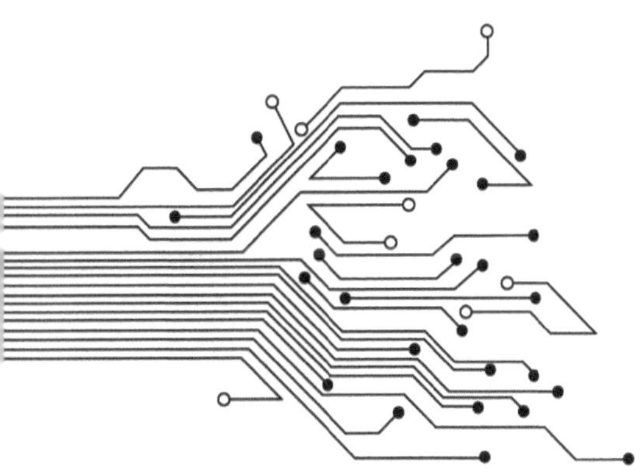

CHAPTER 26

*P*ing. "King Arthur, this is Darth Vader. I've got eyes on a robot. It just came across the travel lane and started blow-torching the first tank in line."

Quentin leaned back from the computer monitor and walked over to the window. He couldn't quite see the tanks, but he could see several more robots making their way up the travel lane. "Roger that. They should be coming in pretty steady now. Keep an eye out for company. I don't know if they sounded the alarm or not."

He turned back to the computer. One technician sat there where Quentin had forced him at gunpoint, typing commands into the control program. The others were sitting on the floor around the water cooler, and he walked back over to them. He ignored the people from downstairs and spoke directly to the other two computer techs.

Retract face shield. "I know how you guys feel right now. I used to be an IT tech for DimCorp back in my dimension." He squatted down so he wasn't towering over them. "I worked for an oil company called IBZ Energy. Then one day I found out that our CEO had a hitman named Carl Holt that went out to these pipeline protests and killed people to break up the protests. Just murdering people that got in their way. How messed up is that?"

No one said anything.

"The next thing I discovered was a portal that led to another world. It turns out that the company I worked for, which is the same company you work for, has slaves working in mines in some dimensions, slaves working on plantations in other dimensions, and I was helping them do it by keeping the servers going and removing malware from computers for a company that supplies oil to them. That made me feel like shit."

One of the techs finally looked up, meeting his eyes. He didn't say anything, but he didn't need to. If he sided with Quentin in front of his boss, the consequences for him later would be bad, but Quentin knew from his face that he was willing to help. He just needed Quentin to put on a show to cover him.

Quentin rose to his feet. "So, at this point in my investigation into my previous employer, I'm trying to save my entire dimension from World War 3, which is being sponsored by DimCorp. So, if you won't volunteer to help me, I will force you." *Deploy weapons 1 and 2. Do not fire.* "Both of you, over to the computers, now." Quentin's forearms sprouted guns with a brief mechanized whine, the barrels pointing at the techs.

The two techs scrambled to their feet and moved across the room. Quentin trailed behind them. "Your teammate has already figured out how to accomplish my task. Get the code from him and start reprogramming the robots. Remember, I'm an IT guy too, so I know what you're doing. If you try to sabotage this, I will hit you with a high-voltage shock. Understood?"

They nodded silently and bent to the keyboards. Quentin watched carefully, trying to convince them and the others that he was monitoring their every move. *External speakers off.* He spoke softly so that only the techs could hear. "This can be fun, guys. I'm sure you've thought about turning these robots into destruct-o-bots before, right? This is your opportunity to play it out."

Two of them smiled, and the third chuckled under his breath. Script poured across the screens, and the stream of robots coming from every corner of the factory increased. The occasional flashes of light reflecting off the ceiling and walls outside the windows became nearly constant as dozens, and then hundreds of torches and welders began burning their way through the tanks. The office was silent save for the clicking of keys as the techs typed commands. The minutes slowly ticked by, and Quentin started to relax. They might just pull this off without any fighting at all.

Ping. "Dude, I've got a pile of heat signatures popping up on the wall across from me. Either we- fuck!" The sound of bullets ricocheting off Eissa's FAT suit rattled the speakers in Quentin's helmet. "Check that. The cavalry has arrived."

Apparently, someone had managed to sound the alarm after all, and the fighting was happening again. This was a moment that Quentin had hoped they could circumvent. He'd spent his whole life avoiding conflict, but fighting with DimCorp was starting to become a regular thing. At least they were prepared for it this time.

"Roger that. If you have to shoot someone, try not to kill them. I'd still like this to be a zero-death event." *That goes for you too, Faith.* He turned back to the techs. *External speakers 20%.* "Keep programming the robots. My onboard computer will be monitoring everything you do, so don't even think about messing with me."

He turned and ran to the open doorway. *Deploy face shield. Threat scan. Thermal scan.* The amount of heat coming from the tanks made his whole screen glow on the right side, and he had to filter the image to pick up the people across the bay. They were behind the CNC machines and 3D printers, hiding from the return fire that Eissa was laying down from just beyond the stairs.

His display picked out an exposed target, probably someone's leg sticking out in the open. *Fire one shot from weapon 1.* His forearm shot out as crosshairs appeared on the screen and zoomed in. A split second later the leg disappeared in a shower of blood. Hopefully that would be enough to keep them from doing anything foolish.

"You hanging in there, Vader?"

"Hell, yeah," Eissa said. "I'm trying to decide if I need to find some cover or not. It feels weird to just stand here and get shot at."

"Well, I just shot one of them in the leg. Hopefully, they'll stop being so aggressive now that they know we're serious."

"Yeah, I don't think that's going to stop them. I popped two for sure. It's hard to tell how many there are since they're all piled up behind the machines."

The phone rang behind him, and Quentin turned back to the room, staring at it. *External speakers.* "Nobody touches that. Let it ring."

Ping. "Dude, look out!"

A streak of red flashed across Quentin's visor, arcing in through the open doorway. The FAT suit reacted faster than Quentin could even think as it spun and extended his right hand, catching the incoming rocket-propelled grenade in mid-air. He took a step forward and hurled it back across the bay, where it struck one of the 3D printers and exploded. The thermal image showed red-hot shrapnel flying everywhere, and as the smoke cleared somewhat, he could see a severed power cable hanging from the ceiling, snapping and arcing as it brushed the ruined machine. The soldiers on the other side scrambled for cover. *Engage targets of opportunity. Shoot to disable, not to kill.* He was trying to be civil about this, but if they wanted to force the issue, he would respond in style. *Two targets neutralized.*

Ping. "Holy shit, Quentin. Did you just throw their RPG back at them?"

"Well, my FAT suit did," Quentin said. His stomach filled with butterflies as he realized what just happened. "I don't think I had much to do with it. Hang on, I'm going to tell them to stop shooting at us."

External Speaker 90%. "Attention, DimCorp Security." The deep robotic voice echoed down the building, drowning out the sound of the robots burning holes in the tanks. "Attention. Cease fire. We have no desire to harm you."

The sound rolled down the walls, coming back in a series of diminishing echoes. Quentin stood in the door waiting for a reply. Some of the heat signatures appeared to be retreating, but after a moment it became clear that they were headed for the tanks.

Ping. "What are they doing?" Eissa asked.

"I'm not sure." They spread out down the line of tanks, seemingly at random. Gunfire erupted in flashes of brilliance across Quentin's screen, and he realized what was happening. "Shit! They're attacking the robots. I'll engage from up here. Can you go try to head them off?"

"On it."

Eissa raced by below him, arms extended with both weapons firing as she ran. Quentin berated himself for not seeing it coming. The FAT suits made them nearly indestructible, so finding another way to stop them was the obvious way to approach it. He hadn't even thought about things from the security force's point of view, and that was a stupid rookie mistake. Had he really thought they would just sit out there and not do anything?

Behind him, the phone rang again. He snapped off three shots at the soldiers on the floor below him, then turned and strode across the room, glancing at the techs. They were busy typing and kept their heads down as he passed. The phone sat at an empty workstation, and he bent over it, finally spotting the button to put it on speaker. He carefully touched it, trying to avoid crushing the phone.

Retract face shield. "Hello, this is the tank factory."

"Who's speaking?"

"You go first," Quentin said.

"This is Carl Holt, Director of Security. Put Quentin James on the phone, right now."

Quentin's heart sped up. "Hello, Carl. How's your head?"

There was a brief pause on the line.

"Quentin James, you are under arrest for terrorist actions. Come downstairs right now and take the suit off. Instruct your partner to do the same. If you comply without resisting, we won't hurt you."

Quentin laughed bitterly. "Really? You just shot a fucking grenade in here, and now you want me to believe you won't hurt me? You could have killed all your employees. You should apologize to them. Go on, they're all listening."

"This is your last warning, James. Give yourself up or die. I'm okay with either one."

Quentin turned around to face Sheila Parker and her team against the back wall. "Do you hear this? This is who you work for. This is who you're protecting. He's willing to kill all of you without blinking an eye. I just saved your life from him. I want you to think about that." He turned back to the phone. "Carl, I'm going to need you to hang out for a few minutes. I'll be done here shortly, and then we'll talk."

There was a muffled discussion on the other end of the line, and then Holt's voice came back clearly. "I think we'll talk now, James. Tell Mrs. Parker to open her email. I'm sending you something that I'm sure you'll find an immediate need to discuss."

"Whatever it is, I'm sure we'll get to it in good time. Be patient. Oh, and please stop shooting at us, it's not very nice." Quentin hung up the phone.

"Uh, sir?"

Quentin turned to the techs, unsure which had spoken. "What?"

The man on the far computer raised his hand. "All the robots are redeployed, although we currently have four that aren't responding. Make that five. Something is taking them offline."

Quentin frowned. "We're working on that. How long do you think it will take to get all the tanks disabled?"

The tech looked back at his screen. "That depends. With all the robots, it would have been thirty-seven minutes to complete the first pass, which is one hole in every hull. The second pass will damage each engine, and that will take an additional sixty-five minutes. If we keep losing units, it will take longer."

Quentin nodded. *Open comms to Darth Vader.* "How's it going out there? We've lost five robots already."

"I'm doing my best," Eissa said. "These guys are getting smarter, though. They're spread out all over the building, taking pot shots at the robots. It's too big of an area for me to cover, but I'm trying."

He flinched at the sound of a bullet hitting her helmet. "Alright, I'll come out and give you a hand." He started for the door.

"Mr. James," Sheila Parker said. "I think you'll want to see this email."

She was holding up her arm, pointing to her watch. He hesitated, torn between saving the robots and seeing what Holt might have sent. "Alright," he said, gesturing to a computer. "Quickly. Bring it up."

She carefully climbed to her feet and moved to a computer. Quentin stepped over behind her and watched as she logged into her email. When it loaded, he spotted his name in the subject line in all caps. She opened the email and expanded the window to full screen, and Quentin's heart stopped.

A picture of Denise filled the screen. She was sitting on the floor of a jail cell with her wrist handcuffed to a steel bedframe, her hair messed up and a confused look on her face. The message under the picture was brief.

WE HAVE YOUR SISTER. THE LONGER IT TAKES YOU TO GIVE YOURSELF UP, THE MORE OF HER FINGERS WE CUT OFF.

"There's a video," Sheila said. "Do you want me to play it?"

Rage filled him like molten lava, making it hard to think. "No," he seethed. "I want you to look at her. She has nothing to do with this. Do you see this? Do you see what's going on here? I'm not the terrorist!"

He stormed to the hole in the wall. With a roar, he bent down and picked up the steel door, dragging the concrete blocks still attached with pieces of rebar. He side-hopped out onto the landing and flung the door across the travel lane and the bay. The door slammed into a CNC machine, burying the soldiers that hid behind it as the momentum shoved the whole thing against the wall. Quentin turned back to Sheila. "I want you to see the truth here, and make sure those tanks get destroyed. I'm going to get my sister." *Close face shield.*

He sprang off the balcony with a scream of rage, landing on the other side of the travel bay at a run. Eissa's blue icon showed that she was still down by the tanks as he charged across the bay in search of Holt.

Ping. "Dude, what's going on?"

"They've got Denise hostage."

"What?"

"Denise, my fucking sister. Holt's got her."

"Oh, shit."

Gunfire erupted all around him, rounds careening off his armor like a hailstorm. Quentin scanned faces as he rounded the first 3D printer, but they were hard to see clearly with their helmets and goggles. He grabbed a soldier and flung him out of the way. His screen was a mess of red squares as Faith tried to communicate all the incoming threats to him. He grabbed the rifle out of the hands of the next soldier, breaking it over his knee like a stick. Holt wasn't in the group, and he moved on to the next machine, throwing the broken rifle at another soldier who was shooting at him. His rear-facing shoulder weapons engaged as he turned his back.

"Don't kill Holt," he bellowed both to Eissa and to Faith. "I'm going to choke him to death myself once Denise is safe."

His screen showed the heat signatures of three people crouched behind the next machine. He leaped on top of it, and as the casing crumpled beneath the weight of the FAT suit, he jumped to the floor on the other side, twisting in the air so that he was facing them as he landed. Instantly all three of them opened fire, spraying his armored chest with bullets. Ricochets riddled two of the three men in seconds, before Quentin did anything more than look at them. The soldier in the middle continued to shoot, a ricochet hitting his own legs, and when the gun was empty, Quentin reached out and took it from him. He grabbed the soldier by the shirt with his other hand, lifting him up into the light. It was Carl Holt.

The heat signature on his screen showed that the gun barrel in his hand was extremely hot, and he shifted his grip, pressing the barrel against Holt's neck as he held him in the air. "Where's Denise?" he shouted. "Where the hell is Denise?"

Holt screamed and kicked his wounded legs, his arms swinging wildly as he tried to twist away from the burning barrel. Quentin threw the rifle away and slammed Holt up against the ruined 3D printer, knocking his Kevlar helmet off. He used the micro-movers to squeeze Holt from head to toe, trying to exert as much pain in as many places as possible. *External speaker off. Retract face shield.* He leaned in close, his nose just inches from Holt's. "You motherfucker!" he screamed. Holt struggled weakly, gasping for air. *Get ahold of yourself, Q. Don't kill him.* He took a deep breath and let it out, reducing the pressure on Holt's chest slightly as he let go with the micro-movers. "We can do this one of two ways. Either I kill you right now, and then I go to Security Headquarters and kill everyone there and destroy the building until I find Denise, or you can tell me where she is."

Holt headbutted Quentin in the face through the open helmet, sending sparks across Quentin's vision as his burning nose began dripping blood. The rage returned, along with a thought that turned into an action before he could stop it: *Shock the shit out of this motherfucker.* Holts body convulsed as electricity poured out of Quentin's palm and into his chest. Miniature bolts of lightning popped out of Holt's back, arcing to the metal framework of the crushed machine behind him. Spittle flew from his lips as his head flung back and forth, and the smell of burning flesh drifted up into Quentin's open helmet, making him feel ill. *Stop, that's enough.*

Quentin leaned back, waiting for the burning in his nose to recede. Holt hung limply in his grip, his chest hitching. The back of his head was bleeding, and the dent in the machine behind him was smeared with blood and blackened burn spots. Quentin reached out with his free hand and lifted Holt's chin. He looked pathetic as his eyes rolled around, trying to focus. Quentin's rage faded as he stood there waiting for Holt to regain his senses. They stared at one another in silence, panting, bleeding, and oblivious to the sporadic gunfire around them.

"Where's my sister?"

Holt licked his lips carefully. He spoke slowly, the words slurring together. "You're a terrorist, James. We're never going to let you walk out of here."

Quentin flushed with righteous indignation. "Do you really believe that shit, Holt? You keep saying it, 'you're a terrorist, you're a terrorist,' but it's fucking absurd. I'm the good guy here."

Holt managed a barking laugh. "How did you convince yourself that you're a good guy? I'd like to hear that."

Quentin stared at him, incredulous. "Let's start with the fact that you kill people who are opposed to DimCorp's corporate interests, and I'm trying to stop you from doing that. You kill innocent people, and I'm stopping you. That doesn't sound like a terrorist to me, that sounds like the right thing to do."

Holt held his gaze, his eyes black. "You are engaged in a violent takeover of a factory. You killed security guards, and maybe other employees. That's what terrorists do."

"We haven't killed anyone," Quentin said. "You're building tanks that are going to North Korea, and that's going to start World War 3 in my dimension. Stopping millions of people from getting killed is not terrorist behavior, arming a fucking maniac with a thousand tanks is terrorist behavior!"

"I don't have anything to do with that," Holt said. "You should have talked to the Board if you have a problem with their business decisions. My job is to protect company assets, which you are attacking. You are a terrorist. End of discussion."

"Unbelievable." Quentin shook his head. "Alright, we're going to get Denise. If she's hurt, I'm going to bust you up in a way you'll never recover from, and I'll make sure you live to suffer." *Close face shield. Open comm link with Darth Vader.*

"Eissa, I'm going to get Denise, and I'm taking Holt with me. Can you hold things together here and give the robots time to finish the job?"

"I'll do my best. Do I need to do anything upstairs?"

"You might check in on them. I think I convinced them to help us out, but it wouldn't hurt to follow up."

"Trust, but verify. Got it. Are you coming back here?"

"Yeah, I'll do something with Holt and get Denise to a safe place, then I'll come back and get you. If it gets out of control while I'm gone, jump back to the island."

"Roger that."

Faith, bring up the Mobile Gate menu.

Save current location.

Jump to Jake's shooting range in Dimension 443.

The factory vanished, and Quentin's face shield darkened automatically in the bright sunshine. The desert sprawled out around them, broken rock throwing glinting reflections into the sky. Holt flinched, closing his eyes against the glare as he hung helplessly in Quentin's grip.

Jump to the DimGate floor, Genesis Dimension.

An instant later, the desert was replaced with dim overhead lighting in the basement of DimCorp. Quentin walked past the DimGate Control Center, ignoring the wide eyes of the techs seated on the other side of the window. His display showed four bodies inside, and none of them were moving. He walked up the hall and through the double door, grinning grimly as Holt's head bounced off the doorframe.

External speakers 30% "Which way?"

Holt spat on his visor in defiance. Quentin slammed him against the wall to the left, then swung him back to the right. His head bounced off the concrete block with a sickening thud. Quentin pulled him back around and lifted Holt's face up to his visor, twisting his grip even tighter on Holt's shirt.

"If I have to ask again, I'm going to fry you until your heart cooks. Which way?"

Holt pointed weakly. "Other end of the hall," he gasped. His head lolled to the side, blood seeping from his nostrils.

Quentin stormed down the hall, his trepidation growing with every step. How bad was Denise hurt? Where should he take her? Would she be better off in a hospital in Dimension 443, or back home in 165? And what about Carl Holt? He finally had him, but he didn't know what to do with him.

His footsteps echoed loudly off the bare walls as he jogged down the long corridor. The hallway ended in a T intersection, and as they approached it, he shook Holt again, accidently banging his head on the ceiling. "Which way?"

Holt's head rolled up, and he pointed to the right. "Past the stairs, third door, left side."

Faith, give me a map with heat signatures. A diagram of the basement popped up on his screen. The second and third doors past the stairs both showed an occupant behind them. There were several people on the floor above them. They passed the arms room just before the stairs, and Quentin recognized where he was.

The heat signature in the first room approached the door, and a moment later a woman in a military uniform stepped into view. The whites of her eyes were enormous against her dark brown skin, her mouth hanging open in shock as Quentin and Holt drew near. Quentin ignored her as she stepped back into the doorway, and passed her by without a glance.

He stopped at the next door and rattled the knob. As expected, it was locked. He dropped Holt in a pile beside the door. The heat signature showed the person was on the back side of the room, but he didn't want to scare her to death, or injure her any worse than she was.

External speakers 60%. "Denise, stay in the corner of the room. Shield yourself with the mattress if you can. I'm going to break down the door." The robotic voice was deafening in the hallway, and he felt a bit of satisfaction as Holt moaned and tried to cover his ears. The red and orange blob on his screen moved around for a moment before condensing into a small round ball.

He took a step back and kicked the door as hard as he could, just under the knob. The door flew inwards, twisting to the right and crashing to the floor as the upper hinge gave way. The lower hinge held at first, preventing the door from flying across the room, but ripped in half as the door hit the floor. Quentin stepped inside the cell.

Retract face shield. Whoever was in the room was hiding behind the thin mattress, as instructed. "Denise? It's me, Quentin." He walked over to the bed as carefully as he could, conscious of his appearance. "It's okay."

A tangled mass of brown curls poked out past the edge of the mattress, followed by a pale white face. "Quentin?"

Under different circumstances, the range of emotions that crossed her face might have been comical; shock, relief, fear, but seeing his sister sitting on a steel bunk in a jail cell, cowering behind a mattress made him want to cry. How did it ever come to this?

He dropped down on one knee, terrified of what he was about to see. If Holt had mangled her, he didn't know if he would be able to control himself. "It's me. Are you hurt? Let me see your hands."

She stared at him, her jaw moving silently. Her head shook from side to side as she tried to comprehend things. "What- where have you been? How are you here? What is this robot thing?"

"We'll get to all that, I promise. Are you hurt? Did they do anything to you?"

The FAT suit picked up voices in the hallway. "Hang on." *Close face shield.* Screens popped up on his visor showing the heat signatures of at least six people in the hallway. One was on the floor by the door, that would be Holt. The next one was kneeling by him. The room next door was empty now, so that would be the female. The other four were in a combat formation, presumably pointing rifles at the door. He had to decide what to do with Holt, and he had to do it fast. He stood up.

Retract face shield. "I need to know if you're hurt, Denise. I know you're confused, and I promise I'll get to all that, but right now, we gotta get the fuck out of here. Do you need to go to a hospital?"

She shook her head, finally extending her uninjured hands. "I'm fine. I just don't know what's happening." She stood up, dropping the mattress back in place on the bed.

Relief flooded through his body like a tidal wave, and for a moment, the FAT suit was the only thing that kept him standing. *Save location coordinates.* He reached out his hand. "Okay, I want you to hold on to me, and close your eyes. We'll be out of here in a second."

She looked at him doubtfully, but slowly reached out a hand. He stifled his irritation with her hesitancy, amused that it only took her thirty seconds to get on his nerves, even here. He pulled her into a hug. *Close face shield. Jump to Dimension 107, location 2.*

The concrete block walls vanished, replaced by the front porch of the cabin. Bob was sitting in his rocking chair, whittling, and jumped visibly as they appeared on the grass in front of him, his knife clattering to the floor.

"Holy hell, boy, you damned near gave me a heart attack." His hand went to his chest.

Retract face shield. Quentin grinned. "Sorry, Bob." He pushed Denise back a step. "Okay, this is going to be a shock. You're not in the same place anymore. Open your eyes. It's safe here, I promise." He glanced up at Bob. "I've got to run back and take care of a few more things. This is my sister, Denise. Can you keep her from losing her mind? I'll be back shortly."

Bob nodded, and he let go of Denise. She staggered as she looked around. "Whaaa?"

Quentin felt a little guilty for dumping her on Bob and Tocho, knowing her current mental state, but at least she was safe here. Obviously, he couldn't take her home, since DimCorp had found her there once already. That was a problem for another time. Right now, he had more pressing things to deal with, starting with Carl Holt. *Close face shield. Return to previous location.*

An instant later he was back in the cell. The six figures in the hall were just as he'd left them a minute before. Stepping out into the hall, he bent down and picked Holt up by the shirt. The woman tending to the cut on his head fell back as Quentin lifted him up, using him as a shield to keep the soldiers from blasting away at him while he tried to figure out what to do.

He was torn by indecision. Killing Holt outright would be a fair punishment for all the people he had killed, no question about that, but would it solve the problem? Holt had said that he should talk to the Board if he had a problem with DimCorp's business policies, and there was certainly an element of truth to that. Not that the Board would change anything, of course, but killing Holt wouldn't change anything, either. There would just be a new asshole in his position tomorrow, doing the exact same things. Besides, killing Vincent Macalister was still haunting him, and he wasn't eager to add another face to his dreams.

"Let him go," the woman shouted, jarring him out of his thoughts. He looked at her.

External speakers 30%. "Who are you?"

"Sergeant Treijo, DimCorp Security. I'm the Director's assistant. Who are you?"

"I'm Quentin James, Protector of the Galaxy." The soldiers behind her shifted nervously, trying to point their rifles away from Holt, while keeping Quentin covered. Quentin took a step back. "I'm going to take him in this cell and have a private discussion. You will wait next door in your office. I can see your heat signatures, so do not attempt to attack me."

"If you're going to kill him, do it right here," Treijo said coldly. "But if you do, I promise you I'll kill you."

Quentin sighed. "I'm not going to kill him; I'm going to talk to him. If I was going to kill anyone, it would have happened already. Now go, before I taser you."

They shuffled backwards into the office, and he turned and entered the cell. Holt moaned as Quentin dropped him on the bed.

Retract face shield.

Holt sat up, grimacing as he leaned against the wall. "You rebroke my ribs. I'm getting too old for this shit."

"That's what everyone says when it stops being fun."

Holt glared at him, his eyes sharpening. "So, now what?"

Quentin squatted down until his face was level with Holt's, but kept a safe distance this time. "That's what we've got to figure out. I don't want to kill you."

"Well, I guess we finally agree on something. I don't want you to kill me, either." Holt's chuckle turned into a cough, and his eyes watered from the pain.

"I don't want to kill anyone," Quentin said. "The whole reason I'm doing this is to stop the violence."

"That's funny," Holt said. "All I've seen from you is

violence. Where the hell did you get that cyborg rig? It damn sure wasn't from some pacifist shop."

A smile pulled at the corner of Quentin's lips. "No, it wasn't from a pacifist shop. Are you saying that you would've stopped the delivery of tanks to North Korea if I'd organized a sit-in?"

"Fair point." Holt held his gaze. "So, you don't want DimCorp to kill people or sell tanks, and DimCorp doesn't want you interfering in its activities."

"The inevitable impasse."

They sat in silence for a moment, regarding one another. *Face shield up.* Quentin confirmed that there were five heat signatures on the other side of the wall, then lowered the face shield again. "Just checking on your people."

"They're good people. I'm glad you didn't shoot them."

"Most people are alright when you get them one-on-one."

Holt shifted his leg, exposing a pool of blood on the mattress. "I don't know what to do. I can't have you running around destroying everything we're doing, and killing you is surprisingly difficult."

"Well, I can't have you running around killing people, either. Killing you would be easy right now, but it wouldn't solve the problem. DimCorp would have someone else in your spot tomorrow morning."

Holt nodded, a rueful grin on his face. "That they would."

"Here's what I'm going to do," Quentin said. "I'm going to keep checking out DimCorp operations. If people are being enslaved, I'm going to free them. If worlds are being threatened, I'm going to save them. If bad leaders are abusing people, I'm going to remove them. If you want to protect DimCorp assets, then you need to make sure they're doing right by people. Then we won't have a conflict."

Holt shook his head slowly. "You're talking about policies that aren't under my control."

"That's not my problem." Quentin stood up. "I'm just telling you how to keep me from showing up here again. In case you haven't noticed, running into me is bad for your health."

Close face shield. Jump to the Diablo Tower, Dimension 443.

His face shield darkened in the sun, but the usual roar of wind and traffic was muted by the suit. *Jump to the tank factory, location 3, Genesis Dimension.*

The face shield returned to transparency. The two men that had been with Holt lay at his feet beside the wrecked CNC machine. His screen indicated that they were alive. He glanced around. There were heat signatures scattered all over the area. Eissa's blue beacon showed her over in the line of tanks.

Open comm link with Darth Vader. "Hey kid, you still hanging around here?"

"Dude, where the fuck have you been? My suit's damaged. I can't use my weapons, I can't jump dimensions, nothing. They're slaughtering the robots."

"Shit!" Quentin charged down the travel lane. *Faith, engage all targets as soon as you have a clear shot. Try not to kill them.* There were red squares all over the building, so he headed for the nearest one first. "Eissa, can you move?"

"Slowly. I'm leaking fluid, not sure what it is."

"Okay, just stay put."

The heat signature showed the first soldier alone behind a pallet of road wheels. Quentin sprinted directly at the pallet and jumped into the air when he was ten feet away. He crashed feet-first into the wheels, knocking the pile over onto the crouching figure behind it. He skidded through the mess, using the momentum to keep his feet as he resumed running. The next heat signature was across the aisle among the tanks.

The soldier was on top of a tank in the middle of the row, firing at the robots below him. Quentin leaped into the air, his screen zooming in on the target as his weapon fired, then switching targets to another soldier a few rows over, who was doing the same thing. The area was littered with damaged robots, and Quentin prayed that he wasn't too late. He hit the ground running, veering to his left to find the next soldier.

Faith, can you call the phone upstairs in the Control Room? Is that possible?

A moment later a ringing phone sounded in his ears. He jumped over a partially assembled turret on a trolley, his right arm tracking down and engaging the target beneath him. He landed in a crouch, and paused as Sheila Parker answered the phone.

"Control Room, this is Sheila."

"This is Quentin James. What's the status on the robots? How many have we lost?"

There was a brief conversation on the other end before she came back in his ear. "We've lost about a hundred robots. There are still twenty responding to commands. Make that nineteen."

"Shit. Where are we on the tanks?"

"I don't know. We really don't have any way to track that at this point, it's all chaos on the incoming data. We need some time to sort it out."

A gun fired twice on the other side of the building. "Okay, I gotta go. Do the best you can to keep them going." *Disconnect call.*

There were heat signatures all over his screen, but it was hard to tell if they were active shooters or neutralized casualties. He decided to follow the gunfire. It had come from the far wall, almost directly opposite of his location. He ran across the travel lane and leaped on top of the first tank, jumping from turret to turret as he made his way across the line of tanks. Below him, several robots were cutting holes in the tanks, the heat signatures blossoming across his screen as he passed. Without warning, a series of bullets slammed into his left side, making him stumble, and his arm pistoned out, firing rapidly at three different targets as he corrected his course. The incoming fire stopped.

Eissa was three rows over from him, down on the floor between two rows of tanks. Her blue beacon had a flashing red circle around it. She popped into his comm screen.

Ping. "Be careful up there," Eissa said. "I fell off a turret, and I think I damaged my suit when I hit the helmet on the other tank."

"Gotcha. There can't be too many left. How many did you take out?"

"Ten or eleven."

He reached the end of the row and jumped to the ground. The heat signature on this end was behind a row of huge spools of wire, and took off running as Quentin approached. Suddenly, the blob of color split and separated, and he realized there were two soldiers, not one. He extended both arms, but nothing happened. He brought his focus back to the screen and realized both weapons were red. *Out of ammo in forward guns.* One of the soldiers stopped and fired a burst at him, and the rounds careened off his chest.

He stepped over to the line and grabbed a spool of wire, flipping it on its side. With a mighty shove, he sent it rolling down the travel lane. He followed it with the next spool, staggering the direction slightly, and worked his way forward until there were a dozen spools of wire whizzing towards the other end of the building like massive bowling balls. The red blips on his screen ran down the travel lane at first, seemingly unaware of what was happening. At the last second, they broke for the side wall, but neither of them made it.

Quentin turned in a slow circle. Technically, the FAT suit had been doing all the work, but he was still out of breath. He scanned the building, looking for any other active shooters. There were still a lot of squares on his screen, but none of them were doing anything. Was it over? The thought made him giddy.

"Alright, Dyke Vader, I think we did it."

Ping. "That one's going to cost you, Q. And by the way, a wounded soldier can still shoot. You might want to go around and collect weapons before you do your little victory dance."

"Good thinking." He made his way back around the building, stopping by each heat signature to destroy their weapons. Only one of the soldiers was still feisty enough to shoot at him, and he didn't even bother retaliating, he just grabbed the rifle and bent the barrel over his knee. By the time he got to the last one, Eissa had made it out to the travel lane.

He began walking towards the control building. "I'm going to check on our progress. I'll be back in a minute, and we'll piggyback you on my Mobile Gate."

"Roger that."

"Da Vinci is going to be pissed that you broke his FAT suit."

"Hey, he knew what we were going to use them for," she said. "I did him a favor by finding the fail point."

Quentin laughed, and carefully climbed the stairs to the control room. The catwalk was bent significantly where he had launched himself over the rail earlier, but it held his weight. Sheila and the rest were gathered around the computers when he walked in. She glanced over at him.

"There are four hundred and thirty-one tanks left to go on the second pass. We're down most of the robots, so that hurts our time, but really, the damage is already done." There was a hint of reproach in her voice, perhaps an unspoken accusation that he had made them do a bad thing.

Retract face shield. "Sounds good. Is everyone in here okay?"

"I think so." She turned to face him, straightening her back. "Mr. James, I'm appalled that you killed all those men out there. I know you think you're doing the right thing, but killing people isn't right."

Quentin raised his eyebrows. "Says the lady who builds battle tanks. For your information, we didn't kill anyone. They're all wounded, but they'll probably live. That doesn't happen with people who get shot by tanks, you know. You should think about what you're contributing to the world."

"Wounded?"

"Wounded. I don't believe in killing people. I don't like violence, but sometimes that's the only way to get people's attention. So, yeah, we wounded thirty or forty people to save the lives of a few million."

She shifted, looking down for a moment. "I guess I always thought that our products were used to protect people."

"Oh, they are. They're protecting the people at the very top. The real question is if those people *should* be protected." He glanced over at the techs. "I know I made this a really bad day for you, but I wanted to say thanks for doing what you did. You might not believe it, but you saved an entire world today. That's a big deal."

No one said anything, and Quentin tried to be understanding of their position. Things would probably be hard for them. Most of the robots and machines had been damaged or destroyed. This factory would be offline for quite a while, and they were probably worried about losing their jobs. It was easy for him to be idealistic in this situation, but they all had bills to pay. Such was life.

"Well, I gotta go. You might call an ambulance for those guys downstairs." He turned to the door and walked out to the catwalk. *Close face shield. Open comms to Darth Vader.* "Alright, kid, I'm coming to get you. Let's go home."

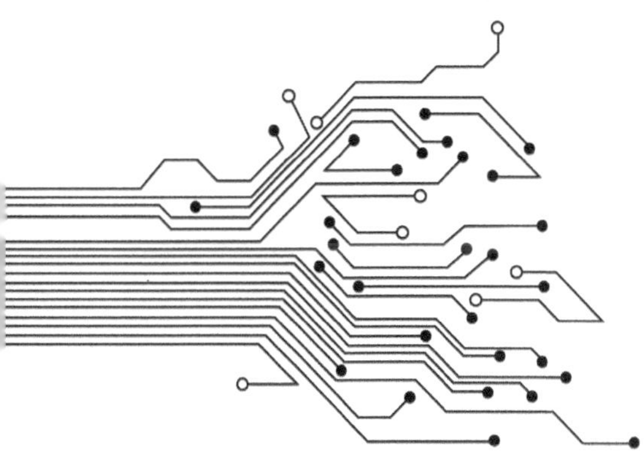

CHAPTER 27

Quentin dove under the incoming wave, popping up on the other side. Eissa floated nearby on a yellow inflatable raft, reading a book under an umbrella. The late morning sun was warm on his shoulders, and he would need to put a shirt on soon to keep from burning. He swam over to the raft, holding it with one hand as he floated on his back.

"You're getting pink," Eissa said, sliding a bookmark between the pages. "Why don't you tow me into shore before we both get fried."

A cloud passed in front of the sun as he floated there, and he closed his eyes, trying to make the moment last. "We'll go back in a minute. I'm trying to soak up as much serenity as possible before I go see Denise."

Eissa laughed. "You're going to need more than an hour in the ocean for that. More like a pharmaceutical intervention."

He smiled. Denise had stayed with them on the island for a few days before returning to Dimension 165 to pack. She was moving across town to an apartment in a friend's name, and Quentin was supposed to be there helping. As expected, Denise hadn't taken the whole alternate-dimension thing very well, and Quentin was in no rush to get there.

"She's had a tough week, for sure. But you have to give her credit for getting a full-time job and keeping the bills paid since I've been gone."

"I'm not taking anything away from her," Eissa said. "I'm just saying that she's a stress monster."

The cloud moved past the sun, and Quentin stood up, grabbing the rope on the front of the raft as he started for shore. "On the bright side, since I'm going home for a bit, I can bring my guitar back. Oh, we've got power now, so I can bring my computer. I just realized that!"

"I don't know if Bob and Tocho can handle listening to you play Wu Tang songs on your guitar. They might vote you off the island."

"One of these days acoustic gangsta rap is going to be a thing, and you'll regret not supporting me more."

"Uh huh. Tow the boat, Mr. Notorious Jack Johnson." She mimed scratching a record. "Wup wup. *My name is Quentin, I thought I might mention, my suspension, because I'm tall, I got long legs, but for my digits, no woman begs, cause I'm a nerd–*"

"Alright, alright. I'm going to push you out to sea here in a minute." He splashed a handful of water at her.

"Hey, watch the book!"

Back on the beach, he tied the raft to a tree and put his shoes on. While he might not be excited about helping Denise move, once that was done, he would be free to go hang out with da Vinci in 443, and that was something he was very interested in. When they had returned the FAT suits, da Vinci asked for a post-action interview so he could find out how the suits performed. Quentin had a few ideas on tweaking things, and he couldn't wait to spend some time in da Vinci's workshop geeking out on tech toys.

Eissa held the umbrella as they walked up the beach to the trail. She was holding up surprisingly well. They had all been concerned that being in a combat situation would trigger her PTSD. They had talked about it a lot over the past few days, and so far, she was holding it together. Still, it wouldn't hurt to start crossing over to Dimension 165 and getting a few sessions in with the therapist. With all they had been through, he was looking forward to that, himself. Therapy was one of his happy places, although how he was going to explain all of this without getting chased by orderlies with butterfly nets was another problem.

Quentin put his arm around Eissa's waist, matching his steps with hers as he hugged her. "I sure am glad you're with me on this adventure. I don't think I could have done any of this without you. You're my person."

"Aw." She leaned her head against him for a moment. "I'm glad I'm here, too. I know we don't talk about it much, but even with the bad stuff that's happened, I feel like I'm doing something important, you know what I mean?"

"We're actually doing something, instead of sitting around talking about what people should do."

"Exactly." She collapsed the umbrella as they approached the trail through the jungle. "And you're my person, too. I like giving you shit more than everyone else I know put together."

Quentin laughed. "You've refined it into an art. Some-day people will be writing acoustic rap songs about your prowess with sarcasm."

She swatted him with the umbrella. "Don't you dare."

The relatively cool darkness of the jungle was a welcome relief from the sun reflecting off the sand and water on the beach. As usual, Quentin's thoughts strayed to DimCorp, and Carl Holt. *What are you feeling, Quentin?* his therapist would ask. *It's complicated,* he would answer. *I'm relieved that I didn't kill anyone this time, but I'm worried that they're going to come after me. I didn't tie up the loose ends.* The fact that he'd left Carl Holt without a firm agreement in place was more troubling than he would readily admit, especially in the dark of night when there was no sunshine to show the light of reason on the problem. He had injured Holt pretty seriously, and basically told him that he would keep doing it until DimCorp stopped doing what it was doing. How would Holt respond to that? How would *he* respond if the tables were turned?

If he were in Holt's position, compromise probably wouldn't be an option. Then again, if he were up against superior technology that kicked his ass every time he encountered it, he would want to avoid going back for more. Perhaps if Quentin stayed out of Holt's face, Holt would turn a blind eye to him, at least until his broken bones healed.

The humidity was building in the stillness of the jungle. Quentin pulled himself back to the present moment with an effort. "Do you want me to bring you anything from home?"

"Starbucks," she said promptly. "I would love an Eissa special. And an omelet from the 43rd Street Deli. I'm starving."

"You could just come with me," he said, not for the first time.

They took a few steps in silence. "I might," she said at last. "I'm just nervous about running into people and having to answer questions."

"Tell them the truth," Quentin said with a laugh. "They'll walk away after a few seconds, rolling their eyes. Problem solved."

"You're probably right about that. Maybe I'll tell them I found an island full of lesbians, and I've decided to move there."

"Definitely a conversation killer," Quentin said. "That's probably a faster way than telling them what we've been up to."

They walked into the clearing. Bob and Tocho were on the porch, trying to put a bookcase together. Bob was arguing about which screw they were supposed to be using to mount the side pieces.

"Alright, that convinced me," Eissa said. "Let me change quick, and we'll go get your sister moved."

Quentin laughed. "And then we'll eat dinner at the 43rd Street Deli."

"Deal."

The End

If you enjoyed this book, please leave a review wherever you purchased it, and tell your friends about it! Quentin and Eissa need your help to take down DimCorp one element at a time, and you can help by spreading the word about the DimWorld series. Visit JBoydLong.com to sign up for notifications about upcoming book releases, and please connect with the author on Facebook and Instagram @JBoydLong.

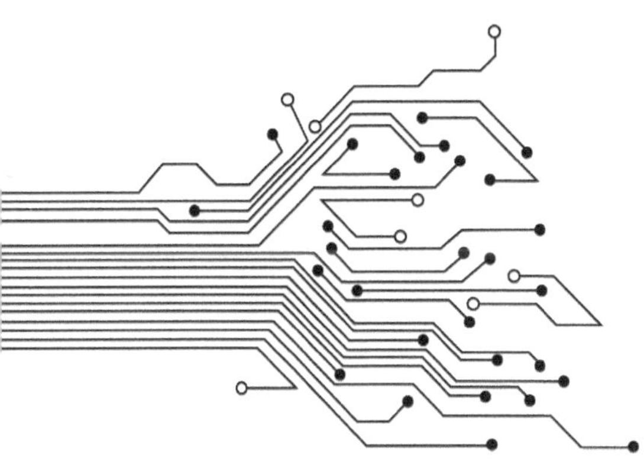

ACKNOWLEDGEMENTS

I am so very grateful to the people who have made the DimWorld Series what it is. I don't know anything about raising kids, but I know it takes a village to create a good book. The determination of whether this one is good is yours to make, but the efforts of my amazing team have made it far better than I ever could have on my own.

I never would have done any of this without the incredible support of my wonderful wife, Dr. Erica Lacher. She has been my inspiration, my taskmaster, my cajoler, and my shoulder to cry upon. She believes in me, which has helped me to believe in myself. That alone is worth more than I could ever repay.

When writing about alternative histories, and what events took place to bring other events to bear, it is supremely helpful to have a friend like Michelle Seitzmeir, who has a master's degree in history from Harvard. She has been instrumental in helping me understand how our world came to be what it is, and what would have to change in order for dimensions like 443 to develop. I wish that I had recorded all my conversations with her, as I think they would make a fascinating podcast.

A special thanks to Eric Wasson for his endless support of my quix, and for contributing a new swear word to the world. I hope it takes off!

I don't know how many hours were put in by Kathy Rothenberger and Robin Vuchnich to make this book both beautiful and functional, but it was a lot. They have both been extraordinary in their diligence and flexibility, and I am endlessly grateful for everything they have done in terms of editing and design, as well as working with my crazy schedule.

Finally, I would like to thank you. Like the proverbial tree falling in the forest (sound, no sound?), I don't know if an unread book has any value. The fact that you have read this book has immense value to me, and I want you to know that I appreciate the hours of your life that you have shared with me. I hope that you have found value in this, as well.

Justin Boyd Long
18 June, 2019

About the Author

J. Boyd Long is a self-embracing nerd who loves crunching numbers, researching interesting things, and listening to podcasts, in addition to reading loads of books. His exposure to Stephen King's books at the age of 10 probably stunted him in some way, but he is still determined to leave the world a better place than he found it. He lives near Gainesville, Florida on a small farm with his incredible wife, 7 horses, 5 cats, 2 donkeys, 2 dogs, and sheep named Gerald.

www.ingramcontent.com/pod-product-compliance
Lightning Source LLC
Chambersburg PA
CBHW051649180726
48284CB00006B/1933